"Heartly God?"

Written by Wil 3.

Published 2017 by Shorehouse Books
Printed in the United States of America

Cover Design by Tony Brandstetter

ISBN-10: 0-9980899-8-2
ISBN-13: 978-0-9980899-8-0

Dedication

Carissimo Rider, mio Figlio:

Subito dopo l'attacco di "9/11", cominciai a scrivere questo racconto. Ci voleva un paio di anni ed a quel punto, lo misi in un cassetto e non lo presi sul serio di nuovo fino che facesti un sfoggio di interesse verso la mia scrittura. Ricordo la tua reazione quando ti leggi ad alta voce alcuni racconti che scrissi, il quale, mi spinse a migliorare il mio stile di scrittura ed in particolare questo libro ed a cercare di pubblicarlo. Penso che questo vecchio lavoro non ti piaccia perche e' completamente diverso che gli altri che scrissi e condivisi con te. Cosi'a cagione di quello, invece di dedicando il libro in tuo onore, ti dedico tutto in cui misi in questo impegno lungo, cioe' il lavoro duro e notturno, il sudore della fronte e finalmente il soddisfazione enorme dopo trovai una casa editrice che lo pubblicò. Sei sempre la mia ispirazione di tutto che faccio ogni giorno e se non per te e tutto che facesti tu, questo racconto restasse abbandonato in un cassetto con i miei pensieri dimenticati e manoscritti incompiuti ed inediti. Grazie mio figliuolo, ti devo tutto, e perlomeno, spero che il mio passaggio sia un essempio di quello che si potrebbe compiere quando si e' ispirato. Ti voglio tanto bene e non vedo l'ora in cui leggero' i racconti che scriverai tu…il quale saranno migliore che il mio.

Con affetto,

Old Daddy…il tuo grande ammiratore sincere

Acknowledgments

The Author would first like to thank T. Scott Frank and Bret Ioli. Without your help, this project never goes anywhere. Your willingness to continually mentor me, to educate me, to listen to my ideas and to give me constant encouragement is overshadowed only by your remarkable friendship you have shown me over the many, many years. I am truly blessed and honored to call both of you my friend.

I would also like to thank my mom, dad and Mark Plain. If I wrote the story of my childhood and what it was like to grow up with the three of you, it would be dismissed as a fairy tale. Thank you all for the love and support.

I would also like to thank my extended family and friends from PH for always looking out for me— Jeah.

Thank you, Donna Cavanagh for taking a chance on this project and thank you Josh Isard for not only your hard work, but for all of your insight which was above and beyond the call of an editor.

Thank you to my W&J family for your never-ending support and to my brothers at Alpha— Perge!

Thank you, Natascha Gerlach, the most beautiful and talented sounding board ever. Thank you for helping me walk.

And finally, thank you, Jodi Irey, for always helping me, but more importantly, for being able to make me laugh, pretty much all the time.

I would also like to dedicate this book to my father, the greatest story teller I have ever known. One day I hope my stories are half as good as the ones you've told me.

Chapter one

Nico Rossi's tired apartment was in Bloomfield, an antiquated neighborhood in the City of Pittsburgh. The low-level drug dealing and prostitution of the evening, common to any working-class city neighborhood, was about to yield to Sunday morning and the smell of fresh baking bread and homemade sauce. Soon, Italian nonnas would don their daily all-black attire and walk to church to light candles for their deceased husbands who passed away many years ago, as was the custom. But it was still too early for that old habit, and the lingering smells of the foul behavior from the night before hadn't yet been pushed aside by the slightly fresher morning breeze that slowly pours across the river.

Sadly, Nico had been out of bed for more than two hours. As he stood before his bathroom mirror dripping wet and wrapped only in a towel, he hoped the cold linoleum floor on his wet feet would help him focus on shaving. Turning the crank on the old window let steam out of the bathroom but did nothing to remove the fog packed tightly in his head. As he slowly pulled the razor across his face, it yielded mixed results.

"Ouch, son of a bitchin' cheap-ass disposable …"

Nico's battle with constant exhaustion and quasi-delirium from sleep deprivation made even the most mundane task a challenge at times.

"Nico, sweetie, is that you … in the bathroom? … What time is it? … When did you wake up?"

Nico pushed the bathroom door open and spied his girlfriend Lucy, who leaned against the bedroom door and wore only a men's oversized T-shirt that came down to her shapely thighs. Her long blond hair was half over her front and half down her back as she struggled to wipe sleep from her eyes. Lucy's striking figure and lack of apparel, combined with the genuine concern in her voice should have been enough to make any warm-blooded man smile. But not Nico. He couldn't concentrate enough to notice, let alone appreciate it.

1

"I'm up … I'm … I don't really know if I slept at all," said Nico as he continued to bang the plastic razor against the porcelain sink.

"Honey, this is the third night in a row. I am starting to worry about you. Why don't you come back to bed and I can help you try to fall back to sleep?"

"No, I have to get ready for church," replied Nico in a very cold, disgusted fashion.

"Of course. It's always church. You know, you go to church more than anyone I know … especially for someone who doesn't believe in God."

Nico slammed the razor hard against the sink and splashed more water onto the floor. "I never said I didn't believe in God. I just said I don't believe that God is listening to me."

Not wanting to argue, Lucy turned around and crawled back into bed, hoping to sleep until at least sunrise.

Nico exited the bathroom and walked through the creaking hallway guided only by a small, solitary nightlight on the floor. He took a seat on the couch in the living room/kitchenette of his tiny one-bedroom apartment and turned on the television. Disgusted that only TV ministers and infomercials showed at this hour, he finally found a *Leave it to Beaver* rerun. As he stared at the small TV screen, he watched June Cleaver cooking breakfast, Ward reading the newspaper and drinking coffee and the Beaver eating a bowl of cereal. Nico slumped down on the couch, put his head back and momentarily fell asleep. Immediately, he started to dream about or remember a similar scene from his own childhood not that long ago, but at this point, it felt like eternity, if not an entirely different life not of his own.

Nico's father sat with young Nico at the breakfast table as he opened the mail. Nico's mother cooked eggs while Nico waited impatiently for his breakfast. "Well, this letter looks interesting … 'To the Parents of Nicholas Rossi' … wonder what this could be?" Nico's father started to read the letter and mumbled "Oh … uh huh … I see." under his breath while occasionally glancing at Nico until he finally put the letter down on the breakfast table.

"What's it say Dad?"

"Oh, it's nothing really. Not that important."

With Nico's curiosity now piqued, he quickly reached across the table, snatched the letter, and began to read it.

"Sorry, Nico, I guess you aren't going to finish second in your class like you hoped," said Nico's father in a very serious tone.

"Oh, my freakin' God!!! I'm going to be the valedictorian!!!"

Nico jumped up from the table as his mother ran to hug him. He remembered that even though his mother was small, the hug she gave almost knocked the wind out of him. With a quick, sharp and almost unexpected inhale-gasp, Nico snapped from his dream and came back to reality. He was awake again—not alert or rested—but awake. He sat alone on his old couch with only the nostalgic glow from a black-and-white TV show illuminating the room. The sun was about to rise momentarily.

Wil 3

Chapter two

The Strip District is another neighborhood adjacent to Bloomfield and downtown Pittsburgh. The Strip is a microcosm of Pittsburgh, and there is not another neighborhood that so accurately memorializes Pittsburgh's past or epitomizes its promising future. The giant abandoned factories and mills that once lined the Strip have been riddled with graffiti and crumble, making them appear more like a still shot from Post-World War II Germany than a neighborhood on the rise. Trees actually grow out of the blown-out windows on the upper floors of some buildings and provide sanctuary for hundreds of the city's filthy pigeons. But recently, seemingly overnight, many of those buildings in the Strip have been razed in favor of modern, *green* condominiums where Pittsburgh's elite reside for a scenic view of the river, the downtown skyline and a quick walk to work downtown—the most green and trendy thing to do.

At night, twenty-somethings from the suburbs fill the cheesy chain nightclubs and singles bars, searching for sex, loud club music, and XTC. Alongside them, staggering drunks pop into cheap dive bars—the only relics left from the steel era—to spend their Social Security checks. The only topics of conversation in those bars are how great it was to live here when US Steel employed thousands of people and the constant rumor that those mills would reopen again soon. Once their meager pittance has been spent on cheap booze and cigarettes, they exit the bars and fade into oblivion, only to resurface after their next check arrives in the mail.

After the drinking and cavorting have stopped and the club lights have dimmed, everybody shuffles back to a car to drive home or to a diner for a late-night greasy plate. The police department frequently appears to assist those who aren't quite able to move or to calm a young man who attempts to defend the honor of his woman … whom he just met that evening. After all the cars have cleared, the produce trucks take center stage in the Strip as working men take to their docks ready to unload fresh produce. Later in the morning, the mothers and fathers of all those who were there the past night arrive to shop for fresh produce, meats and cheeses while their hipster children nurse hangovers and try to remember who they called on their cell phone at four o'clock in the morning. This routine occurs with every transition from Saturday night to Sunday morning.

In the midst of all this organized chaos sits St. Mary's—a Roman Catholic church built by immigrant labor just before the Great Depression, a time when the Strip District was nothing more than a shanty town. Two golden domes sit atop the Romanesque church reminiscent of so many of the great cathedrals in Europe. If it's sunny—which is rare in Pittsburgh—9:00 AM Mass on Sunday is the absolute best time to be there. At that time of day, the sun rises above the downtown skyline and floods the inside of the church with natural light flavored by the pristine stained glass windows imported from Europe. If Jesus Christ ever returned to Earth, most likely he would announce his presence at a sunny 9:00 AM mass in St. Mary's.

St. Mary's was the lifeblood and center of the Strip District when it was a shanty town. It fed all the residents, both physically and spiritually. It housed hundreds of people during the St. Patrick's Day flood of 1936. And its school offered education to the young with the hope that the knowledge it provided would be enough for them to get out of the Strip District and move to a better life. Due to the condos, clubs and trendy restaurants, this once prominent church was almost all but forgotten. Practically nobody even noticed it, unless they were looking for a discreet place to relieve themselves after too much beer at three o'clock in the morning. It was almost closed and consolidated with neighboring parishes until Father Thomas O'Toole, a classic Irish priest, who was stubborn and motivated, took over as pastor.

"Though an Army encamp against me, my heart shall not fear. Though war rise against me, in this I will be confident," said Father O'Toole to himself as he peered out a mezzanine window of St. Mary's to the ground just below. Father O'Toole proceeded down the steps and past the altar. He blessed himself and took a large gulp of communion wine, just to make sure that it hadn't spoiled from the past evening's services. He slowly made his way to the confessional to hear parishioners' confessions before the start of the 9:00 AM Mass.

Outside it was gray and overcast, damp and uninspiring. Inside, the dark wood of the church pews, the dim lighting and cold marble floors cried out more of being old and tired than traditional and classic. Father O'Toole felt the same way. He turned back for one more sip of wine, just for good measure, then made his way into the confessional to sit by himself as nobody was there to confess, or in the least, to keep him company.

Wil 3

Chapter three

The protestors' movement, if it can be deservingly titled as such, was aimed at the removal of Father O'Toole from St. Mary's Parish and the whole Catholic Church. It started with a few unhappy parishioners who didn't take kindly to Father O'Toole's most recent and more progressive sermons. A few unhappy parishioners led to a few unhappy families, who then enlisted the help of other, very concerned, non-parishioners who were equally offended by what Father O'Toole had to say. Although they never actually heard it first-hand, but through their friends, which apparently was good enough to cause them to be offended.

At first, the movement was easily ignored by the remaining St. Mary's faithful and by Father O'Toole. But when it became apparent that it had grown and was not going away, Father O'Toole decided it was time to engage the protestors in dialogue. That was a mistake. The dialogue was short-lived and within a matter of minutes, Father O'Toole's Irish got the better of him and he had to be physically restrained and separated from the group. The "swear jar" Father O'Toole kept in the office behind the altar was contributed to heavily that day by him.

It used to be easy for Father O'Toole to bridge gaps between those who were with him and those who were against him. He made a short career of that in the Army prior to the priesthood. It seemed to him that he was losing that ability due to his old age in the same way that he was losing his hair and his hearing. Sadly, Father O'Toole's lack of statesmanship only fueled the fire of the protestors' movement. The following week, after word got out via social media, the movement doubled in size. The week after that, the local media was at the 9:00 AM. Mass to cover the protestors. A thirty-second clip of the protestors aired on local news the following Monday.

"We are protesting Father O'Toole's ludicrous message! The Bible says that a man should not lay down with another man. That is a sin. It's an abomination against nature! Women who have abortions are killing babies! They don't need forgiveness; they need to be locked up!!"

Once the media coverage of the protestors' movement aired, the Bishop and other higher-ups in the Church became heavily involved in the situation. The Bishop didn't necessarily agree with Father O'Toole's new message or ministry. In fact, he never really saw eye-to-eye with Father O'Toole on much of anything. But more importantly, he did not like to see one of his churches under siege. It was bad for business. Attendance at Mass was down because many of the remaining parishioners felt uneasy trying to navigate amongst the protestors as they tried to get into the church. Accordingly, the weekly collection started to come up short ... very short at times.

The stress on the income stream necessitated constant communication, which Father O'Toole equated to constant aggravation, between him and the Bishop. If he wasn't talking to the Bishop, he was talking to one of the Bishop's underbosses. If it wasn't an underboss, it was someone from the Diocese public relations department. If it wasn't public relations, it was a Diocese lawyer. All the stress and constant watchdogging of Father O'Toole made him physically tired and mentally weak. Making the situation worse was Father O'Toole's acknowledgment that he simply did not have the time to devote to the parishioners who still needed him, or to those unfortunate sick and dying people that he would minister to in three of the local hospitals.

Father O'Toole was no longer a young man. Far from it. He should have retired years ago, by his age. But he grew up in the Strip District, went to St. Mary's grade school and he welcomed the opportunity to become the pastor at St. Mary's when the opportunity presented itself. Truth be told, St. Mary's was on the verge of collapse before Father O'Toole's arrival. The Diocese plan was to let Father O'Toole *run* the parish for one or maybe two years, then close it down and sell it to a developer for a big profit. It was expected that Father O'Toole would retire after that. It was a clever and convenient strategy by the Diocese and their legal think tank. Fortunately, or unfortunately, Father O'Toole actually grew the parish in the short time that he had been pastor. Prior to the protestors' movement, St.

Mary's Parish had become bigger and stronger than ever. Father O'Toole initially felt a youthful resurgence as the parish grew around him, but in the wake of this protest movement, Father O'Toole was not sure how much longer he could last. He was clearly nearing his breaking point.

The easiest way to resolve the problem would have been to reassign Father O'Toole to another parish. However, the higher-ups in the Diocese thought that move would signal the Church's acquiescence to the will of the protestors. Besides, reassignment did not guarantee that the same thing would not happen at a different location. The last thing the Diocese wanted was to engage in war on two fronts. The Diocesan leaders asked Father O'Toole to retire, but that conversation was even shorter than Father O'Toole's attempt at dialogue with the protestors. With all the brain power and money of the Diocese, nobody had any clear solution for resolving the situation. And they also knew that they were dealing equally with a very hard-headed old Irishman who never backed down from a fight before. Thus, they were all stuck and decided nothing could be done other than to ride it out. The situation evolved into a chicken fight between three entities to see just who had the most stamina.

One thing was for sure—the thick concrete walls and enormous oak doors of St. Mary's that once created a spiritual and a physical safe-haven for the parishioners could no longer keep the din and ruckus of the protestors outside. In calmer days, the only sound that might have been heard from the outside during a Mass was the occasional siren on a police car or ambulance. Now, even the sirens couldn't be heard over the protestors' fanatical rants and chanting.

Wil 3

Chapter four

It was 8:30 AM, and the church was empty except for a handful of people. The soles of Father O'Toole's well-made Italian dress shoes sounded like rim shots echoing through the old stone church as he made his way up the marble floor to the confessional. After he sat in silent prayer for a couple of minutes, the light outside the confessional turned on to signal Father O'Toole's readiness to hear confessions. The inside of the confessional was almost completely dark from the mahogany wood and mesh screen that separated priest from penitent. It smelled slightly moldy, but mostly, it just smelled old. Yet Father O'Toole was at peace when he was inside the confessional. It was the one time that he couldn't be bothered by the Diocese and even the noise from the outside could not penetrate the confessional room inside the Church. Hearing confessions and granting absolution was the part of his job that Father O'Toole enjoyed the most. Even after so many years of hearing confessions, he sometimes still felt uncomfortable hearing the devious things people had done. But his discomfort was well worth it when he made the penitent feel better after he afforded the forgiveness he or she truly yearned for.

Confession was an extraordinarily personal and humbling experience for sinners if done properly. Father O'Toole strove to make sure it was spiritually rewarding for those who bared their souls to him. Deep down, however, sometimes Father O'Toole wished that nobody would confess as he did enjoy the few minutes of serenity by himself in silent prayer of the dark room.

Dylan Ray knelt quietly in a church pew. He held his rosary beads so tight that his hands started to swell. He did not make eye contact with Father O'Toole when the priest walked past him on the way to the confessional. Father O'Toole didn't seem to pay Dylan Ray any attention either even though he was a stranger in the church where Father O'Toole knew just about everyone. A few minutes after Father O'Toole had entered the confessional, Dylan Ray rose to his feet and shuffled down the old marble aisle to the confessional booth. His footsteps were not as loud as Father O'Toole's, but they were loud enough to snap Father O'Toole from his silent prayer and caused him to sit up straight and ready himself for the job at hand. The rickety old confessional door squeaked and chirped and screamed out a need for its hinges to be oiled as it was slowly opened and shut. The light outside the confessional went dim.

"Forgive me, Father, for I have sinned … I think that is right? It's been a while," said Dylan Ray.

"Relax, my son, there is no script. Just tell me how you sinned so that His Most Gracious Lord can pardon you," said Father O'Toole warmly.

"Father," asked Dylan Ray, "Does God forgive all sins?"

"Of course, He does. Our Lord gave His only begotten son, Jesus Christ, up for death so that all of mankind's sins could be forgiven. Now, between you and me, I have been doing this for a good number of years, so you probably can't confess anything to me that I haven't heard before. Just relax and get it off your chest."

"Father, are there some sins that are worse than others?" asked Dylan Ray, almost sarcastically. Father O'Toole paused. He was briefly distracted by the sound of the oak doors of the church opening. Parishioners had started to arrive for Mass and he could also now hear the protestors outside as their ranks had grown since he first spied them from the mezzanine earlier that morning. He quickly looked at his watch and hoped that no one else would come to confess because he had a strange feeling that this confession was going to be difficult and maybe time-consuming.

"Well, son, all sins offend God. But practically speaking, I suppose that some sins are worse than others."

"Father, is it a sin to steal a loaf of bread to feed your starving family?" asked Dylan Ray, again sarcastically. Father O'Toole had heard this question, disguised sometimes as religious quandary for years, but he never thought much about it or if it had deeper meaning. However, maybe the way the Dylan Ray asked it brought Father O'Toole back to a time when he and his older brother Matthew would steal bread so that they would not starve to death in shanty town.

Father O'Toole did not enjoy this bad memory and he certainly did not appreciate the tone in Dylan Ray's voice as the hair on the back of his neck started to stand.

He wanted to yell at him to stop playing games and confess already, but he calmed himself and responded, "Son, a sin is a sin regardless of the reason for committing it. Are you seeking forgiveness and absolution or are you seeking justification?"

"Well, Father, I guess that is for God to decide now," said Dylan Ray defiantly as he pushed open the confessional door and proceeded toward the exit of the church.

Father O'Toole sat in silence for a moment then said, knowingly to himself, but out loud, "Very well, go in peace" as he made the sign of the cross. The light outside the confessional remained off.

Outside the church, Nico Rossi parked his 1978 BMW R100s motorcycle in the parking lot opposite the protestors. It looked like it had seen better days, but the hum of the engine indicated that it was extremely well-maintained and could still hang with any motorcycle half its age. Nico took off his helmet and sunglasses and navigated through the protestors. The early morning motorcycle ride to church woke him up slightly. In his sleepwalking-style gait, he did the best he could not to *unintentionally* bump anyone, at least not too hard. As he opened the door to the church, Dylan Ray exited past him. Neither person noticed one another.

Wil 3

Chapter five

When Nico entered the church, he picked his head up just enough to notice that the church was less than half full. Being half full was the new norm. He remembered what St. Mary's was like when he came back to it, shortly after Father O'Toole's arrival, when the attendance had skyrocketed. Nico thought the agitation caused by the protestors was keeping people away or maybe it was from constant road closures and detours from the revitalization of the Strip District. Or perhaps Father O'Toole was just too tired and unable to do was what necessary to sustain a congregation that had grown. Whatever the reason, the reality was now there were three times as many protestors outside chanting and holding signs than there were parishioners inside praying and holding rosary beads on Sunday mornings.

Nico half sleep-walked, half death-marched across the marble aisle to the altar. He paused for a moment, blessed himself in front of the enormous golden crucifix on the back wall at the center of the altar and proceeded to make his way to a small room behind the altar. He noticed the light on the confessional was not lit, so he assumed Father O'Toole would be there getting ready for Mass. He was surprised when he opened the door to the back-office room and nobody was there.

The back room behind the altar was a glorified storage closet. Nico had converted half of it into his own personal closet to keep his church clothes. Otherwise, there was nothing there but a small table, a small couch, some folding chairs, the unconsecrated communion wafers and communion wine, and a small sink for washing the chalices after mass was over. Nico went to his clothing rack and put on a button-down shirt over top of his Ramones t-shirt after he threw his black leather jacket onto the small table. His back was to the door as he put on a pair of dress pants when Father O'Toole came into the room.

"Hey, my son, thanks for coming today," said Father O'Toole.

17

"Yeah, Padre, it is a madhouse out there today. Did you see it?" said Nico with his back still turned to Father O'Toole as he buckled his belt.

When he turned around to greet the priest, Father O'Toole exclaimed, "Jesus, Mary and Joseph! Look at you! It looks like you haven't slept in a month of Sundays, praise the Lord!"

"Maybe a month and a half, but who is counting?" replied Nico who struggled to comb his helmet hair up from his head.

"Seriously, how long has it been since you have slept … I mean … really slept?"

Nico stopped and paused for moment. When he continued to finish dressing, he half muttered an exasperated response, "Maybe a year … or so. Maybe more. I dunno. I don't much think about it."

"Oh, I see. About a year, eh? About the same time you stopped receiving Holy Communion. Isn't that about right?"

Nico turned quickly to face Father O'Toole to respond to the query, "Communion! You know I shouldn't even be in church, let alone getting communion. I definitely shouldn't be on the altar. But the only thing scarcer than priests these days are altar boys … so you are just lucky I feel bad for you, that's all," said Nico with a look more of desperation than defiance.

"Well, son, I am glad you are here and I am thankful for your help, praise the Lord. And if it makes you feel better thinking that you are a hypocrite, then fine. Have it your way. But you haven't sinned, not in the way you think. I am pretty sure that I am the authority on this one."

Nico and Father O'Toole both walked together to the back of the church to start the procession to the altar for Mass to begin. The massive pipe organ bellowed loudly with fewer and fewer parishioners in attendance to absorb any sound. It was good, though, because it was the only time the noise from the protestors could not be heard. As Nico walked with Father O'Toole, one thought could not escape his head: "When is ambivalence *not* a sin?"

Chapter six

Nico and Father O'Toole waited a few moments at the back of the church while the pipe organ music concluded. The organist then instructed the congregation to open their Hymnals and join in singing the processional hymn. As the two began their procession from the rear of the church to the altar, Nico led the way by carrying the readings, which were bounded in a weathered, red leather cover and adorned in bright golden Latin inscriptions. Father O'Toole simply held his hands together in prayer while "How Great Thou Art" bellowed through the pipe organ. Each week, the music from the pipe organ seemed louder and louder while the voices from the pews sounded less and less. Today was no exception.

At that exact moment, Nico experienced his first taste of lucidity for the day. He noticed the snapping and cracking sound of Father O'Toole's shoes on the marble floor could not be heard even though he was only a couple feet behind him. And despite few parishioners in attendance, the pipe organ didn't completely drown out their voices, although not one true or distinct voice could be heard. The sound that emanated from the gathering was one of warmth. It was more of a feeling than a sound. Nico felt the vibration from their voices and from the pipe organ and the warm feeling of an occasional sun ray on exposed skin when they sometimes found a piece of stained glass to move through. Most importantly, Nico realized that the ruckus of protestors outside the church was eclipsed by this warm feeling of sound, but he knew that wouldn't last. Even if for just one fleeting moment, the entirety of the world outside the church was muted by warm earmuffs and Nico tried his best to enjoy it.

Nico was completely puzzled why these seemingly instant moments of clarity occurred, and furthermore, why they never lasted more than just a moment. He also struggled to understand why he had absolute focus of presence, but at times, he completely lacked all comprehension or meaning as to what he was experiencing or what was happening around him. In his mind, he equated his situation to looking at abstract art through high-definition lenses; sometimes, he could see every brush stroke down to the individual bristle; he could see every pin-sized paint drop; he could see the minute wrinkles in the canvas and under each wrinkle, each single pore that remained free of paint. Yet, he did not know what he was looking at or what the artist had hoped to create.

As the tandem made their way to the altar, both bowed and moved the final steps forward. Nico took the left side of the altar and stood in front of his very ornate, oversized wooden chair that looked like a king's throne. Father O'Toole took his place behind the altar. When the music and singing stopped, Father O'Toole addressed the congregation.

"Welcome, brothers and sisters. Thank you for celebrating with me today ... especially in what is turning out to be a turbulent time for our little parish. Before we begin today's Mass, let us take a few moments to remember that Jesus said blessed is he who is persecuted in my name. And if anyone strikes you on the left cheek, turn and offer them your right. And especially remember that we all are God's children, including our brothers and sisters outside. And we all lose our way sometimes. And we all sin. And we all need forgiveness," said Father O'Toole as he pointed in the general direction of the protestors outside the church.

"Please join me as we pray, I confess to almighty God, and to you, my brothers and sisters that I have sinned through my own fault, inn my thoughts and in my words, in what I have done and what I have failed to do. And I ask the Blessed Mary, ever Virgin, all the angels and saints, and you, my brothers and sisters, to pray for me to the Lord our God. Amen."

When the opening prayer concluded, Father O'Toole motioned to everyone, including Nico, to take their seats as he made final adjustments on the altar before heading to his own oversized, wooden, king-like throne opposite Nico. Nico took his seat and quickly sank deep into the plush, velvet cushions of the throne chair. He sat peacefully as he smelled the tapestries around him that were seasoned with incense burned over the course of many, many years.

Nico remembered when he stood in a museum and held the hand of an energetic, bouncy girl who was quite happy to be there with him. Although he could not see her face, her long hair flowed down her back, allowing him to detect the faint hint of incense, most likely from a burning the previous night. He remembered the feeling of being in love and started to feel that warmth once more. He reached for her hair to take a closer smell when a security guard standing next to him cleared his throat. Nico looked at the security guard, then turned back to his girl, but she was gone. Her unexpected absence caught Nico off guard and caused him to take a scared, sudden deep inhale, which snapped him from his daydream.

Again, Father O'Toole cleared his throat to get Nico's attention. Nico focused his sight on Father O'Toole and noticed he was attempting to discreetly signal to Nico that it was now his turn to take the podium at the front of the altar to do the First Reading.

Chapter seven

Nico attempted to look deliberate as he slowly rose from his seat and made his way to the altar to stand beside Father O'Toole. When he was just about two or three feet away, a commotion in the pews drew his attention from Father O'Toole as both men looked out into the congregation. There, about three quarters of the way from the back of the church, Dylan Ray, the almost-repentant visitor who attempted to confess to Father O'Toole before Mass, was pushing people in the pew out of his way. He quickly made it to the aisle and immediately charged down the marble pathway toward the altar.

Without breaking stride, Dylan Ray pulled a stainless steel .45 caliber 1911 semi-automatic pistol from his waistband and squeezed off two shots from about twenty feet in front of the altar. The unabated echo throughout the cement interior of the massive church made it sound like many more than two shots were fired.

Horrified parishioners screamed in fear and shock. Many of them were simply too old to do anything more. Younger parishioners burst through the main door at the back of the church. Thinking they were now being attacked by parishioners, some of the protesters dropped their signs and ran, although some dropped their signs and threw punches at the fleeing parishioners. When shouts of "He's got a gun!" could be heard outside, everyone ran in all directions. Many people were nearly struck by unsuspecting motorists who were looking for a place to park for Sunday morning shopping and fresh produce. Several men and women suffered black eyes, bloody noses and fat lips from the collisions between fleeing people blinded by fear and those who simply shopped for their goods in stores and markets adjacent to the church. Car doors slammed and tires squealed as screams and cries filled the air. Pandemonium ensued. At some point during this terrifying mess, a few people had found enough composure to make frantic calls to 9-1-1.

It had been several years—a long time as a matter of fact—but once again, pain, fear, overwhelming sadness and a little bit of bloodshed had made its way back to the Strip District.

Chapter eight

Detective Ben Martin and Detective Francis Kelly sat in their unmarked police car about one mile away from St. Mary's Church.

"Shots fired in the Strip District" was the first call through police dispatch, but the exact locale was not specified.

The two detectives readied themselves and waited. Less than thirty seconds later, the second call came through and indicated that shots were fired from *inside* St. Mary's Church. The detectives attempted to drive to the scene. But by that point, fleeing parishioners and other patrons in the Strip District were already in their cars driving at speeds beyond reckless in both traffic lanes, and at times, on sidewalks, in a desperate attempt to put distance between themselves and the church. Within a short time, the sound of the deep hum of spinning rotary blades was heard from the police helicopter that circled the vicinity.

Inside the church, Nico found himself with his arms and hands over his head as he lay on the altar floor. At first, he wasn't sure what had happened. He tried to focus himself and wondered if he just had an *episode* and if so, how long was he out? At that point, he thought it best to open his eyes and start from there. He saw Father O'Toole, who was also on the ground clutching his rosary beads.

"Father," said Nico in a very loud whisper, "Are you okay? Did you get hit?"

"No," said Father O'Toole, "I … I think I am alright."

Nico eventually started to raise himself from his belly until he locked eyes with Dylan Ray, who sat on his legs in the middle of the aisle about twenty feet away from him. Momentarily, Nico thought he should charge the shooter, but then the sight of the chrome .45 in Dylan Ray's right hand suggested that was probably not the best idea. So, he froze. And as the two continued their staring contest, Nico's thoughts started to become clearer as he recognized the gravity of what just happened and what still was happening. When Nico fully realized the shooter still held the gun, he became paralyzed by fear and thought he was incapable of any type of physical response if it was necessary. He simply hoped the shooter would not take any further action.

After a few moments, Dylan Ray sat up off his legs and kneeled up straight. He then lowered his head, almost to the floor in the direction of Nico, and started to cry. His cries quickly turned into full-blown sobs. Then, half sobbing, half yelling in anguish, he called out to Nico, "Forgive me, Lord, I didn't mean it … Forgive me Jesus, I didn't know what I was doing …" Ray soon broke down into uncontrollable weeping, just after he slid his gun on the floor toward the altar in the direction of Nico.

Nico knew that he needed to get that gun, so he struggled and tried his best to push the paralyzing fear aside. Quickly, as much as was possible under the circumstances, he pulled himself to his feet and moved toward the gun, all the while keeping his eyes on Dylan Ray. Dylan, on the other hand, only continued to weep more and beg Jesus for forgiveness.

Nico bent down and picked up the gun. Although he had never handled any kind of gun before, he instinctively raised it up and somewhat aimed it in Dylan Ray's general direction as it shook and wobbled in his unsteady hand. He then saw what appeared to be a single bullet, without a brass shell casing around it, lying on the ground about three feet from the altar, directly in front of where he stood when the shots were fired. He did not go toward it for a closer look, but rather, started to slowly move sideways toward Father O'Toole. After one or two shuffle steps to the left, Nico stepped on something hard like a stone. Nico picked up his foot and underneath it, he saw a second bullet on the ground, which was beside the first one, a little less than two feet away. This bullet also did not have a brass casing around it. Nico bent down and picked it up, while keeping his eyes on Dylan Ray. He continued to shuffle toward Father O'Toole as he also tried to keep one eye on Dylan Ray and the other on the bullet that he now held in his hand.

"What the fu- …," mumbled Nico to himself in astonishment.

As the woeful cries continued to come from Ray and with the gun now in his hand, Nico sensed that the danger most likely had passed. His physical abilities started to come back to him as his body began to relax a bit, although the hand holding the gun still shook. He moved across the altar to where Father O'Toole was still lying and helped the old priest to his feet. Dylan Ray then changed his position so that he remained facing Nico as he continued to wail and lament and ask Jesus for forgiveness. Neither Nico nor Father O'Toole said anything to each other. Nico walked to the back of the altar and grabbed the chalice of communion wine. Before he could offer it to Father O'Toole and say "Blood of Christ," Father O'Toole grabbed it from his hand and gulped the whole chalice down.

"Freeze, nobody move! Pittsburgh Police!"

Ben Martin and Francis Kelly, the two City of Pittsburgh detectives, were the first to arrive on the scene as they stormed into the back door of the church with their guns drawn. For the most part, their command to freeze was wholeheartedly ignored by all. Dylan Ray continued to weep and wail, Father O'Toole refilled the chalice with wine and started to drink it and Nico Rossi laid the chrome .45 on the altar, then took a seat on Father O'Toole's chair. Ben Martin and Francis Kelly approached from the back of the church and moved hastily toward the altar.

Chapter nine

Shortly after the arrival of Martin and Kelly, uniformed Pittsburgh Police officers, the SWAT unit, firetrucks and ambulances appeared. It was quickly determined that any active shooter situation was not at hand, and as such, most of the secondary responders dispersed. Some uniformed police officers remained on hand to secure St. Mary's as it was now a crime scene. The officers taped off the outside of the church as well as the more immediate vicinity around the altar. Crime scene investigators marked and photographed four distinct spots on the floor—two spots where the brass shell casings were found and, maybe for the first time in their careers, two spots where the actual intact bullets were located, approximately ten feet away from the discharged brass casings. Several officers also began to canvas the Strip District to find actual parishioners who were present during the shooting and surveyed any incidental damage to other businesses caused by the panic of the churchgoers and protestors.

The local media was also quick to arrive on the scene. Without any official statement yet to be offered, speculation was rampant among both the media and patrons of the Strip District. Was the shooting an act of extremist terrorism? Was it an act of domestic terrorism? Was is simply the signs of repeated failure in the mental health system? Was this a gun issue, and most importantly, were more attacks forthcoming? After waiting for the official police spokesman to issue a statement and having obtained an initial sense of security, the media also began scouring the area to get statements from witnesses for news footage.

Inside the church, Detective Kelly had Dylan Ray on his feet with his hands cuffed behind his back. Two uniformed officers each had ahold of Dylan Ray under his shoulders as they received final instruction from the senior detective. "Take him back to the station for questioning. Hopefully, he will calm down a bit. I haven't gotten anything from him at all, not even his name. He just keeps screaming for Jesus to forgive him," said Detective Kelly. Detective Martin started the initial interview with Nico.

"I know this is difficult, but you and the priest are probably the best witnesses to what exactly happened. So please, just tell me what you remember. I mean, it was a shooting, it happened about fifteen minutes ago, not much has changed between then and now." said Detective Martin.

"Yeah, I got it. Like I said, I got up from my seat over there and I went to the altar over here. When I was about three … maybe two feet away from Father O'Toole, I heard a noise, like rustling or something, but it was sort of loud … I turned to see what was going on and I just saw that screaming lunatic running up at the both of us," said Nico.

"Hey Padre," said Detective Francis Kelly, "do you mind walking over here for a bit and talking with me?" Father O'Toole, now with a bottle of unconsecrated communion wine in hand, walked over to Detective Kelly to discuss the events.

"Was he screaming when he shot?" continued Detective Martin.

"No … I don't think so. I remember … commotion … disturbance from the pews … it was the sound of people moving unexpectedly. But I don't remember him screaming or saying anything … there was just … noise. Then a gunshot … I guess he really didn't start to scream until after he shot."

"Just one shot?"

"Uh … no, no … I guess there were two shots … I thought at the time, maybe there were more. Sounded like more. But, I mean, I saw the bullets on the ground … I can't say that I remember both shots … Like I said, just noise, then a bright light, then complete silence."

"A bright light? You didn't say anything about that before."

"No, I guess I didn't …"

"Well, what was that about? Where did it come from? What caused it? Was it a muzzle flash, maybe?"

"Could have been, I guess, I don't know. All I know is that there was a lot of noise, then a bright light … a feeling of being warm

… then I picked up my head and the church was empty. Then the loon was just sitting in the aisle screaming for Jesus to forgive him."

Detective Francis Kelly started to question Father O'Toole in a tone that was significantly warmer and more respectful than that of Detective Ben Martin. Father O'Toole was visibly shaking. Three-quarters of a bottle of unconsecrated communion wine did nothing to calm his nerves. Detective Kelly put his hand on the old priest's shoulder. "Father, please excuse my language, but what in God's name happened here today?"

After a long pause and another big swig of wine, Father O'Toole responded. "Sir, please excuse my language … but how the hell should I know?"

"Well, just tell me what you saw or what you remember. We can fill in the rest later."

"I was at the altar. My helper, Nico, was with me today. It was his turn to do the First Reading, but I could see he was daydreaming. So, I tried to signal him. I got his attention, but he started to walk towards me instead of walking to the podium to read … then an explosion or something and a bright light … then I was pushed to the ground."

"Is the shooter a parishioner, a visitor, a guest of somebody, do you know him?"

"I don't know," said the shaken priest after taking another chug of wine, "he did… he said something, I dunno, it all happened too fast for this old man, praise Jesus."

"What did he say?"

"Huh, well … this morning, before Mass, a man came into the confessional … then, before you arrived and cuffed that guy, he was screaming about only wanting to steal one loaf of bread."

"What? Not sure I get that? What did the man say in confession?"

"I can't say."

"Oh, I get it. Protected communication, like lawyer-client privilege. Well, listen Padre, I respect your willingness to follow the rules, but if you want us to make sense of what happened, you might have to bend the rules a little and tell us."

"No. I can't say because I want to protect him; I can't say because he didn't make any sense. He asked a few questions about what it means to sin and about stealing a loaf of bread to feed starving children … but he really didn't say anything more that made sense. When he started screaming about only wanting one loaf of bread, before you guys got here, I remembered the confession from this morning, and I thought maybe it was the same guy."

"Was it? Was the shooter the same as the confessor?"

"I can't be sure. I can't see faces through the confessional screen wall."

"Thank you, Father. You can go now. I know none of this makes any sense to you. It is too early for us to arrive at conclusions. Right now, all seems to be safe for you and your church. Try to get through today. I know, it will be rough. If you need me, call me. Here is my card with my cell number on the back. Otherwise, I am sure we will chat in the future. Don't worry, we know how to find you."

Chapter ten

Father O'Toole put what little remained in the wine bottle down on a table, exited the church, and headed to the rectory. His head spun so much at that point that he neglected to check on Nico before he left. He entered the rectory and just stood at his living room window that faced out over the Strip District. As he watched the chaotic situation develop and unfold around him, Father O'Toole started to take stock of his life once again. He had been going through that mental exercise more frequently in recent years, but he never thought much of it. Reviewing past successes and failures, regrets, opportunities not seized and other various bucket list items was a common thing to do by anybody of his age. But having one's life pass before his own eyes in an instant, at any age, was traumatic, to say the least. Following his near-death experience, the review of his life's work was performed in a less-cursory fashion.

The large amount of wine consumed before 9:00 AM on a rather empty belly added an additional ingredient to the soup that already sloshed in his head. He moved from the window to his couch and stared up at the old plastered ceiling. "How did I get here?" he said out loud to himself. He wasn't thinking about the immediate shooting, though. In time, all those answers would be readily available. But how or why did he… become a priest?

Father O'Toole thought about his parents, which was something that he rarely did. Colin O'Toole and Mary Margaret Flaherty emigrated just before the start of the Great Depression. In later years, any time someone would reference the "luck of the Irish," Father O'Toole would indignantly tell the story of how his very lucky Irish parents were fortunate enough to leave the blight and famine of their family farms and meadows of their native land only to relocate to the blight and famine of the cobblestone, potholed streets of the shanty town, now known as the Strip District. One of the last things he remembered his father telling him was that living here was much like living in Ireland—everyone was still poor, dirty, cold, hungry and scared to fall asleep at night because they did not know if they would wake up the next day. But, as luck would have it, here in America, they also got to experience discrimination as the Irish were clearly on the lowest rung of society's ladder. So, in at least one regard, they did have more than they had back home in Ireland. God bless America.

Thomas' parents didn't know each other until they accidentally met one day, while each wandered the streets in search of ... something. Soon both realized they lived at opposite ends of the shanty town where they both resided in shacks—literally. Within a couple months of their meeting, they were married. The marriage of Thomas' parents wasn't necessarily based on love so much as it was based upon the need for survival. There was strength in numbers, so Thomas' father rented a clean suit and his mother did her best to make a white dress—which she sold to another young Irish woman almost immediately after the wedding ceremony—and the two were married in St. Mary's Parish by the new priest, Father James R. Cox, who eventually went on to fame leading "Cox's Army" in the Strip District and across the country.

Immediately following the wedding, Colin O'Toole returned his rented suit, put on his dirty, raggedy old clothes and trudged to the other end of the shanty town to take any items of value or use from Mary Margaret's shack. The few spools of thread and sewing needles easily fit into his pocket, which allowed him to carry the oil lamp. He then removed a two-foot by three-foot piece of tin from the roof that would be useful in patching the roof of the new family's homestead at the other end of the Strip. Colin felt bad about leaving a gaping hole, so he used his hands to remove clay and weed—almost sod—that was on the ground to fill in the gap. If nothing else, hopefully the next Irishman that inhabited the abandoned shack would feel more at home with a *sod* roof over his head.

The lack of financial resources or adequate housing never stopped the Irish from procreating. Irish Catholics felt it was their holy obligation to have as many children as possible, God willing. Within a very short time, Colin and Mary Margaret were blessed with three sons born in less than four years—Irish triplets. Colin eventually acquired another shack and physically pushed it through the Strip

District until he could abut it against his existing shack. He removed the now two interior walls between the shacks and used the extra wood that became available to make one bed for all three children to sleep. The walls of the shack were simple uninsulated plywood that rattled and shook in the windy winter months. It was far less than adequate, but it was home. And even if it wasn't full of food or heat, it was filled with love—love of family and love of God and the genuine belief that with God, love and hard work, all things were possible. Colin and his family did the best they could to make the most of it with smiles on their dirty faces.

As time passed, the O'Toole family seemed to be more cursed than blessed. Tragedy and death were the norm throughout the shanty town, but even more so with the O'Toole family. Thomas was the fourth-born child and was three years younger than his brother Matthew, the last of the original three children. The blessing of his birth quickly turned tragic as Mary Margaret died from complications following delivery, despite the best efforts of the midwife. Thomas never knew his mother. They only met once, very briefly.

In fact, by the time Thomas O'Toole was old enough to appreciate the bleak circumstances he lived in, only Matthew and his father were still alive. Shortly after his birth and the death of his mother, the Strip District and numerous immigrant families were rocked by a horrific explosion in the local textile mill/sweatshop that employed James, the first-born O'Toole son, as well as many other immigrant boys and young men. But Thomas O'Toole was too young to realize it. Likewise, and equally thankfully, Thomas O'Toole was too young to appreciate the death of the second oldest child, Mark, who was killed by a train, most likely in his attempt to gather coal that had fallen off the hopper cars. Thomas O'Toole was alive, but too young to experience or appreciate any of those tragedies. But the story of his family's humble beginnings, as well as the death of his mother and two brothers, were relayed to him second hand several times throughout his youth by teachers and friends who knew the family.

Unfortunately, Thomas was five years old when Matthew died in the family shack from a mysterious wound that had become infected due to not being properly treated. Thomas remembered holding his father's rough hand at the grave site. Father Cox was the only other person there. The fresh mud and dirt visible over the old, dried mud and dirt on his father's clothing was a clear sign to Thomas that his father had dug the grave, probably because he didn't have enough money to pay someone else to dig the hole.

Unlike the other deceased members of his family, Thomas thought about Matthew more regularly, though still not often. When Thomas thought of Matthew, he distinctly remembered his voice and a few of the conversations they had while they were standing in a soup line or after they had stolen food from a local vendor. And over the years, Matthew had found his way into Thomas' dreams. And despite the tragedy of his demise, the dreams that Matthew invaded were never scary or even sad. Matthew appeared always as Thomas remembered him—as a little boy about eight or nine years old. Sometimes he smiled, sometimes he didn't. But the odd thing was that he never spoke. Not one word. Ever. Thomas wasn't sure why Matthew didn't talk in the dreams, but he remembered that after he woke up following a Matthew dream, he always felt good.

"Maybe I will be with them soon?" Father O'Toole said to himself. But now, after the quick trip down tragedy lane, Father O'Toole was confronted with a more immediate question—why am I still here? It was no longer the broader, big picture question of "How did I get here?" But rather, the question of why he was still alive following the shooting. It made perfect sense to him: if he was truly an O'Toole, which he was quite certain that he was, then shouldn't his death result from an unforeseen, extraordinarily tragic event? Wouldn't assassination by a deranged lunatic while attempting to conduct a Catholic Mass fall squarely into that category? "How am I still alive?" muttered Father O'Toole again to himself.

Wishing to think no more about … anything, Father O'Toole rolled over on the couch and pulled a blanket down on top of himself for a nap. He napped for a little more than an hour until he was jarred from his slumber by the shrill sound of a telephone ringing. When Father O'Toole opened his eyes, he knew a constantly ringing phone would be expected in the days to come.

Chapter eleven

After spending the entirety of his shift at St. Mary's Church, Detective Kelly hitched a ride with a uniformed cop back to the police station so he could start drafting the initial report. His partner, Detective Benjamin Martin, stayed behind to continue with the investigation, which was sure to last deep into the night and for days to follow. When he arrived back at the station, Detective Kelly decided to go home instead of starting the paperwork. That could wait until the morning.

Detective Francis Kelly was the last of a dying breed of "old school" law enforcement officers. He was tall and strong as a young man. After he graduated from high school, he went to work full-time in the steel mills. Although the money was good, especially for a person right out of high school, he had a couple of close calls that almost resulted in his permanent disfigurement or death. Francis realized he was being put into dangerous situations because of his size and strength. He believed he would always be able to make money, but he only had one life to live. So, Francis did whatever he could do and made many promises that he could not yet fulfill to every single politico that gave him five minutes of their time. Eventually, a call was made and Francis was accepted into the police academy.

While at the academy, instructors worked with Kelly more so than other cadets because they saw in him the opportunity to create a true "super cop." Once he received formal instruction and learned how to use his size and speed to maximize his success, he quickly rose to the top of his class in all fitness components. Upon graduation from the academy, Francis Kelly was assigned as a beat cop in some of the worst city neighborhoods.

After the glow of becoming a police officer had worn off, Patrolman Kelly realized that he was being used solely for his physical ability and again, was being put into some bad situations— not unlike his days in the steel mill. Worse yet, the superior officers, who he now reported to and who assigned him his duties, were nothing more than politically well-connected individuals with guns. Most of his superiors never achieved the level of his success he had when they were in the academy and none ever worked the streets. Their shortsightedness and use of Kelly as a "one man wrecking crew" were only going to get him killed…quickly.

Francis Kelly had strong faith, though. He firmly believed that the majority of people, for the most part, were good and he could serve and protect those in his community better than anyone else. He just needed to find a better way to accomplish that task without risking his life at every turn. Instinctively, he fell back on the only true weapon that he had in his arsenal—his body. His imposing stature commanded respect and everyone that crossed paths with him assumed that he was a complete badass looking for a brawl. His size, combined with a gun on his hip, made it rather easy for him to get people's attention. And when he had people's attention, he did something that really wasn't taught in the academy—he talked to them.

All the time. Not just at a crime scene. Good guys, bad guys, neighborhood guys or interlopers, it didn't matter. Kelly talked to all of them, which soon earned him the reputation for being one of the "good cops." He watched out for people, especially the innocent ones. He knew who the bad guys were and what their racket was, but he also would not hassle them, so long as he had no reason. And that was his message—don't give him a reason to come back here angry.

After a few years on the streets, Francis Kelly had indeed turned into everything his instructors at the academy hoped he would become—a super cop. As a reward for his progress, he was eventually promoted to the rank of detective. Although he received this promotion with smiles on the outside, inside he hated it. He would no longer be walking the neighborhoods and instead, would be sitting in a squad car of some sort. He would be doing investigations only. He would now have to report to more supervisors with even less intelligence who were even higher on the political food chain. The whole thought of it turned his stomach. But what was he going to do? He certainly couldn't turn down a promotion, so he just did what he needed to do to get by.

As the years went by, some faster than others, Detective Francis Kelly found himself doing less policing and much more paper pushing. He had spent more years as a detective than he did as a beat cop, but the memories of walking the streets during his beat cop years were fresh in his mind as he struggled to forget the things that he saw as a detective, which haunted his dreams. But he couldn't dwell on that. He was too close to retirement.

The shooting at St. Mary's Church bothered Detective Kelly in a profound way. It didn't matter to him that nobody was killed. He always believed that schools and religious places were off limits for violence. Everyone should be entitled to one or two truly safe places, especially if a home was no longer one of them. Unfortunately, violence in schools and in religious institutions had now become commonplace. Perhaps when he was younger, he would have felt a desire to put all that to an end. Now, his only desire was to stay away from dealing with any of it. He realized he was tired and had become ineffective at his job. Retirement couldn't come soon enough, he thought as he crossed out one more day with a big red "X" on his calendar that hung in his bedroom.

Although he was not a deeply religious man in a traditional sense, Detective Kelly routinely said two prayers a day: He said the first prayer when he holstered the exact same standard service revolver that was issued to him following his graduation from the police academy. It was a simple prayer where he asked, well, no one specifically, to watch over him and see that he returned home at the end of the day without having to use his gun. Upon his return, as he hung his holster in his bedroom closet, he would thank, whomever, for his safe return.

Wil 3

Chapter twelve

Detective Ben Martin was a new, 21st century law enforcement officer. He was highly motivated to surmount every obstacle in front of him. He was a tireless worker and he never gave up, regardless of the situation. He was sleek and streamlined, like a European sports car.

If a person didn't know better, he would have thought that Detective Ben Martin was a blue-blood through and through, but in fact, he was a second-generation Italian-American. His grandfather, Gaetano Martino, came to this country by himself as a young teenager with only the clothes on his back and no understanding of the English language. Fortunately, the Italian slum section at the center of the tiny mill town thirty miles west of Pittsburgh was full of Italian immigrants who excelled at taking care of their own, especially the young ones who had no other family in America.

After a year or so of living on the streets, Gaetano was eventually *adopted* by Jovanni and Mary DeLuca, Italian immigrants who had no children of their own. In exchange for taking Gaetano into their home, he started to work with Jovanni, who was the foreman of a general contracting business. It wasn't so much of an official business, but rather, an amalgamation of a few skilled laborers—a painter, a carpenter, a plumber and an almost-electrician—who worked for one boss. The boss was a decent man who always made sure that his crew was paid, albeit poorly, for their services. The boss was not Italian and it was rare in those days for anyone to hire immigrants, so they were all loyal to him and were thankful for their employment.

In only a couple of years, Gaetano demonstrated that he was the hardest worker and the most skilled at detail work and was added to the crew full-time. By age twenty-five, Gaetano had risen to the rank of foreman, the position previously held by his adoptive father. The heavy lifting was reserved for Gaetano as well as the more skilled work too, as the rest of the crew showed their age from the years of hard labor. When the crew's boss unexpectedly died one day from a heart attack, the men were both shocked and saddened by the loss. But mostly, they feared the immediate future and wondered how they would now support themselves? Gaetano, on the other hand, seized the opportunity. He used the money that he had saved over the years and started a new business—Guy Martin Contracting and Remodeling. The original crew was brought on as the labor force. In less than three months under Gaetano's direction, more than a year's worth of jobs were lined up. The significant increase in workload, combined with the increase in revenue, necessitated the hiring of additional workers, which allowed the original crew to work as supervisors and not laborers.

When Gaetano married Camelia, he bought a house two blocks away from Mary and Jovanni, so the family he hoped to start would always remain close. Gaetano's three children were raised as proud Americans with strong, traditional Italian culture and family values. Rarely would a day pass without a visit from the grandparents. Sundays also included the entire family going to church together and of course, the traditional Seven Fishes meal every Christmas Eve.

The youngest of Gaetano's children and only boy, Jovanni "Joey" Martin, followed in his father's footsteps and became a builder as well. When the time was right, "Big Joe" Martin, as he was known, started his own business—Martin Custom Homes. Big Joe employed Guy Martin Contracting and Remodeling as his subcontractor on every job. Big Joe's business had become very profitable for all involved. Things only improved for the family when Big Joe bought two adjacent parcels of land in Fox Chapel, a wealthy Pittsburgh suburb.

Big Joe used his own men to build the only home he would ever own. It was a beautiful three-story brick home that Big Joe said was a gift to his fiancé. When construction was complete, he built a second, much smaller ranch house on the adjacent plot which he gifted to his parents so that they could always stay close. At first, Gaetano did not understand why his son wanted to live in a community full of *mangia tortes.* However, that decision turned out to be quite serendipitous when it was discovered that the *mangia tortes* of Fox Chapel had no problem paying big money for custom-made homes and renovations. Big Joe's business grew at a staggering pace.

Big Joe and his wife, Alyssa, settled into their new marriage and new home and soon, she became pregnant. Alyssa gave birth to a healthy baby boy—Benjamin Martin. Unfortunately, the birth of Benjamin was not the continuation of a storybook life that started with one young immigrant all alone in this country. Rather, it signaled the start to the end of an era. After delivery while she was recovering in the hospital, Alyssa contracted an aggressive antibiotic-resistant staph infection and was rushed to the ICU. Her body was weak from the pregnancy and delivery and she was not able to fight off the infection. She died in the ICU two weeks after the delivery of her son.

Alyssa's death was not only emotionally devastating for Big Joe, it also brought new problems that Big Joe was not equipped to handle. How could Big Joe run a multi-million-dollar company as well as raise an infant son without a mother at home? At first, Gaetano and Camelia tried to fill this void, but it quickly became clear that they were not up to the task and needed assistance of their own to make it through a day. Fortunately, Big Joe's wealth allowed him to hire various people on a full-time basis to care for his elderly parents and his infant son.

Big Joe stopped speaking Italian when his father passed and he stopped going to church with Benjamin on Sundays as well. Benjamin, who was now five years old, was not growing up with family, but rather, with employees as cooks and nannies tended to his needs while his father ran his company. His summers were filled with organized sports and memberships to exclusive athletic clubs. Benjamin had no knowledge of his Italian roots, any language skills or any customs. Gaetano's death closed that chapter of Martino family history and it was now in Benjamin's future to start a new era. Being only five years old, he had no understanding, let alone appreciation, for what that meant. He could not comprehend what a loss of culture and identity meant. He eventually grew up like the other upper-middle-class, privileged *mangia torts* that lived in the same elite suburb.

Benjamin Martin was educated in the most prestigious private schools and attended an elite private college. He grew up only with a general understanding of the concept of God. Any faith that he developed was in knowledge he acquired and his ability to think, reason and how to use technology to problem solve. Without the hang-ups of trivial things, such as heritage, customs, or traditions to maintain, his mind was free to concentrate on a singular purpose— winning. Benjamin Martin could have pursued any professional occupation. He chose law enforcement as he believed it presented the most challenges and would provide him ample opportunities to surmount obstacles ... and win.

Chapter thirteen

Not exactly sure what he should do or should be doing following the shooting, Nico thought it best to get a sandwich with his girlfriend Lucy. He left the church and walked to the Primanti Brothers bar where Lucy met him. Primanti Brothers was mostly empty, it being a Sunday night combined with the fact that a church shooting occurred about three blocks away earlier in the day. Nico sat at the stainless steel bar with Lucy as the two of them conversed with the bartender/cook, Jerry, while Nico ate a capicola and egg and Lucy worked on the "No. 2 Best Seller." Although she was not in the church at the time of the shooting, Lucy was clearly more shaken up than Nico, who appeared to be his usual, slightly aloof, possibly bored self. The local news was on the television above the bar and, in the absence of any real crowd, was easily heard throughout the place.

"Tensions have been increasing at a local Pittsburgh Catholic parish over the past few months. Angry protestors have been gathering outside this church every Sunday before Mass to protest what they believe to be the quote 'Beyond liberal views and stance of Father O'Toole that threaten to destroy the traditional fabric of the Catholic Church.' This morning, those tensions peaked when it is believed that one of the protesters went into the church during a service and allegedly fired shots in what seemed to be an attempted assassination of Father Thomas O'Toole, pastor at St. Mary's Parish."

The TV footage showed a previously recorded statement from a man in his sixties who wore a weathered Steelers jersey and spoke with a heavy Pittsburgh dialect. "I was just sittin' in the pews prayin' for a Stillers win like I do every Sunday when some lunatic jumps outta the pews and starts shootin' up at the priest. Then that other guy jumped up all quick-like and knocked them bullets outta' the air before they could hit the priest. I haven't seen a miracle like that since seventy-two when Franco beat the Raiders."

The footage then cut to an elderly woman with a babushka on her head and rosary beads in her hand. "That young man saved our priest's life today by stopping those bullets. God was with him. It's a miracle."

The taped footage ended and went back to live coverage. "Many parishioners now claim they have witnessed a miracle. A spokesperson for the Diocese of Pittsburgh briefly commented on the events today by stating quote, 'Those people who choose to protest Father O'Toole crossed the line today from legal protest into attempted murder. The protestors' actions are nothing short of a hate crime and the Diocese of Pittsburgh is hoping that federal authorities will be investigating this matter. It is amazing that no one was injured or killed today.' Live from St. Mary's Church in Pittsburgh, this is Rob Willis, Channel Two News."

"Well, there you have it. A miracle. Right down the street," said Jerry as he mindlessly wiped down the bar.

"I don't think so," said Nico. "I mean, the guy was probably a terrible shot or maybe he just had some cheap gun that he bought off the street. I guess we just got lucky today, that's all."

"But weren't you scared?" asked Lucy, seemingly in awe of her boyfriend.

"No, sadly, I wasn't. I … I really didn't notice what was happening until it was all over and people were running. I haven't really been sleeping well, you know … so I just didn't realize the danger, I suppose."

As the TV news shifted to the weather, Jerry turned down the volume. Silence filled the room and started to become almost uncomfortable as Nico and Lucy finished their meals while Jerry continued to wipe down the bar. After cleaning up the few French fries that fell off the sandwich, Nico balled up the wax paper and pushed it across the bar toward Jerry.

"Well, in spite of this absolutely riveting conversation, I must get home. I have a big day tomorrow … Teaching kids how to add two-digit numbers and then maybe even how to carry a number. Jerry, how much do I owe you?"

"Nothing. It's on me."

"Are you serious?"

"Sure, it's not often one of my patrons, I mean, friends, performs a miracle in front of an entire church full of people. And all along I thought you were just some jagoff school teacher."

"That's permanent substitute teacher," said Nico condescendingly.

"Yeah, well I guess I was right about one part," replied Jerry in an equally condescending tone.

"Well, there you have it. Now that is a miracle. A comp'd meal. Where are the cameras when you need them?"

Nico shook Jerry's hand and Lucy gave him a hug. As the two started to exit the bar, one of the patrons on hand approached Nico.

"Excuse me, sir, but ain't you the guy who performed the miracle in church this morning, stopping those bullets, n'nat? I just want to shake your hand, if I may?" The nervous patron grabbed Nico's right hand and vigorously shook it. Nico clearly did not know how to react or what to say. He was taken aback by the fact that he had been recognized by someone in the public, and furthermore, that he was being credited with performing a miracle.

"Well, yeah, I guess ... I mean, I was there when the shots were fired. I was on the altar. But I am not sure that I had anything to do with it, I mean with stopping it." After a few moments of what progressed into full-arm ratchetting, Nico forcefully removed his hand from the bar patron. Not knowing what else to do, Nico stepped back and made the sign of the cross in the air in front of the patron. "Well, may God be with you."

"Oh, thank you. Thank you for the blessing. God stay with you!" Nico, upon seeing who he believed to be the guy's wife nervously standing behind him, stepped to the side and threw a blessing to her as well.

"Peace be with you as well, ma'am."

Nico and Lucy finally made it outside without any further involvement. Lucy's car was parked in front of the bar. "Hey, look at that. You got a parking space right in the front. Another miracle!" said Nico sarcastically. After Lucy unlocked the car, Nico jumped into the passenger seat. As he looked out of the car and through the bar's storefront window, he saw the two patrons talking to Jerry. A memory inexplicably flashed back into his mind as he remembered being on the podium at his high school graduation for his valedictorian speech.

"In conclusion, a lot of adults think that we are nothing but a bunch of unmotivated slackers who will drain society. Well, I—for one—don't believe that at all. Some of us will be going to college, some will be working, others will be going into the military. But all of us have a great opportunity to make a difference, regardless of where we end up or what we do next. I think that is our mission. Let us not waste this great opportunity that we have earned. So, as your friend and classmate, I will leave you with a final thought—let's all find that way to make a difference. Let's show everybody that we are not slackers. Let's make everyone proud of us and let's be proud of ourselves. Class of ninety-seven, we did it!" The crowd erupted into applause as Nico flipped the tassel on his graduation cap to the other side.

His vivid and truly unexplainable memory came to an end when Lucy shut her car door. As she sat next to Nico, she didn't utter a word. She only put the key in the ignition and started the car. After more moments of uncomfortable silence, Nico turned to her and said, "Hey, are you good to come over tonight? It is still kind of early."

"Actually, I think I would rather just go home by myself tonight."

"Oh … okay … yeah, I mean, whatever you want." Nico turned away from her and buckled his seatbelt. Lucy stared in a trance-like manner out of the windshield while more awkward silence followed. Nico turned on the car radio to a local sports talk radio program that happened to be on at that time.

"Yeah, J.J., thanks for taking my call. I want to talk about that miracle that happened today at St. Mary's"

"Whoa, whoa, whoa, hold up!! Were you there?" said the obnoxious radio host.

"No, I wasn't. But my neighbor's brother-in-law …"

"So, you weren't there, but you have already concluded that a miracle happened?"

"Yeah, but …"

The sports talk show host hung up on the caller. "But nothing. You are an idiot! You are an idiot just like all the rest of the morons and idiots who are calling me tonight to talk about church. This is sports radio. Save your miracle talk for NPR or some other crap ..." Nico quickly turned off the radio.

"You know what, silence is good right now. Let's just drive in silence." Lucy pulled away from the bar and soon dropped Nico off in front of his apartment.

Nico was completely exhausted as he dragged himself up the interior staircase to his second- floor apartment. After he entered his place, he took off his clothes and left them on the floor where they landed. He saw the light on his old-school answering machine was blinking. He played the message on his machine from a nervous grade school principal, his boss.

"Mr. Rossi ... this is Principal ... This is Steve Alders ... Ahh, look ... I heard what happened today at your church and that you were involved ... First of all, thank God you or nobody else was hurt or killed today. I can only imagine how you must feel right now."

"No, you can't," said an annoyed Nico at his answering machine.

"Look, Mr. Rossi, take some time off. In fact, take this whole week off. You need to decompress. I am sure that there are a lot of police officers who will want to talk to you anyway. But don't worry, this time off won't count as sick days or anything like that. Don't worry about it. Call me if you need more time than a week, I'm sure it won't be a problem ... Thank you ... Thank you, Mr. Rossi. And so glad you are okay."

Confused and dazed, Nico stared at his answering machine. "Maybe I am alright, but I'm certainly not okay," he muttered to himself. After he stripped down to his boxer shorts and undershirt, he walked to his kitchen table and poured a glass of table wine. He took two pills from a prescription bottle and washed them down with his wine. Nico then shuffled himself to his bedroom, got into bed and stared at the ceiling. He didn't move from that position all night, but he didn't fall asleep, either. Just before the 6:30 AM alarm could blare, Nico turned and shut it down before the vexatious ring let loose. Even though Nico did not have to go to work today, he nonetheless got out of bed to start his day.

Chapter fourteen

Nico dragged himself into the shower and stood in the water for an extended amount of time. He wasn't singing, thinking or even bathing. He just stood there as the pulsating water from the oversized shower head smacked his body. After several minutes, the hot water tank was emptied and the shower started to turn cold. The cold water brought him some sort of awareness and he realized that he needed to employ soap and shampoo before the cool water turned ice cold. After his shower, he walked through his apartment and put on the same shirt and pants he wore the night before. At least now, his clothes were off the floor.

After dressing, Nico took two frozen waffles from his freezer. He placed them in the toaster and started a pot of fresh coffee. While he waited for his meal to be finished, he stepped into his living room and turned on the television as he sat on his tattered couch. The local TV news was on, and, of course, the shooting from yesterday was being reported. Nico quickly turned off the television and with a remote, turned on his stereo. "I Wanna be Your Boyfriend" by the Ramones played and a few seconds later, Nico was fast asleep on his couch. He started to dream of a time from several years ago, when he was in Philadelphia:

A young Nico, dressed in pressed khaki pants with a button-down shirt and perfectly combed short hair made his way into a local bar by himself. He quickly discovered how out of place he was as the bar exclusively catered to a punk-rock crowd. "I Wanna be Your Boyfriend" was being performed live by a Ramones cover band. Nico muscled his way up to the bar and placed an order.

"Hi, yeah, can I please have a Philly cheesesteak and a draft of whatever is on special?"

"Kid, you're in Philly. Just order a cheesesteak, I'll know what you mean," said the gruff bartender.

The bartender shouted back his order to the cook as he pushed a Yuengling draft in front of him. While Nico sipped on his beer, he noticed a rather cute girl staring at him. Not thinking anything more of it, Nico just assumed he was being checked out because he was so out of place in this crowded punk bar.

A short time later, the bartender put a huge cheesesteak sandwich loaded with peppers and mushrooms in front of him. "Wow," said Nico, "That's a big Phil ... a big steak sandwich." Before he could dig in, the cute girl, Jessica LaRue, took the bar stool next to him. She was dressed in a Dead Kennedy's T-shirt underneath a red flannel, long denim skirt and sandals. She appeared to be a mix between a punk and a hippie, especially with her naturally long reddish-blond hair.

"Hi darlin'. I'm here to save you," said Jessica confidently. Nico, surprised by her actions, stumbled on his words.

"Okay ... well, yeah, hi. How are ya? I ... I didn't know that I needed to be saved."

"Yup, you do. If you eat that entire sandwich, you will be up all night with heartburn. That is no way to start your time in Philly," said Jessica even more confidently. She reached across the bar and grabbed a knife. Placing her whole hand on the sandwich, she cut it in half and began to eat it. Nico was completely stunned by this girl's brashness and he could do little more than watch her eat.

"Okay, so ... I'm Nico, by the way."

"Hi Nico, I'm Jessica," she said with a mouthful of cheesesteak as she reached for his hand to shake it.

"So, how did you know that I am not from here?"

Jessica forcefully swallowed her mouthful of food and delivered a judgmental look. "Are you serious? Look how you're dressed. What are you, from Iowa, or something? Do you work for Republicans?"

"Actually, I'm from Pittsburgh, and I just started a graduate program out here."

"Pittsburgh, huh?" said Jessica as she took another bite. "That's like Pennsyltucky, right? Pretty close to Iowa."

"So, are you going to help me drink my beer as well?" said Nico jokingly.

"Nope. But you can buy me one." Before Nico could even get the bartender's attention, another cold draft was placed in front of Jessica.

Jessica picked up her beer and toasted Nico. "Cheers, Nico from Pittsburgh."

"Salute, Jessica ... the sandwich eater?"

The two spent the next couple of hours eating and drinking together in the bar as the Ramones cover band continued to play. Nico and Jessica eventually decided it was time to go. They left the bar and walked up the city sidewalk in the direction of Nico's apartment.

"Well, this is where I must leave you," said Jessica, "I am going in a different direction."

"Okay ... Well, look, I really enjoyed talking to you. Do you want to give me your phone number, or something? I can call you sometime and maybe we can split another sandwich?"

Jessica took Nico's hand and put it on her face. "No, darlin', you don't need my number. I will see you again soon."

Nico was again stunned by Jessica's inexplicable actions. "What? How? When? I mean, this city is huge and—"

Cutting Nico off mid-sentence, she chuckled and turned away from him as she started to walk in the other direction. The excitement of having met someone new and completely interesting quickly turned back to confusion and disbelief. Nico said goodbye under his breath and waived to her, although he knew she could not see it or hear him. Nico slowly turned and continued his walk back to his apartment.

A few moments later, Nico felt a strong tap on his shoulder, which startled him. He turned around to see Jessica standing in front of him.

"I never thanked you for the sandwich," Jessica said sweetly as she pushed Nico against the wall of a building and gave him a very passionate kiss on his lips before she kissed his ear and whispered, "Thank you, darlin'." She smiled and took one step away from him as she held both his hands.

A loud knock on his apartment door startled Nico and woke him from his sleep and dream. He groggily got up from his couch and opened the door to find Detective Martin standing in his hallway.

"Good morning, Mr. Rossi. Do you remember me? I am Detective Martin. Remember, we spoke yesterday?"

"Yes, of course, how could I forget."

"Well, I stopped by your school and the principal told me that you would be taking some time off this week. I hope you don't mind me stopping by uninvited and what not," said the detective in a very stern and serious manner.

"No, of course not ... well, where are my manners? Do please come in." Nico opened the door and the detective entered his small apartment. His eyes immediately started to canvas the area.

"Can I make you some Eggos?"

"Excuse me?"

"Eggos ... you know, toaster waffles. They are great with powdered sugar."

"No, no thank you."

"How about a cup of coffee? Made it fresh a few minutes ago?"

"No, I am fine without."

"Wow. A cop that doesn't drink coffee."

"That is Detective, Mr. Rossi."

"My apologies, Detective Martin," said Nico, who was now annoyed after only a few moments of the unexpected contact. Nico walked back into his kitchen and poured maple syrup into a small bowl and started to break pieces of the waffle apart and dip them into the syrup with his hands.

"So, Detective, I appreciate you checking up on me," said Nico sarcastically in between bites, "But I am fine. I will be fine. And I really don't have any new information to add other than what I told you yesterday in the church."

Detective Martin continued to scan the apartment, seemingly ignoring the words Nico spoke. "What is this?" said Detective Martin as he held Nico's sleeping pill bottle in his hand.

"Prescription sleeping pills for insomnia."

"How long have you been an insomniac?"

"I don't know. Too long. What's your concern?"

"Son, you were involved in a shooting that occurred in a church of all places. Why wouldn't I be concerned?"

"Involved? More like nearly murdered."

"I guess that is one way to view it. Look, I am glad you are fine and not injured. Why don't you tell me again what happened and I will leave you alone. Sometimes witnesses don't always give the best statements at the scene of a crime. Maybe the dust has settled enough and your thoughts are clearer?"

"Fine. Again, I was on the altar with Father O'Toole, daydreaming. O'Toole tried to get my attention and when I started to walk to him, that crazy loon jumped out of the pew with a gun in his hand. Then, I just pushed O'Toole to the ground and covered my face. I heard shots and heard everyone in church scrambling for the doors. I turned around. O'Toole was on the ground and I could see he wasn't hit. I looked up and saw the shooter about twenty feet away. He was on the ground whimpering like a little bitch and then he just sort of side-armed slid his gun at me on the floor. So, I picked it up. You and the other cop showed up eventually. End of story."

"Okay, good. Almost the same as yesterday. Did Dylan Ray say anything to you specifically?"

"Who is that?"

"Ahh," said Martin with a slight chuckle, "he is the shooter."

"I didn't know that was his name. He failed to introduce himself before or after the shooting. He just moaned and whimpered, mostly. But he did scream out to Jesus for forgiveness a couple times, I guess."

"I see. Well, last question, you did go to grad school at Penn, right?"

"Umm, yes, for a short time, but I dropped out. How did you know that?" asked Nico.

"Oh, well, just standard police work. You know, do quick backgrounds on people involved in crimes. See if any of them have a criminal history, where they work, where they live, pretty standard stuff for those involved."

"Well I'm really not sure why my background is of any interest—probably wouldn't be if I had caught one in the chest. But I will save you some time. I don't own a car. I have a thirty-year-old motorcycle that I drive everywhere until the weather gets bad, then I take a bus or walk. I live in this tiny, old-ass apartment with used furniture because it is the only thing I could afford on my salary. And I probably have insomnia because my mattress is so bad. I was a Golden Domer as an undergrad and I went to U Penn for grad school until I dropped out. I moved back here once I left Philly only to find my church under siege by protestors. My bad luck, I guess."

"I don't believe in luck. People's circumstances are determined by the choices they make in life," said Detective Martin coldly.

"Umm, yeah, I guess. Look, I don't get it?"

"Excuse me?"

"I don't get it ... this line of questioning about my background. And you keep saying I am 'involved.' Do you think I had something to do with this mess?"

"Oh, well, probably not. We all know Dylan Ray was the shooter. No question about that. But it is way too early to arrive at any other conclusions. But that was all I needed. I just wanted to hear your story one more time ... and to make sure you were okay, of course. Eat your breakfast, I can show myself out. Thanks again for your time."

Once he was gone, Nico finished his waffles and instinctively went to his table, poured a small glass of wine and popped a couple of sleeping pills. He then went back to bed.

Outside Nico's apartment, Detective Martin received a call on his cell phone from Detective Kelly who was ready to begin the first interrogation of Dylan Ray at the police station. "Yeah, what's up, Kelly? What do you got?"

"Not much so far. It is still too early for conclusions. But very weird stuff. The crime lab was able to do some quick ballistic work on the gun. The gun is good. I mean, it is a top-of-the-line Sig Sauer .45 cal. Great working condition. No obvious defects. The remaining rounds in the clip were fired through it and it works fine. Ray should have put holes in people big enough for a fist to go through at that distance. The bullets recovered at the scene look like they most likely were fired through that gun, but Crime Lab needs more time for a full ballistic analysis. Hell, the guy even bought the gun legally and registered the damn thing in his own name. Just plain weird, that's all."

"Okay, that is strange. I got nothing on my end. I am heading back to the station now. I will meet up with you after the interrogation."

Chapter fifteen

Dylan Ray spent the better part of the day and all Sunday night in the holding cell following the shooting. It was clear when he was brought into the interrogation room that he hadn't slept a wink. He sat shackled to the plain metal table in the middle of the room as he shook and tried to drink very weak coffee from a Styrofoam cup that he was handed upon his entry. Detective Kelly, one of the two lead investigators, talked to high-ranking brass of the Pittsburgh Police Department behind the two-way mirrors that looked into the interrogation room. For obvious reasons, all the top-ranking officials were interested in the progress of the case.

"Any theories on this case or this guy yet, Kelly?" said the Chief of Police.

"No sir, not yet. The only thing we know for sure is that this guy is from Philadelphia and he has a zero-prior record score. He seems to fit the profile of a religious zealot and not as a terrorist. But any theories that I may have had just went out the window after this preliminary ballistic report. I have never seen anything like this … officers on duty last night said that the only thing this guy did the whole night was scream to Jesus to forgive him, but he was being very strange about it."

"What do you mean 'strange?' What was strange about asking Jesus for forgiveness, besides the obvious fact that he just shot up a House of God?"

"Well, the boys said he was specifically asking Jesus to forgive him … almost like he specifically targeted Jesus himself."

"Well, didn't he? Isn't Jesus supposed to be inside the House of God?"

"No, I get that. But the boys said that the way he was asking for forgiveness was as if he literally shot at Jesus in the flesh and was sorry. Not in the general sense of shooting God's house or a place that God dwells. They said it was like Jesus was the intended target. I know, it's hard for me to explain … hard for even me to understand it, too. And I don't think the boys down there understood it either," said Detective Kelly, sheepishly.

"Look, Kelly, just do your job. Quite frankly, this guy shouldn't be very hard to break. We got him at the scene with a gun in his hand and witnesses that can ID him. He is dead to rights and we all know that. We could go to trial tomorrow if we had to. Just make sure that he knows he can have a lawyer with him. If he lawyers up, be cool and proceed when he has counsel. We don't want to lose this guy over some ACLU bullshit. The main thing is to just try to find out if he does have some affiliation with a terrorist group, and if he does, stop what you are doing, let me know and I will call the FBI. They're already up my ass over this guy, but they're also at a loss because they have no records on him and he was never on anyone's radar."

"Got it, Chief. No worries. I'm clear with the directive," said Detective Kelly as he entered the interrogation room to question the suspect, Dylan Ray.

"Mr. Ray, my name is Detective Kelly of the Pittsburgh Police Department. This room is heavily mic'd. Everything that you say and I say is being recorded. As such, I want to reiterate your rights as you were previously advised yesterday. You have the right to remain silent. Anything that you say may be used against you in a court of law. You have the right to an attorney. If you cannot afford an attorney, one will be appointed to you at no cost. Do you understand your rights?"

"Yes, I do," said Dylan Ray in a very shaky tone.

"Do you want an attorney present during this questioning?"

"No, I want … I need Jesus to forgive me," said Dylan Ray as he broke into a full sob.

"I can't help you with that. If you don't want an attorney to be here, then I will start the questioning."

"I don't need questions, I need forgiveness. Jesus, forgive me, I didn't know! I didn't realize! I am sorry," screamed Dylan as he continued to sob uncontrollably.

"Sir, I have to question you. We need to know what happened yester—"

"I already told you yesterday what happened. I already admitted it. I tried to kill the priest, but Jesus stopped me!"

"Okay, okay, let's calm down a bit. Slow yourself," said Detective Kelly in a calm voice as he lit a cigarette. "Do you consider yourself to be a religious person?"

"Absolutely."

"What is your religious affiliation?" asked Detective Kelly as he took a seat at the table across from Dylan Ray.

"I am a devout Catholic."

"Catholic?" said Kelly after a long pause. "I don't get it. If you are a devout Catholic, then why would you try to kill a priest?"

"Because that man is not a priest," screamed Dylan Ray. "He preaches about homosexuals and whores who have abortions and how they should be accepted and forgiven. It is a slap in the face to God. He is destroying our Church. God never said those things were acceptable."

"So, you thought it would be okay then to kill a priest in the House of God?"

"Yes. I thought that is what God was telling me to do. But I was wrong, I was wrong. And Jesus stopped the bullets from hitting the Priest. Jesus forgive me, I am sorry!"

"Alright, okay, get ahold of yourself, will ya'. Let's go a different direction." After making some quick notes on a tablet, Detective Kelly continued his questioning. "How long have you known Nico Rossi?"

"Who is that?" asked Dylan Ray as he wiped the tears from his face with his shirt.

"He was the altar server who was with the priest when you tried to kill him yesterday."

"There was no altar server," said Dylan in a puzzled manner.

"Yes, yes there was. In fact, in your statements you made yesterday in the church, you said—"

"I know what I said. I never said anything about an altar boy."

Detective Kelly flipped through his notes. "Alright, you said he stopped the bullets. You said—"

"I said that Jesus stopped the bullets. There was no altar boy with the priest," said Dylan defiantly.

"You are right, you did say that … Okay … let's just … I mean … just tell me what happened yesterday."

"For the hundredth time, I was outside of the church before Mass. I entered the church and sat in a pew. My gun was loaded and was in my waist. My shirt was untucked and it covered the gun so nobody could see it. Typical Catholic stragglers came late to the Mass and disrupted the pew a bit. I had to slide closer to the middle of the pew from the end where I first sat. When I thought that the time was right, I jumped out of the pew, put the priest in my sight and squeezed the trigger twice. But as soon as I shot, my Lord and Savior, Jesus Chris,t moved in front of the priest. He stretched out his hands and there was a bright, blinding light coming from behind him. Jesus, Lord, forgive me! I am so sorry," cried out Ray.

Detective Kelly tried to maintain his composure, but it was clear that he had lost total control of the interview. "Okay, ahh … tell me about the gun. Where did you get it?"

"What?" asked Dylan Ray, seemingly confused by the new line of questioning.

"Where did you get the gun?" repeated Detective Kelly.

"I got it at that sporting goods shop on Fifth Avenue. I forget the name of it. But that is where I bought it," said Dylan Ray very matter-of-factly.

"Did you ever shoot it before? Do you regularly shoot guns?" asked Detective Kelly who visibly struggled with his interrogation.

"Well, I never owned a gun before. I asked the clerk at the store to suggest a reliable gun that is easy to use. He asked me if I wanted a gun for target practice or self-defense … I thought that self-defense was a better answer. He then gave me the bullets to use for self-defense. He said that the self-defense bullets were more expensive than the target bullets, or something like that. I think he said they were called hollow points, or something. So, I bought two boxes of bullets. I took my gun to the state game lands that has the shooting range and I shot one whole box and part of the second box."

"How did you shoot? Hit the targets?" asked Kelly.

"After a few shots, I was able to hit the target regularly at fifteen yards. But why does that really matter?"

"What?"

"Jesus Christ stopped the bullets. They only went ten feet! I watched them fall to the ground. I watched as Jesus Christ made the bullets fall to the ground! I saw them fall with my own eyes. Jesus forgive me! I am sorry! I am so, so sorry, Lord!" And with that, Dylan Ray again broke into a full-blown, uncontrollable sob.

Detective Kelly turned back to the two-way mirror where the brass watched the interview. The expression on his face said more than words could ever convey. In all his years, with all his training, with all his experience on the streets and even from the hundreds of suspect interviews he conducted throughout his career, he was not prepared for the interview with Dylan Ray. Nobody was. Everyone who witnessed the first interrogation just shook their heads in disbelief. Dylan Ray was insane or delusional was the only reasonable explanation for him. But insanity did not explain why Father O'Toole or Nico hadn't been shot. Nobody spoke openly about it, but a collective belief started to form for the alternative explanation—a miracle had just occurred. It was the only option on the table. Regardless of the state of Dylan Ray's mental health, the undisputed fact was undeniable: Dylan Ray tried to kill the priest, and for some unknown reason, he failed to do so because perfectly good rounds fired from a perfectly good weapon only traveled ten feet before miraculously falling harmlessly to the ground.

Chapter sixteen

Later that evening, Nico continued to try to make sense of all that had occurred over the past two days. He could not decide what was stranger—the actual shooting or the police reaction. How could anyone, let alone trained law enforcement officers, believe that he had anything to do with what transpired, he thought to himself, and at times, wondered out loud.

He noticed that it was now past dinner, not that Nico bothered to eat anything, and it was odd that Lucy had not called him today. Normally, the two talked a couple times a day or exchanged a few texts, especially on days when they did not plan to see one another. Under these extraordinary circumstances, Nico was at a loss to explain why she hadn't called him at all today. He pulled his cell phone out of his pocket and made a call.

"Hey Luce, what's up? … I'm fine, it's cool. Well, sort of … just weird stuff happening, I don't really know how to explain it. The cops showed up today at my apartment … Just one cop. He had some more questions … It was very strange … Well, he said he was checking up on me, but he kept saying I was involved and it seemed like he was investigating me … No, I'm serious. He was even asking me about when I was in Philadelphia … That's what I said, it doesn't make any sense … Yeah, well, look, why don't you come over tonight? We can hang out here or go somewhere. I can debrief with you and then maybe later you can debrief me, what do ya' say? … No, it's cool, I understand, you have a lot going on right now … No, no, it's alright. Listen, you know how these things work, this will all blow over soon enough. I mean, sooner or later some Pittsburgh Steeler will do something, will break a law or fail a drug test and my saga will no longer be news. Only a matter of time … Well, maybe we can get together tomorrow … Ok, great. We'll talk tomorrow. Have a good night."

With nothing else left to do, Nico begrudgingly turned on the television to watch the local news. Since he hadn't really spoken to anyone, other than Detective Martin, he thought watching the news, though painful, may be necessary. In the back of his mind, he hoped that the story would not be covered anymore. Clearly, his hopes were in vain.

"This is Rob Willis with Channel Two News, and I am here with a gentleman who claims that he was healed by Nicholas Rossi, the altar server who many witnesses claim stopped bullets in midair that were allegedly intended to kill the priest of Saint Mary's Parish yesterday morning. Sir, tell us your name and explain just what in the world you are talking about."

"Oh, for the Love of God!" Nico exclaimed out loud as he watched the news report.

As the television news camera focused in, Nico immediately recognized the man who was about to speak as the same guy who shook his hand in the bar last evening.

"My name is Stanley Chaplinski. For the last twenty-five years, I have been workin' on the docks dahn-nare in the produce yards, you know, loadin' and unloadin' pallets of produce every morning. Well, you see, I need to take aspirins and other stuff everyday 'cause I developed some arthritis in my joints."

"Okay, so far so good," said the reporter as he seemed to be prodding him for more relevant information.

"Well, last night, the Mrs. wanted to go out to eat. I didn't want to, 'cause I was all tired and sore from workin' so much. But she wasn't going to cook anything, so I thought we should just go to the bar for fish sandwiches, n'nat. While we was sittin' at the bar, she's like, 'Look, Stanley, that guy over there is the one who stopped them bullets from killin' the priest at St. Mary's.' And I'm like, nut-ah. And she's like, 'Uh-huh, swear to God it's him. I heard him talking about it to the bartender.'"

"So, what did you do?" questioned the reporter.

"Well, I went up to him and I says, 'Hey, ain't you the guy that stopped them bullets from hittin' the priest at St. Mary's yesterday?' And he was all like, 'Yeah, that was me. I stopped them bullets, n'nat'. Then the guy shakes my hand and is like, 'God Bless you, Stanley. Go in peace.'"

"What the Hell? I never said that! I don't even talk like that," said Nico out loud in utter disbelief.

Stanley Chaplinski continued. "Now, here's the thing, when I woke up this morning, I felt like a million bucks. I mean, I wasn't sore or stiff or nuttin'. I went to work, worked a whole day plus a couple hours O-T and I never once took a pill. My joints feel great. Haven't felt this good in years. I feel like I could work a double tomorrow if I had to, no problem."

"So, what are you saying, Mr. Chaplinski? Are you suggesting that Nicholas Rossi cured your arthritis?" questioned the reporter.

"Damn straight he did!" said Stanley Chaplinski with great advocacy.

"Well... you heard it here first. Could this healing be the second miracle performed by Nicholas Rossi? I guess we must wait and see. But stay tuned as Channel Two continues to provide coverage on this ever-developing story that started out with a church shooting in the Strip District. Live from the Strip District, this is Rob Willis, Channel Two News."

Nico turned off the television in disgust. It was now apparent that even the most notorious Steelers scandal would not bump him from the front page. He walked to his kitchen table and took two sleeping pills, along with an even bigger glass of wine. He crawled into bed to begin staring at the ceiling.

Chapter seventeen

Nico tossed and turned as usual until he eventually fell asleep at some point. He wasn't sure how long he slept, but he was sure that he was sleeping because he woke from his slumber before his alarm clock rang. *Figures.* He thought to himself.

A group of about ten senior citizens had gathered on the sidewalk in front of his apartment. They sang church hymns loud enough to wake him. Nico got out of bed and moved his bedroom window curtain just enough so that he could peek through to see what was going on. From his view, he thought that the group appeared to be praying to him—which was exactly what they were doing. A few candles had been lit and placed on his stoop. Most of them held rosary beads as they sang their hymns and asked Nico specifically to heal their ailments.

Prior to this gathering, the situation was beyond Nico's comprehension. Now the situation was also clearly beyond his control. He quickly dressed, left his apartment through the backdoor fire escape, and jumped onto his motorcycle. He drifted it away from his apartment for a few yards before he started it. He drove directly to the rectory and parked behind the building.

Nico frantically rang the doorbell. Father O'Toole, who lived in the rectory by himself, answered the door. Nico barged in, agitated and almost manic.

"Sorry, Father, I had to get in here before anyone saw me. Got coffee made? I smell it. I will help myself." Nico sprinted past the priest to grab a cup of coffee.

"Well, good morning to you, my son. And just where have you been? I tried to call you three times yesterday," said the priest who seemed eerily calm under the circumstances.

"Yeah, well, I shut my phone off. Too many people calling me." Nico vigorously sipped his black coffee while the old priest tried his best to keep up with Nico who bounced off the walls.

"I don't think you need coffee. Whiskey, maybe, but not coffee."

"Father, what the hell, excuse me, is going on?"

"Damned if I know," retorted the old priest.

"Are all these people insane?" asked Nico with an exasperated tone.

"Son … sit down. Sit down and calm yourself. This situation will resolve itself in due time. Look, religious zealots are what they are. And every one of them is a little skewed in their beliefs and their actions follow …"

"No, no, I'm not talking about the guy who tried to kill me."

"He tried to kill me," said Father O'Toole defensively.

"Yeah … right … the guy who tried to kill you. I'm not talking about him. At least I understand him. I don't agree … but I understand. He is a religious nut job. I got it. I am talking about everyone else."

"What do you mean?"

"Did you see the news report yesterday; did you see this Chaplinski guy?"

"No, I didn't watch the news yesterday at all. I was a bit preoccupied with—"

Nico cut the priest off mid-sentence and continued to talk over him. "The night of the shooting, I went to the bar with Lucy for dinner. When I was done, this old Chaplinski guy comes over to me and shakes my hand. He recognized me somehow. Then last night, on the news, this old Chaplinski guy is saying that because I shook his hand, I healed his arthritis."

"They put that on the news?"

"Yeah. They sure did. But it gets better. This morning, at the crack of freakin' dawn, about ten senior citizens were camped outside my apartment. They were singing and praying to me. They were asking me to heal them, too. So, I escaped out the back door and came here," said Nico, still very frantic, still drinking his coffee.

"I see, this is very concerning," said Father O'Toole in contemplation.

"Concerning! That is not the half of it. Have you spoken to the police since the shooting?"

"No, like I said, I was a bit preoccupied with—"

"Well, get this. The one cop came to my apartment yesterday morning. My principal dimed me out and told him that I was taking some time off from work. So, the cop … Martin, Detective Martin, he came into my apartment and started asking me questions. I said I already told you what happened. But he keeps questioning me and questioning me. He asks me about Philadelphia and if the shooter said anything to me. And he was so strange about it that it made me think that he was investigating me, like I was working alongside the shooter to have you killed, or something."

"What? Are you sure? He couldn't have meant that. That doesn't make sense!"

"I know, right. That's what I said," exclaimed Nico. "I mean, if I wanted to kill you, I would do it here when nobody is around, not in a church with people in it. How would they not see that? Um, well, you know what I am trying to say."

"Son, no more talking. Go to my office." As the two left the kitchen and headed to the priest's rectory office, Father O'Toole took Nico's coffee mug from him. He walked to his desk and pulled out a bottle of Jameson from the drawer and poured a mouthful into Nico's mug before he gave it back to him.

"Sit on the couch, son. Try to calm yourself for a bit. You need to listen now. Our Loving Father designed us all with two ears and one mouth for a reason. Just listen to me for a moment." As Nico sat on the couch and drank his spiked coffee, Father O'Toole began to talk slowly as he paced methodically around the office before eventually sitting at his desk.

"Since the shooting, my phone has been ringing off the hook, as you can imagine. Unlike you, I have answered the calls. Most of them have been from the parishioners, you know, just seeing if I am okay and if there is anything that they can do for me. My freezer is full right now from all of the food that has been dropped off to me over the past two days. Then, of course, the newspapers are calling me. Not just local, nationwide. This is quite a story … But the most difficult of all the calls … are coming from the Diocese."

Nico piped up, no longer being able to remain silent. "Oh, figures. What do those bureaucrats want now?"

"Ha, yeah, true enough, sonny, they never call you to ask for something, but they always seem to call when they demand something from you," said Father O'Toole begrudgingly. "The Diocese has informed me that they are launching their own investigation into this incident. They are launching their own investigation and they need to speak, in person, to me … and to you. Thus, one of the reasons that I was calling you yesterday."

"What! What for? I don't get all this investigation. What is there to investigate? The damn shooter confessed in front of you, me and two cops at the scene of the crime! Case closed. Investigate what? And, besides, shouldn't the cops investigate, I mean, that is their job, right? Since when does the Diocese investigate anything? Shouldn't they be shutting down churches or holding fish fries or capital campaigns? There are a lot of other things the Diocese should be investigating, but they don't. Isn't it their job to turn a blind eye …"

Father O'Toole glared at Nico with that comment and Nico realized that he needed to tone it down a bit. Father O'Toole was a dear friend, but he was also a priest. After a long pause, Father O'Toole continued, though he fumbled with his words a bit. "They have to investigate … they want to investigate … look, the fact of the matter is had I been shot, it would be a matter for police to investigate … but because I … or you … wasn't shot … and there is no good explanation for why … they have to investigate …"

"Oh, my God! Don't even say it …"

"They have to investigate the possibility that a miracle did in fact occur. Divine intervention that prevented both of us from being killed on the altar, praise Jesus," blurted out Father O'Toole. "Yeah, let that sink in."

After sitting in silence for a few moments, Nico began to pace about the office and peek out the window every time he walked past. "A miracle, huh?"

"The possibility of a miracle."

"Look, Father, I do believe in miracles. I am sure they happen. I want to believe they happen. I mean, you are clearly more of an expert on the subject than I am, but from what I know about miracles, they only seem to happen to good people … people that deserve … people that need a miracle. I'm not the one. I don't deserve anything. I'm not a good person, certainly not worthy of any miracles."

"Your opinion."

Nico continued, "The Diocese, well, the Diocese, okay, see, they can tell you what to do. You work for them. I don't. I don't work for the Diocese at all, except for the school, but I answer to a principal, not them. I am a volunteer here. Your volunteer. I am not a volunteer to the Diocese. I don't have to do anything. They have no power over me," said Nico defiantly.

"You are right, son, you are right. And your agitation against the Diocese is not lost on me. I get it. But, look, Nico, you were there. You were there along with me. Now you can avoid them all you want. Maybe you will be successful, who knows? Maybe after I meet with them, they will lose interest in you, maybe in this whole matter. But maybe they won't. Now, I am not the Diocese. I am your friend, a good friend. And you are mine. You are more than my volunteer. As your friend, I am asking you to please meet with the Diocese. Let me make the arrangements. We can go together."

"For what? For what purpose? I don't know what happened, but I am sure it wasn't a miracle. I don't care what the Diocese says it was," said Nico even more defiantly.

Father O'Toole looked long at Nico and sat up straight in his chair. "So, you are sure that whatever happened, there must be an explanation, right? You are convinced that whatever it was, it was certainly not a miracle. Okay. Well, please son, please enlighten me then," said Father O'Toole in a very condescending tone.

"What?"

"Yes, please enlighten me. I mean, it is clear that you have a complete understanding of how God works. You clearly understand His ways and I guess the rest of us just have to go through life pondering God's mysteries. But not you. Clearly, you are an expert in miracles and you understand them and how they work. That is the only way possible that you can conclude that a miracle didn't occur. So please, explain it to me as well as the other mysteries of God. And when you are finished, I can line you up with hundreds, probably thousands, of holy men and women of all different faiths and religions that have studied and prayed their whole lives for a fraction of the understanding that you so clearly now possess. Go ahead then, you have my attention."

Nico realized that he was digging a hole for himself. He also realized that the last thing he ever wanted to do was alienate himself from Father O'Toole. In light of the bizarre totality of all these circumstances, Nico quickly concluded that things would be better with Father O'Toole and not without him. After another sip of spiked coffee, Nico continued apologetically and more focused on his word choice.

"Look, Father, that is not what I am saying … All I mean to say is that if a miracle occurred, wouldn't I realize it? Reverse it for a minute. If I was the one saying a miracle occurred, then I would believe it. And if the Diocese agreed with me, then great. But if they didn't, I wouldn't care. Wouldn't matter to me … I just … I just think that if a miracle occurred, I would know it without the need for a Diocesan stamp of approval. I don't know what happened, but I know that I don't feel a miracle. I mean, look at all the stories in the Bible about people who directly experience God's intervention, or a miracle, if you will. Don't their lives immediately change? Don't they all get a different perspective and start to live and feel better? Well, that didn't happen to me. I didn't feel a thing. And I don't feel any better now than I did right before Mass, that's all."

"You don't feel anything. You haven't felt anything in years. Perhaps you are not the best barometer for feelings anymore," said Father O'Toole.

Nico finished his drink and looked out of the rectory window to the Strip District below. With a deep sigh, Nico turned around and sat back on the couch. Father O'Toole, who never took his eyes off Nico, sat at his desk and waited for a response. When Nico said nothing, Father O'Toole gave it one last effort.

"Look, son, I have to admit that I somewhat agree with you. We don't need the Diocese of Pittsburgh to validate our beliefs. But right now, I don't know what to believe or what to think. I … I am just not as sure as you are at this point, that's all. But forget the Diocese. They are not as important, agreed. But the people … the people … they are what is important. The people are the Church. The Church is not the buildings or the Diocese or even the Pope. The people are the Church. There was a shooting in our church and the people are scared and they want answers. We owe them that much, at least. And if the people believe a miracle occurred, regardless of what the Diocese says, then maybe that is what is most important. Perhaps believing in a miracle will bring people back to the Church. Not just to our church, but all the churches. If that happens, wouldn't you agree that would be a miracle?"

"So … is that how you plan to handle this? Push the Diocese to conclude that we are not victims of an attempted assassination but rather undeserving recipients of a miracle?"

"No, son. That would be disingenuous. I am merely going to comply and let this thing run its course. I make enough waves with the Diocese as it is. Not over this, though, not over this. Whatever they find, I have already accepted it. What I tell people on my own accord … well, let's just say that is between me and the Lord. I will answer for all my actions, as will you, in due time."

Nico relented. He agreed to meet with the Diocese, not because he had to and not because he thought it was important, but rather, because his friend asked him to. Nico was always one for not letting his friends down.

"Okay, son, thank you," said Father O'Toole. "Why don't you plan on spending the day here, huh? Go to the kitchen and take out one of the frozen trays of meatballs and pasta and put it on the stove. We can have lunch later, okay?"

Nico smiled. He stood up, walked to the priest and gave him a hug. He then made his way to the kitchen. When Nico left the room, Father O'Toole took the Jameson bottle out one more time and took a healthy swig before putting it back in his desk.

When Nico got to the kitchen, he called Lucy. "Hey, Luce, how are you? Sorry for calling you so early. I know that you are probably trying to get ready for work. But listen, I really, really, really need to get out of the house today. Could you see who is around tonight, I mean, can you see if anyone wants to get together around dinner, after dinner, any time, somebody's place other than mine? Let's have some beers or something … Can't host, not at my place. Can't do it. It's crowded … I will explain later … Yes, I'm alright … Lots to talk about, I suppose … Do you mind doing this for me, please? … Okay, great, pick me up at the rectory … Yes, the rectory. I am spending the day here."

When the call concluded, Lucy hung up her phone and placed it on her bed. She had been on her knees praying all morning. A candle was lit beside a small statue of the Virgin Mary. She was holding rosary beads that belonged to her grandmother.

Chapter eightteen

After he got the frozen meatballs and pasta ready for the stove, Nico returned to Father O'Toole's office. "Anything you need, Father, while I am here today?"

"Yes, actually, there is one more thing that you can do for me," said Father O'Toole, somewhat bashfully. Nico could tell something else was up. He returned to his seat on the couch.

"I got another call last night that I did not get to tell you about …. The shooter, Dylan Ray … His name is Dylan Ray. He called me last night."

"Wait, what? They let that wingnut have phone privileges? What did he call you about? Should be calling a lawyer."

"He wants me to come pay him a visit … and, more importantly, he wants me to bring you with me," said Father O'Toole as he prepared for another go-round with Nico.

"Bad idea. The guy tried to kill me."

"No, he tried to kill me."

"Whatever, I got nothing to say to him."

"Look, son, even Pope John Paul II, God Rest His Soul, went to prison to visit the man who shot him …"

As Father O'Toole began to get onto his soapbox, Nico fell into a full-blown daydream flashback on the couch.

Nico was again with Jessica LaRue as she took him by the hand and led him through the Philadelphia Museum of Art. "Just so I know, is this our second date or our official first date?" joked Nico.

"Agggggghhhh. You engineer types have to define everything, don't you now?" said Jessica playfully. "Just go with the flow for a minute." As she led him through the museum, they stopped at the Pablo Picasso exhibit. The two viewed the masterpiece *Bullfight— Courses de Taureaux*. Jessica continued as the tour guide. "Picasso is definitely my favorite. He painted what he felt, not what he saw."

"I know," said Nico in agreement. "He is my favorite, too."

"Yeah, right. C'mon, dude, you are just saying that."

"No, I'm serious. Picasso once said that there are no accidents, only encounters in history, or something like that … I thought a lot about that after I met you in the bar the other night."

Jessica's demeanor changed from giggly to very serious and impressed. "Oh my God, you do like Picasso."

"Maybe there is more to me than just numbers, kid."

Jessica moved very close to Nico and looked deeply into his eyes. Nico stared back, but the intensity in her eyes forced Nico to look back to the painting. Jessica started to gently rub his back for a few seconds as he continued, "Take this painting here, *Bullfight*. I mean, sometimes, this is how I feel. Like the bullfighter, sometimes I am in total control of everything around me. And other times, I only think that I am in control, when in reality, I am heading for complete disaster, just like the bull."

"I come to this museum about once a week. It never gets old. I get inspiration here. My dream is to one day come in here and see my art hanging next to a Picasso."

"He can who thinks he can, and he can't who thinks he can't," said Nico very proudly.

"I get it, I believe you, you know Picasso. You don't have to keep quoting him," said Jessica as she started to slowly leave Nico's side. "Anyways, that is my dream. What is your dream, Nico from Pittsburgh?"

Nico turned away from her and refocused intently on the painting. After a few moments, he turned back to his left and said, "To be with you forever," but she was no longer standing there. A solid tap on his right shoulder caused him to gasp.

As Nico gasped and turned to his right in real life, he snapped out of his daydream.

"So, as with the Diocese, I can't force you to go with me, but perhaps you will consider it as a nice warm up for the meeting with the Diocese," said Father O'Toole, who was oblivious to the fact that Nico was completely daydreaming and did not hear a word of what he said.

"Yeah, okay—whatever, whatever you need. No more arguing. Go to the jail, talk to the Diocese. I got it, I'm good," said Nico who now struggled with reality.

"Son, go lay down in one of the many, many unoccupied guest rooms. Try to sleep. I will wake you up for lunch."

Nico stood up, shook his head in agreement and without saying anything further, went to a guest room to try to nap.

Chapter nineteen

Nico managed to get a few minutes of sleep in a rectory guest bedroom. The smell of homemade sauce and meatballs cooking in the kitchen lofted up to the bedroom and gently woke him. Although he could have used more sleep, it was a pleasant way to wake up. It reminded him of being in his grandparents' house when he was a small child. Nico joined Father O'Toole at the dinner table and the two shared a meal. Very little was said, other than "Pass the parmesan."

It was a very short drive to the county jail from the rectory. Still, neither person said a word to one another. Father O'Toole was exhausted from dealing with Nico, the Diocese, and the newspapers. Nico was exhausted from apparently having given up on sleep, besides the brief respite experienced in the guest bedroom, which was nice, but not nearly adequate. The silence between these two good friends was odd at first, but deep down, both welcomed the relative peace they were experiencing, albeit if only for a short time.

Nico and Father O'Toole underwent the rigorous screening process at the jail so that guards could be certain that neither possessed any contraband or any object that could be seized by an inmate and turned into a weapon. Having been properly screened, Nico and Father O'Toole were led to the non-contact attorney conference room, which was a small room separated from a slightly larger room by a thick piece of glass with holes in it for talking. The visitor's section of the room was only slightly big enough for one person. There was only one chair, which Nico yielded to Father O'Toole as he squeezed in behind him. After waiting about ten minutes in silence, a jail guard led Dylan Ray into the inmate section of the non-contact visiting room. When he saw both the priest and Nico there, Dylan Ray immediately burst into tears and pleaded as he fell to both knees.

"Forgive me! Forgive me! Please! I didn't mean to try to kill you, my Lord," screamed and moaned Dylan at the top of his lungs.

"It's okay, son, it's okay. I forgive you. God will pardon your sins if you properly confess," responded the priest in as warm of a manner as he could muster.

"No! No! Jesus, please forgive me, Jesus, please forgive," shouted Dylan even louder.

"Yes, my son. Jesus and our loving mother Mary will forgive you. I will forgive you, you just need to—."

"Oh, would you shut up! I don't want your forgiveness. I want his!" screamed Dylan Ray as he pointed at Nico, who was stunned.

Father O'Toole, now feeling insulted, got up quickly from his chair, which he caused to slide back and slam into Nico's knee. "Wait a minute! You bring a gun into my church! You shoot at me twice! But you don't want my forgiveness—you want his?" yelled Father O'Toole who was completely outraged.

"Don't you see? Aren't any of you looking? We are in the presence of our Lord and Savior, Jesus Christ! He has come back to save us all!" Dylan Ray screamed as he again pointed at Nico, who was rubbing his knee from where the chair hit him. Dylan then threw his entire body at the window, seemingly with the hope of trying to fit through one of the talking holes. "Please, Jesus, I know I do not deserve it, but please forgive me ..." The commotion of his body crashing into the dividing glass caused the closest two guards to quickly enter the room and restrain Dylan Ray.

"We are done here," muttered Father O'Toole as he shoved his way past Nico to get out of the visitor's room. Nico followed with a slight limp.

Outside of the jail, Father O'Toole lit up a cigarette as the two walked toward the car. Nico removed the cigarette from Father O'Toole's mouth and took one deep drag. "Well, Padre, guess that really didn't go as planned, huh?" He took another drag and handed it back to the priest.

"I don't know what to say. Perhaps he is trying to plant the seeds for an insanity defense," said the completely frustrated priest.

"He is a complete nut job. How am I the only one who sees things for what they are?" Nico's phone rang. He answered the call from Lucy. "Hey, Luce...Yeah, look, I will be at the rectory in ten minutes … Yeah, please get me there … Great, see you then." Nico hung up the phone and continued to walk with Father O'Toole to his car. Neither said another word on the walk or the short car ride back to the rectory.

Wil 3

Chapter twenty

A short time later, Nico's girlfriend Lucy arrived at the rectory. Nico ran to her car and jumped into the passenger seat. He lunged across the seat and smothered her with an enormous hug, but when he tried to kiss her, she turned her head and instead, Nico kissed her cheek. He then noticed a religious article hanging from her rearview mirror.

"When did you get this?" asked Nico, inquisitively.

"The scapular, oh, I've had it for a while, years, actually. From my grandmother. I just put it up there today, though," said Lucy.

"Huh, you don't say…Well, I have Allstate, so I'm in good hands," said Nico. The two took a short drive through the city until they ended up at their mutual friend James's apartment. James was famous for hosting both planned and impromptu gatherings that involved watching a sporting event or listening to good music. But whatever the cause, the events were always flush with beer. This night was no exception. Beastie Boys music could be heard outside of the apartment as the people gathered inside drank beer and argued about rap music in historical context.

"See, you hear that? That is Led Zeppelin. Not just a sample, but the whole damn beat. Only a genius would think of mixing that element of classic rock and making it fresh again with innovative rhyme schemes. That is why *Licensed to Ill* is the greatest rap album of all time," said Rick, a partygoer.

"You are so full of it and what the hell, truly, is wrong with you? Greatest ever my ass! Look, these kids, and they were kids at the time, were just punks who couldn't make it in the dying New York punk rock scene. This album was a joke. In fact, I think I read somewhere that it was made as a joke. Rapping over Led Zeppelin was not meant to be taken seriously. Genius? Hardly," quipped James, the host, who loved to argue.

"That so, huh? Well, then, if you think that the Beastie Boys were a joke, why were they called the white Run DMC back in the day? Don't tell me you think DMC is a joke, too?" retorted Rick.

"Rick, that is just it. Back in the day, they were compared to Run DMC. Today, with their activism, they're called the U2 of Rap Music. They are always compared, tenuously at best, to someone else or some other group. They never stand on their own. I.E., joke," declared James.

"C'mon, James. Where's the love? How do you not like these guys? I mean, look, they're Jewish, you're Jewish, how about giving some props to your people," said Rick jokingly. The others in attendance started to laugh out loud after that remark as well. The doorbell rang.

James tried to talk over the laughter and fired out one final response on his way to the door. "Yeah, well, 3rd Bass were Jews, too. You don't see me saying that they put out the best albums, either." When he opened the door, the music stopped as Nico, followed closely by Lucy, entered the room.

"Well, hey, I'm not the cops. Nobody said turn down the music. Don't let the party stop because of us … But hey, how long do I have to stand here before someone shows me where I can get a beer?" said Nico. In a rush, three people ran over to Nico with cold cans of beer in their hand. Nico took one, gave one to Lucy and put the other in his pocket. He opened one and took a big drink. The silence continued. "Let me guess, I will bet that Rick has just suggested that either the Beastie Boys are the greatest rap group of all time or, alternatively, *Licensed to Ill* is the greatest rap album of all time, right?" said Nico condescendingly.

"Um-hum, yeah, right, sure did," the group responded.

"How'd I guess … I must be a prophet," said Nico jokingly.

"That is what the newspapers say," said James.

"Well, you can't believe everything you read in those goofy corporate tabloids." Nico took another drink. "This debate has been going on for what, five years now, at least? I will now end all debate," Nico took a quick look around the room before he continued and was stunned that everyone just stared at him in silence. "Public Enemy's

Fear of a Black Planet is the greatest rap album of all time. Right from the start, with the immediate intro, you get hit with all those samples, drum beats and record scratches at the same time, plus a very healthy dose of awesome bass. Kids could blast it in their cars and liberal academics could study the message in each song. That album did for rap music what *Sgt. Pepper's Lonely Hearts Club* did for pop."

After a few moments of nobody saying a word, Nico turned to Rick. "That's it? No response? No argument?"

"No, I think you nailed it. Public Enemy is the greatest," said Rick timidly. The rest of the crowd all voiced support for the conclusion. The music was turned back on, though at a low volume. A minute later, *Fear of a Black Planet* played on the stereo. Nico said nothing further and just rolled his eyes. He took a spot on the couch with Lucy. After sitting on the couch drinking beer for a little more than an hour, Nico signaled to Lucy that it is time to go. She agreed to go with him back to his apartment, but first swinging past the rectory so that Nico could retrieve his motorcycle. On the drive to the rectory, Nico shared his story about his encounter with Dylan Ray at the county jail with Lucy, who just listened.

Wil 3

Chapter twenty-one

Nico quickly circled the block in front of his apartment while on his motorcycle and, to his delight, nobody was gathered in front of it. He parked his motorcycle behind the apartment, then walked out front to meet Lucy, who sat in the car and waited for him to arrive. As Nico unlocked the front door to the apartment, he turned back to Lucy, who still sat in her running car.

"You coming up?" asked Nico. Lucy just looked at him. Nico could tell by the way that she sat and by her noticeable lack of words, she considered not coming up to his apartment. *But why not?* He thought to himself. Eventually, she turned off her car and joined Nico at the front door. He led her by the hand as the two trekked up the two flights of stairs to his second-floor apartment.

"Ahh, home sweet home," said Nico. He kicked off his shoes and jumped onto his old couch. Lucy continued to stand silently just inside the doorway as she looked around the apartment. "Lucy, what was up with those guys tonight?" asked Nico as he lay on the couch.

"What do you mean? They seemed fine to me," said Lucy who had grown anxious.

"Well, yeah, they were fine, I guess … but no matter what I said, everybody just agreed with me. Not one disagreement, let alone an argument or debate."

"Maybe when you're right, you're right and there is no need to argue?"

"Yeah, but that is just it. We were discussing sports and music. And there are rarely, if ever, correct answers that everyone agrees with. Ha, and yeah, what fun is it if everyone agrees with everything you say? Where is the challenge? … Lucy, what are you looking at?"

"Your apartment … it's so … it's so … organized," said Lucy, who still had not moved from the doorway.

"It is. And clean too!" said Nico, very proudly. "Actually, I was hoping that you would be in the mood to help me mess it up a bit.

You know, start by taking off your coat and dropping it on the floor after you actually come in here and shut the door."

"Sorry, Nico, I don't think I can stay with you tonight," said Lucy apologetically.

"What? Why not? You haven't been here for a few nights now. We haven't been together forever, it seems."

"It's just ... I just ... can't. That's all."

Nico sat up on the couch as he thought to himself about all the confusing situations and circumstances that recently presented, Lucy's new attitude certainly must top the list. "I don't get it. Do you not like me anymore? You want to break up or something?"

"No, Nico ... honey ... that is not it at all ... It's just ... I love you, Nico."

"You love me? Well ... Lucy ... I ... love ... you ... too? Is that it? Is that what you need to hear from me? I love you, Lucy. Now, if you would just stay here, I can show you how much love I have for you. Please, allow me to demonstrate."

"No, that's just it, Nico. I can't stay. We can't ... get together," said Lucy as she struggled to find the right words in the stressful situation. "Premarital sex is a sin. We can't do that anymore."

Nico literally jumped from the couch. He was both agitated as well as confused. "A sin? It hasn't been a sin for at least a year. It wasn't a sin before you met me ... You're not even Catholic!"

"Please calm down, honey, you are getting all worked up,"

"I was getting all worked up, but not now, don't you worry about that." Nico stomped across the room and grabbed his sleeping pills. He took two of them and swallowed a mouthful of wine right from the bottle. Lucy just watched him in silence. He took another mouthful of wine from the bottle, then turned to Lucy as the expression on his face changed from confusion into total disbelief.

"Oh ... my ... God ... Lucy. Don't tell me that you actually believe in this miracle Jesus Christ nonsense?"

"I don't know what to believe anymore. I don't know who to believe ... It's just, I know that what we did was a sin and we can't do it anymore. That's all. Look, I should go. Stay there," said Lucy as she removed herself from Nico's apartment. Nico heard her shoes echoing off the cheap linoleum in the staircase and the tight hallway. Mockingly, Nico threw a sign of the cross to her as the entrance door opened and closed.

Nico returned to his couch and sat there for almost five minutes with his head in both his hands. He was not thinking, he certainly wasn't talking, he just sat there and tried to calm himself. After a short time, he got up from the couch and picked up his old-school landline telephone. He called his principal, who he knew would not be in the office at that time, and left a message.

"Hey, boss, it's just me, Nico Rossi. Sorry to be calling you so late. But listen, I don't need a whole week off. Two days was more than enough. I think all my obligations with the cops and what not should be done by this point. I want … I need to come back to work. I am starting to go stir-crazy being all cooped up in my tiny apartment. I will be there tomorrow. I just didn't want to shock you showing up unannounced. Thought that I should let you know so that you didn't order up a sub in the morning, okay? Thanks for your understanding. See you in the morning."

Nico walked into his bedroom and opened his closet which was full of boxes of old stuff. He removed the boxes and pulled out a mysterious oil painting in a cheap frame that was buried at the back of the closet. The painting was signed. It was odd in that one half of the painting was bright and cheerful while the other half was dark and foreboding. As Nico stared at the painting while he sat on the bed, he lapsed into another flashback.

The dark, off-rust colored portion of the painting transformed into a very weathered industrial metal door that had seen better days. Nico stood back from the door in a small hallway as Jessica LaRue pulled an enormous key from her purse. The door made all kind of noise when the lock tumbled from the key and the hinges squeaked painfully as Jessica, who had to noticeably use force, started to pull the door open, then jumped to the other side to push it the rest of the way. Jessica grabbed Nico by the hand and led him into a dark room until she could make her way to the light switch. The very old, 1970s-style fluorescent lighting mounted near the top of the industrially high ceilings artificially lit up the room and revealed several paintings, sculptures and other creations that sat quietly underneath the buzz from the ballasts of the fluorescent lights. Nico was speechless as he scanned the room.

"Well, go on. Get a closer look. Don't worry, you won't break anything," said Jessica proudly.

"This ... this ... all this stuff is yours? You painted these and ... sculpted all of this art?" said Nico with impressed wonderment in his tone.

"Yes, silly, this my studio."

"I thought you said that you were bringing me to your apartment?"

"I did ... and I did ... I live here, too. Get it? Studio apartment," said Jessica.

As Nico continued to walk around the studio in amazement, Jessica followed closely behind. "So, Jess, do you sell any of this?"

"Not as much as I would like to. I mean, if I sold more, then I could stop bartending and waitressing and just focus on my art. But I don't, so I will continue to sling beers. But hey, I don't paint or sculpt for money, I do it because I have to. I have to get it out of me and on to canvas or clay ... That is why I do my art, that's just who I am."

Nico said nothing as he methodically moved through the studio apartment and examined pieces of artwork. He also looked elsewhere at places where objects were void. Eventually, his silence was too much for Jessica to handle.

"Well, Nico, what do you think ... what are you thinking about?" questioned Jessica nervously. "You ... ahh...kind of quiet over there."

"Needs a few more things," said Nico in a very matter-of-fact tone.

Nico's daydream flashback then took him to the same art studio apartment a few days later. Jessica was putting the finishing touches of stain on an antique, large roller desk from the 1930s. Nico dragged an old, beaten up futon couch-bed into a freight elevator. A queen-size bed with no headboard, a la punk rock style, had replaced the old, rickety futon piece.

The "burning rubber" from a car outside of Nico's apartment ended his memory dream. He realized what just happened as he continued to stare into the painting. "I thought I was your ying," he said to himself as he put the painting back into the closet and piled the boxes back in front of it. He made one final trip to his kitchen and consumed two more pills and one more healthy drink of wine. It was important that he slept tonight, even if it was from prescription pill use. He set his alarm clock for 6:30 AM and crawled into bed.

Wil 3

Chapter twenty-two

Nico succumbed to the double dose of sleeping pills and booze, but his sleep was not filled with his usual drug-induced crazy dreams. He just slept, then was awake with nothing in between. Not a great sleep, but at least it was rest. He probably would have slept through his alarm had it not been for the people gathered outside his apartment who woke him with their serenade of church hymns. Nico gently slipped open the curtain on his bedroom window just enough so that he could peer out. To his dismay, he discovered the group had grown in numbers. Instead of being just a handful of senior citizens, at least twenty people of all different ages, including young children who came to sing before they themselves had to go to school, were now gathered.

Nico made sure to keep the lights off. He went into the kitchen and started the coffee, then jumped into the shower. By the time that he was finished showering, enough natural light in the apartment allowed him to dress. He put on his working man's khakis and plain white button-down shirt with a brightly colored Jerry Garcia tie. Just as before, Nico exited his apartment via the fire escape and drifted his motorcycle several yards before he fired it up and rode to school.

When Nico entered the school, he immediately met Steve Alder, the principal, in his office. The principal's office was directly across the hallway from the school cafeteria where all students gathered in the mornings. Although the cafeteria doors were shut, as was the door to the principal's office, the noise emanating from the cafeteria grew at a steady pace and could be heard by both Nico and Principal Alders. The two sat together for several minutes and talked.

"Mr. Rossi, we are all just so grateful that you are alive and well. It is just mind-blowing that something like that could happen … and in a church, no less," said the principal.

Nico was tired. He looked tired. He tried his best to feign interest in the conversation, but even the principal could see that Nico was probably most tired from having these conversations with other people.

"It was strange. That's for sure. Either God was with us or we just got lucky. Either way, I'm okay. Ready to start teaching again."

"Calling that shooting strange is by far an understatement. So many people are just sick these days—so sick and disturbed. It is quite a shame. And honestly, I admire your willingness to go back to work so soon. I don't know if I …"

As the principal rambled on nervously, the growing sound of the students caused Nico to sink into another full-blown daydream. The noise from the cafeteria soon became the noise of the open-air market that Nico remembered.

Nico found himself with Jessica LaRue in a very gritty, industrial section of Philadelphia near the shipyards. The ground was half-dilapidated blacktop, half cinders with potholes, puddles and weeds growing everywhere. It smelled of a mixture of diesel fuel and fresh baked goods, which shifted slightly as the salt water breeze came and went. The sound of many people bartering or buying and selling goods eclipsed the noise from the working men on the nearby ships.

Vendors on the street sold everything from homemade foods to car parts and everything in between. Although Nico had never been here before, he felt somewhat at home as the place reminded him of the Strip District. The only difference was that there were not any actual stores. Every booth seemed to be makeshift and was outside. Nico wasn't sure if this place was regularly conducting business in this manner or if these people all just assembled in swap-meet fashion like a band of transient gypsy salesmen. However, Nico thought it would be best to limit his questions and just go with it.

"What did you bring me here for, again?" asked Nico as he struggled to keep up with Jessica, who was being particularly bouncy as she bobbed and weaved through the throngs of patrons and merchants.

"Silly, if you are going to start going to clubs with me, we have to get you some proper clothing."

"You know, we must have driven past two or three malls before we got here. I'm sure we could have found something there."

"Yeah, probably. But I think you have enough J. Crew and clothes from Macy's. You need club clothes, non-Republican clothes." said Jessica, partly being playful but also sincere. "Wait right here," said Jessica as she disappeared into the crowd.

Nico stood around, as told, for a couple of minutes, until he smelled, then located, a vendor selling hot sausage sandwiches. He tussled to get through the crowd to make his way to the vendor. He looked around once more for Jessica, but could not find her. Nico was just about to order a sandwich when a strong tug came to his right hand. It was Jessica and she held a Clash T-shirt in her hand with the iconic picture of Joe Strummer smashing a guitar on stage, being the *London Calling* album cover.

The unexpected tug on his hand made Nico gasp. In real life, he turned to the right and gasped as he awoke from the daydream.

"Nico, Nico are you still with me?" asked the principal.

"Yeah, sorry, I just … Look, I wasn't shot. And from what I know, I wasn't even the target. Just my bad luck for being at the wrong place at the wrong time. But I am ready to teach now."

"I see. Well, how about you at least let me buy you a doughnut and we can get some coffee in the cafeteria?"

Nico looked at his watch. "Sure, we still have a few minutes before first bell."

Principal Alders led Nico from his office into the cafeteria. By that time, the noise from the cafeteria had become quite loud, which was commonplace, as the kids tried to get the last word in with one another before the first bell rang. When the principal entered, there wasn't much of a reaction. However, when Nico entered the cafeteria, a few steps behind his principal, the entire cafeteria became immediately silent. The silence was quite unnerving. Neither Nico nor the principal had ever heard such a lack of noise in any room of any school at any time in their careers, including study halls in the library. Students that sat soon rose to their feet. Students that were in line all parted so that Nico could easily and quickly get to the front of the line. Some students even bowed their heads as Nico walked past them. Both Nico and the principal looked at each other with amazement. Sadly, Nico had started to adjust to all the weirdness that now surrounded him. "Why should it be any less weird at his place of employment?" Nico thought to himself.

Later that afternoon, Nico was teaching in his classroom. He had just presented a lesson and had answered the questions. With only the last ten minutes remaining in class, he allowed his students time to get their homework started, as long as they didn't talk. Nico walked around class to monitor his students' progress and noted, oddly, that they all worked quite diligently. A loud knock at the door startled a few students and stopped Nico where he stood. He moved to the front of the room to open the door.

"Oh, it's you again."

"Good to see you again as well, Mr. Rossi," said Detective Martin with flat affect.

"Forgive my manners once again, but I am kind of busy. Whatever you need, can't it wait?"

"Oh, well, maybe it can, maybe not. Your principal said that it was okay for me to pull you out of class for a couple of minutes."

"Well nobody asked me. And that is not okay. Don't you know what happens when you leave schoolchildren unsupervised? One of them may have already started a fire or something while you distracted me."

Detective Martin pushed slightly past Nico and opened the classroom door to its fullest. All the students still worked quietly. "I don't see any problem here."

"Yet," quickly retorted Nico. "Look, I don't bother you when you are working, now do I?"

"I am working now,"

"Yes, I know that. But I am not bothering you, now am I?"

"No. I guess not. But you are not cooperating either," said Detective Martin with an air of frustration.

"Fine … okay man, whatever. I can see you won't leave." Nico intentionally and slowly cleared his throat. "How may I assist you, Officer Martin?"

"Detective Martin."

"Oh yes, of course, how could I forget? How may I assist you, Detective Martin??"

"Thank you, Mr. Rossi. I understand that you visited Dylan Ray in jail last night," said Detective Martin as he stared down at his iPad.

"That really isn't a question at all. But yes, you are correct. Father O'Toole and I visited Dylan Ray in jail last night. The visit lasted less than five minutes, if that. Just fulfilling my Christian obligations, I suppose," said Nico as he tried to remain calm.

"Christian obligations, huh? Don't you think your obligations stem more from your friendship?"

Nico responded very sarcastically and with disgust, "You got me. You are right. I baked him a cake that had a metal file in it, but the guards were clever enough to confiscate it from me before I could give it to him." Nico continued, in further disgust, as he looked down at the ground when he spoke. "I keep telling you, I never met that dude before he shot up the church. Yesterday, Father put me on a guilt trip and basically made me go with him to visit that guy in jail. I didn't say one word to him in the short time we were there. You are just wasting your time if you keep going down that path. I mean, that's cool, it's your day. But don't waste mine."

"So now you are going to tell me how to do my job, is that it?"

"Look, detective, what do you want from me? I have told you everything that I know, at least two or three times. Nothing has changed. You are harassing me now," said Nico, defiantly.

"Watch it now son, you are on thin ice," said Detective Martin with a cold edge in his voice

"No, you watch it and I'm not your son. You can't keep showing up at my apartment or showing up where I work just to ask me senseless questions. I know my rights and you are hassling me for no good reason," said Nico even more defiantly.

"Would you prefer to come downtown to answer my questions then? I thought I was being nice, extending you this courtesy."

"Yeah. Sure. I'll be right there. As soon as you show me a warrant or you arrest me. I will be there with a lawyer. That how you want to handle this?" Nico peered back into his classroom. To his amazement, the students still worked hard even though they were unsupervised. "Now, we are done here. Please excuse me before one of them really does start a fire."

Nico pulled the door closed quickly, but stopped just short of slamming it. "*Maiale*," he muttered under his breath. "Sorry for that interruption guys. Does anyone have any questions?" said Nico to his students.

Outside the door, Detective Martin finished writing a note and then took handcuffs out of his pocket. He was just about to open the classroom door when the bell for the end of the day rang and within seconds, Detective Martin was surrounded by excited students eager to go home. Detective Martin put the handcuffs back into his pocket and exited the school in the flow of the students.

Chapter twenty-three

The first Sunday morning following the shooting came to Nico as a complete blur, which was par for the course. Nico rode his motorcycle to church and for the first time since the shooting, he took some time to reflect on the entire situation, not just the bizarre new reality that had engulfed him. Sometimes Nico did his best thinking on his motorcycle, so he chose the long and out-of-the-way route to church that provided him a lot of opportunity for reflection.

The week ended … oddly, he thought to himself. It paled in comparison to how it all started, but still, it was quite odd. Lucy told him that she loved him and did not want to break up with him, yet would not have sex with him. And she still never returned any of his calls or text messages and he hadn't seen her since she left his apartment Tuesday night. What kind of love is that, he thought? It was strange that he hadn't spoken or seen Father O'Toole since the incident in the jail with Dylan Ray. Nico usually spoke to him at least once a week, besides church, of course, and they generally spoke about either the Pittsburgh Pirates or the state of Major League Baseball. Father O'Toole was a huge baseball fan. Nico figured that he must be swamped on his end dealing with parishioners and the Diocese. But at least he hadn't heard anything more from that goofy detective with his even more bizarre line of questions since he surprised him at the school. And at least nobody had taken any more shots at him.

Behind the rectory was a very old, seemingly abandoned alley. It was too narrow for any car to drive down. But for Nico's motorcycle, it was perfect. He always parked back there and walked across the rectory lawn to the back of the church, where Nico could use a church key to enter through a door that led directly behind the altar.

Following his normal course, Nico parked his bike and walked to the church. As he turned the corner from the rectory, he could see a large group of people gathered in front of the church. The protest has grown larger. But as he got closer, he noticed that something was different about this week's protest. There was more standing around and less commotion. Less organization. No signs or chants. As he got closer still, he realized that the people gathered out front were not protesters, but rather, were parishioners and other people who had no place to sit or even stand inside the church. Nico walked past the church door so he could get a look at the parking lot. The parking lot was filled beyond capacity with cars double-parked and blocking other cars. Up and down the street they led to the church, cars were parked on both sides as far as he could see. Nico had never seen the church this full. Not even on any Christmas or Easter. Even the church festival never gathered such an enormous crowd.

Nico entered the church through the rear door, which was already unlocked. Father O'Toole had just finished putting on his vestments. "Hey, good morning, Padre, looks like you could use a hand today, that's for sure."

"Well, top of the morning to you! Yes sir, we are packing them in today," smiled the priest, as he was both happy to see Nico and happy to see so many people in church.

"Hey, I got something for you. A good luck charm. You can wear it under your vestments." Nico laughed as he tossed a blue plastic bag to the priest. Father O'Toole opened the bag and pulled out a T-shirt with a huge red bullseye on it.

"Jesus, Mary and Joseph. It looks like you haven't lost your sense of humor, as sick and twisted as it is," said the priest with a smile. He put the shirt back into the bag and gave it a good toss right back to Nico, who also laughed.

As the two exchanged pleasantries, reminiscent of older times when things were less strange, an unexpected guest and his entourage came into the room from the back door, which Nico neglected to lock behind him.

"Your Excellency! I wasn't expecting you today. I ... I would have prepared something," said Father O'Toole who was completely surprised to see the Bishop and two of his assistants standing there.

"No need, no need. I am sorry for arriving unannounced," said the Bishop. Nico turned away from the Bishop as he muttered "whatever" under his breath and continued to dress himself for the altar. Father O'Toole kissed the Bishop's ring. Eventually, Nico followed suit.

The Bishop then turned from Nico and squarely addressed Father O'Toole. "Well, I'll keep this short as I know that you have a Mass to celebrate. As you can imagine, my phone hasn't stopped ringing. Everyone wants to know the Church's official position on what exactly happened here last week as to whether or not it was a true miracle." He paused for a moment as if in deep contemplation, then continued. "Miracles take years to confirm and actually require action and validation from the Vatican, as you are well aware. The Vatican has been fully informed of this situation—both the fact that a shooting occurred as well as the belief that a miracle may have equally presented itself since nobody was injured or killed. They are forming, as we speak, their own committee to investigate this matter, which will run independent of the Diocese investigation. That all being said, since what occurred is not a typical miraculous situation, i.e. your weeping statutes or images of the Blessed Virgin appearing …"

"Yeah, like that lady who found the image of the Blessed Mother in a bag of Cheetos. I think that item is still on eBay. You can bid on it if you want, Your Holiness, I'll give you my password if you like," said Nico.

"That is enough out of you, Nicholas," scolded the priest.

"Indeed. Yes, as I was saying, even if what happened was a miracle, it will take years to confirm. In the meantime, I believe that we should seize upon this day and this opportunity to further promote the Church …"

"Whoa! Whoa! Whoa! Hold up, now. Are you trying to spin the fact that we both were almost killed last week to promote the Church?" questioned Nico, who was very sincere, yet still could not lose the smart tone to his voice.

"Young man, did you just accuse me of trying to 'spin' this situation which is both terrible and potentially miraculous at the same time?" said the Bishop indignantly.

"Stop it, Nico. Show some respect. You know better than to speak to his holiness in that tone. I apologize, your Eminence," said Father O'Toole, who was trying his best to show restraint.

"Yes, Your Holiness, that is exactly what I said."

"Nicholas, so help me God, when I get my hands on you ..." Father O'Toole, now seemingly without any self-control, started to approach Nico. He halted, however, when the Bishop put his hand up with the international stop sign signal.

Nico continued. "What exactly is the message that you are trying to promote? That our priests can't be shot and killed? What kind of message is that? To me, that sounds like a challenge to any other possible whack-job out there who may be thinking the same thoughts. I mean, did you happen to see how many people are out there today? There has to be at least as many people outside of the church as there are on the inside. Who knows which one of them might be next to take a shot at us. Next time, we may not be so lucky ... or fortunate ... or blessed ... or whatever we were last time we got shot at."

"Bless you, my son. And you too, Thomas," said the Bishop in a very genuine manner. His words had a very calming effect upon the priest. Nico, not quite so much. "I understand your frustration and anger over what has happened and I don't pretend for a minute to understand how you truly feel inside. All I know is that you and you, Father Tom, are very strong for even returning to the altar a week after what has transpired. Yes, there are many people in the church and no, I do not know if any of them has the intention of trying to harm either one of you. But as Christians ... as Catholics ... we can't focus on the hate or the evil that is out there. We can only try to bring our faith to the masses for the betterment of all of us. For the betterment of our entire community, including that which extends beyond the walls of this sacred place."

After a few moments of silence, Father O'Toole spoke up. "Forgive us, both, your Excellency. The recent week has been rather trying. What would you like me to do?"

"Thomas, you continue to run the church, as you have. Nothing beyond that, besides making yourself available to the investigators, as needed. But as for you, Mr. Rossi, we will ask that you speak to the media about these certain events." After the Bishop made that statement, one of his assistants walked across the room and handed Nico a manila folder. Nico opened the folder and quickly scanned the documents inside. He noticed that all the pages were prepared statements, presumably put together by the Diocese's PR department.

"I ... I don't understand. I mean, the gunman was trying to kill Father O'Toole. We are all clear on that. I wasn't a target. Tell him, Padre, just like you told me. You were the target, not me," said Nico in a very confused manner having been tasked with such an assignment.

"We are all aware of that. We know that you were not the target. Father O'Toole, because of his ... stances and ministry ... was the intended target of assassination. But all the newspapers are printing the fact that Dylan Ray has consistently said that you, that Jesus Christ stopped the bullets from hitting his intended target. And oddly, the media is not commenting on the mental state of Dylan Ray. Not one mention of a clearly insane person. It is ... it is almost as though the newspapers believe him. Rather, it seems as though the news media doesn't believe he is insane or delusional. It is as though they believe that Jesus Christ worked through you and stopped the bullets."

"Of course, they do. Why wouldn't they? A miracle story sells more papers and gets better ratings than a loon with a gun storyline," said Nico.

"Perhaps. Perhaps you may be right. But I, rather we all, believe that it is important that your story gets out there in a way to allow people to arrive at their own conclusion while the Vatican conducts its investigation. Let the people decide if a miracle did occur. Maybe, with any more luck, they will believe. Then they will come back to the church."

Nico quickly shot a glance at Father O'Toole, who was looking back at him and shrugged his shoulders at Nico as if to say: *Hey, this is a complete shock to me too.* But both people knew it wasn't a shock; Nico remembered already having that conversation with Father O'Toole on Tuesday before going to the jail.

"Your Eminence, with all due respect, I already told Father and I'll tell you the same—I will cooperate with any investigation, be it the Diocese, the Vatican or the cops. Hell, I'll cooperate with the FBI if they want to get involved. I agreed to go visit the shooter in jail because I was asked to. And I will continue to be an assistant to Father O'Toole for Mass or for whatever else he needs. But talking to the media, I mean, I am not a good Catholic. I sin on a daily basis, usually multiple times. Ask father, he will tell you. I don't take communion, I haven't been to confession in years. I mean, I don't think you want me as your poster boy spokesman for all that is holy. I'm not a poser and I don't want this spotlight. I never asked for any of this," said an exasperated Nico.

"Be that as it may, my son, please remember that the Good Samaritan was not always good. Likewise, Saul was a terrible, terrible murderer of Christians until God converted him, thus becoming St. Paul, our beloved. And our Mother Mary, she certainly did not ask God to be the mother of our Lord and Savior as a young teenage virgin. I cannot give you explanation—theologically or otherwise—as to why God has chosen you. But he has. And when God has chosen you, you cannot ignore Him."

"I did that once before," said Nico, seemingly ashamed.

"Then in His infinite wisdom, He has given you a second chance. Do not make the same mistake again."

Nico paused and thought about what he was just asked to do and how he would handle it. He thought about how he used to take pride in his ability to reason and how, with minimal effort, he easily convinced people to agree with his point of view, which was always based upon logic. But now, no matter what he said, his argument and reasoning were being stonewalled. It didn't matter if it was the police, Father O'Toole, the Bishop or even Lucy. Not one single person viewed this situation like he did and none of them even slightly validated his own opinion. Was his reasoning that flawed? Did his dependence on prescription medication and constant insomnia deprive him of his once great ability to get through to people with logic?

Maybe everyone else, including Dylan Ray, was normal and he was the one who was crazy? Crazy people never know they are crazy, he remembered once being told. Or maybe this situation was so far off the charts that normal, logical playbooks were simply insufficient? To top it off, he was being asked to be some sort of spokesperson to the media on behalf of St. Mary's Church.

Stillness filled the room and Nico felt everyone's eyes upon him. He felt weird and different. Not his normal off-self, but he felt like he had changed somehow and the feeling made him uncomfortable. As he looked around the room, Nico didn't just feel their eyes, but rather, he felt the weight of the entire situation physically resting on his shoulders. And not just the weight of being a spokesperson for St. Mary's, but the weight of the entire Roman Catholic faith and the weight of all the crosses that needed to be carried to get through what happened last Sunday.

Yes, it was the weight of the cross Father O'Toole carried, which included his own struggles against the Diocese over the years; the weight of the cross for both the Diocese and the Vatican as they desperately tried to stay relevant in times when people were just about to give up on organized religion; the weight of the good people inside and outside of the parish who just wanted so desperately to still believe in miracles, or at least believe that good people and sacred places still existed; the weight of Detective Martin's cross as he only wanted to bring sense, sanity and protection to people, even if his actions were contradictory; even the weight of the cross carried by Dylan Ray—although his motives may have been mistaken, Nico was sure that Ray's belief was sincere; and finally, the weight of his own cross—the cross he carried for such a long time that suffering had become the norm and his new status quo of existence.

Nico desperately yearned for answers as he thought to himself: *How could I have spent my entire life building for an amazing future only to see it ripped away when it was inches from my grasp? And now I am in such a dark place and do nothing but ... nothing but kick a can around, yet these guys want to put me on a pedestal? They think I am some sort of linchpin or pathway to understanding? How is that possible when I don't understand it myself?*

"What exactly do you have in mind, Bishop?" asked Nico.

"There is a reporter from *The New York Times* who is waiting in the rectory to interview you after Mass is finished," replied the Bishop.

"*The New York Times*!" exclaimed Nico, "Seriously? Guys, c'mon, this is too much. It doesn't get any bigger than that, unless you want me to do a sit down on CNN and talk about almost getting shot."

"Please, Nicholas, please. I know that we … I know that I have asked a lot from you recently. But I agree with the Bishop. I think that you need to tell the story. I know you are not a model Catholic, but you are sincere and people recognize that in you. If you tell the story, it will be better received coming from you than from any of us holy men whose motives would be subject to questioning, as you have pointed out. Please, Nico. It's the right thing to do," said Father O'Toole.

Maybe it was *Catholic Guilt*? Maybe it was Nico's inability to turn down a friend's request? Or, maybe Nico subconsciously decided to forget normal logic and just going with the flow afforded the best opportunity to find answers? But Nico eventually acquiesced to the will of the Bishop and Father O'Toole. Nico slowly approached the Bishop with his eyes to the ground.

"Your Excellency, I will do as you wish on one condition … That you stay here and celebrate Mass with us," said Nico softly.

"Agreed, and it will be our pleasure." The Bishop continued, "Now Nico, the reporter is waiting to meet you in the rectory after Mass. We have provided you with some pre-prepared statements. Feel free to answer questions, but if you get stuck, refer to something that has been prepared. It will allow you to get through the interview smoothly. Maybe read them over quickly in advance, just in case. Do you have any questions?"

"Just one," said Nico with a half smirk.

"Yes, my son?"

Nico pulled the bullseye T-shirt from the plastic bag. "When you take your place on the altar for today's mass, could you wear this T-shirt and stand about twenty feet away from Father O'Toole and me?"

"For the love, Nicholas, what's wrong with you!" scolded Father O'Toole.

"What wrong with all you? That was funny!" chuckled Nico, though he still dreaded the thought of being interviewed by *The New York Times*.

When the conversation and instruction concluded, Nico, Father O'Toole, the Bishop and his assistant made their way to the back of the church to start Mass. Nico carried the readings high above his head and led the holy men to the altar while the opening hymn played on the pipe organ. Father O'Toole conducted the Mass. He made no mention of the shooting. He made no reference to miracles. It wasn't until he took his place at the altar that he fully comprehended how many people were in the church—and that made him nervous for many different reasons. When it was time for the communion rites, he stepped aside and allowed the higher-ranking Bishop to continue.

"The Prayer of St. Francis" bellowed through the pipe organ when ushers released people from their pews to receive communion. Father O'Toole and the Bishop took the center aisle, one of the Bishop's assistants took the right aisle and Nico took the left aisle to distribute communion to the large congregation. As the people were released, every single person made their way to the left aisle to get communion from Nico. The priest, the Bishop and the other Eucharistic minister were totally ignored. It was not a sign of disrespect to anyone, but rather, it was awe and desire to be in Nico's presence. Even those people who would otherwise not have received communion still proceeded through the line and approached Nico with arms crossed, simply asking to be blessed by him. The priest and the Bishop were stunned as they just stood there. They assumed their next job function, which was that of a runner to make sure that Nico's chalice stayed full of communion wafers.

Wil 3

Chapter twenty-four

After Mass, Nico and the others reconvened in the small office behind the altar. Father O'Toole removed his vestments and likewise, Nico removed his altar boy apparel in favor of his street clothes. Nobody said a word because nobody knew what to say. Everyone, besides Nico, simply tried to comprehend the fact that Nico, a non-priest or deacon, just distributed more than one thousand pieces of Holy Communion and offered at least two hundred blessings to parishioners who were not receiving communion while the priest and the Bishop stood idly by and watched.

When Nico finished changing his clothes, he forced a smile as he wished everyone a happy rest of the day. He grabbed his motorcycle helmet and the manila folder with his prepared statements and reluctantly walked to the rectory with his shoulders slumped and eyes to the ground.

Nico met Chris Michaels, a reporter from *The New York Times*, in the foyer of the rectory. The reporter had now been waiting for almost two hours. The normal fifty-minute Mass took twice as long because so many people received communion and blessings. After brief pleasantries were exchanged, Nico and the reporter proceeded to the living room where Nico took a seat on the couch. Chris Michaels sat on a chair at small table with a couple of notepads and a recorder in front of him.

Michaels picked up the recorder and started the interview process. "Nico, again, it is a pleasure to meet you. Personally, this whole story fascinates me. I have heard bits and pieces about it here and there, but nothing firsthand. I thank you for the opportunity to speak with you today for the real scoop on just what went down. And, I always find it easier just to record conversations, then write from the recording later, although I may take a note from time to time as well. Do you mind if I record the interview today?" asked Michaels.

"No. Not at all. I do, however, have a question for you before we start, if you don't mind?" asked Nico.

"Sure, yeah, whatever you need," said the reporter.

"Well, it's just … Father O'Toole has been a priest for what, almost fifty years, and he is the only man running this entire parish, which is unheard of by today's standards. And right over there, in the church, is our Bishop, the Bishop for the whole Diocese of Pittsburgh. Now, why do you want to talk to me? I'm a nobody compared to those two. I know, the Bishop wasn't there that day, but Father O'Toole was. And, if you don't know by now, I can assure you, Father O'Toole was the intended target of the gunman, not me. So, why talk to me?"

Chris Michaels was taken aback by Nico's question. He was previously told by the Diocese that Nico was slightly aloof and easily distracted. Michaels prepared himself for a "pulling teeth" style interview, but in the first few minutes of meeting Nico, he knew that wouldn't be an issue. After a moment, he responded. "That is a fair question. Ha, I'm not used to being the one to field questions. I guess I agree with you in part. I agree that Father O'Toole and the Bishop completely outrank you. I agree that if I was going to write a story about Church actions or policy, both would be better, more credible sources than you, a lay minister."

"More like an altar boy, not quite even a lay minister. So, the angle to your story that you're writing about is the whole miraculous aspect of what happened last week?" said Nico interrupting the reporter mid-sentence.

Chris Michaels looked down at his recorder. He now intentionally chose his words more carefully when he spoke to Nico. "Maybe. I don't know yet. As I was saying, I agree with you in part and disagree with you in part. My disagreement is that you said you are a nobody compared to the priest and the Bishop. Not true. You were there, you were a witness to a shooting inside of a church while active protests were ongoing outside of the church. That is the story which you are very much a part of. Now, as for miracles, I guess I should be truthful with you and let you know that I am not much of a churchgoer and as far as miracles happening, personally, I think I may start to believe they are possible once I catch a leprechaun or see a unicorn. But that is me, personally. I am not here to judge; I am here to report. My opinion doesn't matter."

"Ha! Old-school journalism. I like it!"

"Yes, well … Look, just so we are clear, I am not promising you that this story will ever get published. First, I have to decide that it is worth my time to write about, and second, the editors will have to approve it for publication. So, there is a good chance that nothing will come out of this interview, at least as far as a published article is concerned. Got it?"

"Yeah, no sweat," said Nico pleasantly.

"Great. Let's begin then. Before we jump into what happened at the church last Sunday, why don't you tell me a little bit about yourself. Who is Nico Rossi?"

"Not much to tell. I live in the Bloomfield section of Pittsburgh. I teach second grade in the Diocese of Pittsburgh School District as a permanent substitute, which is a full-time teaching position with half the wages and no benefits. I'm an airhead with an old BMW motorcycle. And yeah, I have this girlfriend. Well, I think she is still my girlfriend, I'm really not sure about that either. She has been acting strange lately, but then, everybody around me has been acting strange. 'Everybody funny, now she funny too'," said Nico, paraphrasing a George Thorogood verse.

"When you say that everyone is acting strange, I am assuming you mean since the shooting? Can you give me some examples of how people treat you differently, or strangely, as you said, since the shooting?"

Nico leaned back deep into the couch. Subconsciously, he put down his prepared statements beside him. He focused his glance, which quickly became a stare, on an old metal crucifix hung on the living room wall. "Well, take this cop, I mean, there is this detective who is investigating the situation. I never met him before this all happened …"

As Nico talked to the reporter and continued to stare at the crucifix, he fell into another daydream flashback. The crucifix was replaced by a cross on the *Affliction* T-shirt worn by one of the movers.

The moving company hired by Nico to get his things out of his apartment and into Jessica's studio was nothing more than a bunch of scrub undergrad students who worked for a couple of bucks and a case of good beer. They collected their wages as they exited the apartment and carried with them their case of beer. After shutting the door, Nico went back into the apartment where he sustained a surprise attack by a flying Jessica. He soon found himself on his back with arms pinned to the new bed and Jessica straddling over top of him.

"Jesus, you are like Cato or something," said Nico as he laughed.

"Who's that?" asked Jessica.

"Never mind." As Nico stared up at her, he could not help but realize how lucky he was to have a girl like Jessica. He loved her crooked smile and the way her eyes were slightly different color. He loved her hair, which now partially tickled his face, and how it seemed to go in every direction because it was often in a ponytail for extended periods. Her intricacies and numerous unique traits were different and perhaps some people might have described them as flaws. But to Nico, she was perfect. Her free-spirit attitude and lifestyle certainly were the opposite of a soon-to-be graduate of a master's program in engineering. Maybe that is why he liked her so much. Maybe it was true that opposites attract. Or just maybe, he found the girl of his dreams.

"How do you do it, Jess?"

"Do what, sweetie," replied Jessica playfully.

"How do you … move … you don't actually walk. You sort of glide, no wait, hover. How do you hover like that?"

"Huh, whatevs, you are being silly, Nico."

Nico freed one arm and playfully pushed Jessica away from him onto the bed. He then sat on the edge of the bed and Jessica quickly scooched up beside him as the two continued their talk.

"I'm serious, Jessica. I look at you, and man, I mean, you seem like you just float from place to place. I've never seen anything like that before," said Nico sincerely.

"Well … I dunno. I'm just a girl, that's all. Nico, you have dated other girls before, haven't you?"

"Me? Oh, yes, of course. I mean, some … a few."

"Oh, only a few? Handsome guy like you and you have only had a few girlfriends? Pity."

"Hey, now, I've done okay and I have had my fair share of girlfriends. But not like this, not like you. You are different than the others … you I really like," said Nico who was embarrassed to admit how much he liked her so early in the relationship.

"Let me guess, all the girls you dated were probably very similar to you, am I right? Probably all of them were high achievers in school with a professional career path in front of them and probably all of them understood when you said that you couldn't spend any time with them on the weekend because you needed time to study for a big test or something the following week, right? And probably none of them ever gave you any grief for that either."

Nico didn't say a word in response. He didn't have to. The half smirk that came across his face was all Jessica needed to see to validate her assessment.

"I see," said Jessica after a slight pause in the conversation. "So, you like me, huh? Why? I'm certainly never going to be a doctor or a lawyer or an engineer, God forbid. I slap paint on canvas and play with dirty clay all day. I live in a warehouse, for God's sake."

"Yeah, well, I live in a warehouse now too, so there," said Nico, which made Jessica smile a bit. "And what about you? How many boyfriends have you had?"

"Including you?"

"Yes, including me."

"Okay, well … I'm thinking … yeah. Just one. Just you. Pretty much you are the first one," said Jessica seriously.

"Oh, as if. C'mon, you expect me to really buy that?"

"Yes, Nico. I do, because it is the truth. Sure, I have had interest in other guys. I've been out on many dates over the years. It just never seems to go anywhere. I lose interest or they lose interest, whatever. I can honestly say that I have never had a meaningful, serious relationship that has lasted. Yet here I am now, living in a warehouse with some guy I picked up in a bar. Figures. I should have stayed in school myself, I guess. So, you never answered my question, honey."

"What was your question, I must have missed it."

"Why is it that you like me, unless you misspoke, of course, in which case you can take it back," said Jessica confidently.

Just as Nico was about to speak, Jessica softly put her hand on the side of Nico's head and gently kissed his cheek and ear. She then put both hands together in her lap and looked Nico in the eye as he tried to answer the best he could. "Well, I don't know. I mean, I do know, but not really. Know what I mean?" said a very befuddled Nico.

"Well I thought that engineers were supposed to be smart, but that answer sounded like something a six-year-old would say," said Jessica who chuckled.

Nico tried to continue. "You are right, you are different than other girls I have dated. That is for sure. But you are also ... you are also different from anyone else I have ever met. You are better."

"How so?" asked Jessica as she sat tall on the bed eagerly waiting for the next words that Nico was about to speak.

"Yeah, see, that is just it. I have a hard time describing it because I have never experienced it before, not with an old girlfriend, not with anyone else, ever. It's like ... It's like there is an aura around you, or something like that. Has to be."

"Really?"

"Truly. I mean, when you are near me, not even this close, just being in the same room, I get such a warm feeling. I get such a feeling of goodness. I have had feelings for other girls, for other people, but I have never been around anyone who emanates good feeling the way you do. It is almost like they are physical sensations that you are sending to me. That is about the best way I can describe it. It is weird, I know, it sounds weird to me as well. But, look, it is like the way I said that you hover and don't walk. I know you don't actually hover. I know you use your legs the same as everybody else. But it is just that I get this feeling when I'm around you and when I see you, it makes it seem to me that you are just floating and gliding while the rest of us just stomp our feet."

They both sat in silence as Jessica tried to digest what she just heard. She took Nico's words as a compliment and in fact, it was probably the most sincere and honest compliment that she ever received. The truth was that she was just as fond of Nico as he was of her, but the intensity of the young relationship frightened her a little, even though she concealed those feelings from him. Jessica slowly got up, walked over to Nico and stood in between his legs as he continued to sit on the bed. She took both of his hands and placed them in hers as she continued their conversation.

"Sweetie, I am an artist, a true artist. I am not saying that I will be a famous artist or a rich artist one day, but I am an artist. I paint, I sculpt, I create, not for fame or money, but because I must. I don't know no any other way. There is nothing more that I ever want and there is nothing else I can ever do. All artists suffer from uncontrollable emotions. Mine run wild, all the time. And when they are dark, they are real dark. You won't have any doubts about that. But I don't ever want that to change. I need it to be that way. If I start to keep my emotions in check, then my art will suffer. And I can't have that. So, if you think that I float, you are probably right. I probably am floating. When I am with you, I am happy. It is because of you that I float, Nico."

"Wow. This is all … Wow. Lots of pressure now," said Nico half-jokingly attempting to lighten the intense conversation.

"Well, it shouldn't be. Compared to what you do on a daily basis, this should be easy. Maybe it was too quick that you moved in with me, maybe that causes you pressure? But it's cool, daddio. This is my place and I was here way before you. And if things are no longer to your liking, then you can leave. Anytime. No big deal. You may be my first real boyfriend, but you certainly will not be the first person to break my heart if that happens. I will survive it. I'm tough like that."

"No," said Nico, "that is not what I mean." Jessica, was still holding his hands, as she looked into his eyes. "I have no issues moving in. That doesn't worry me. But there is a lot of pressure to keep you floating. And I want to keep you floating. All the time. I really, really like when you float."

"Ah, yes, all good when I am floaty, I suppose. But I can't be like that all the time. If I was, I would be reduced to comic books or children's book illustrator."

"Certainly. I know you are, uh, complex. And deep, too. But I am not looking for the other shoe to drop. I like it here too much ... being floaty with you, Jess."

"Nico," said Jessica very softly and close to his face, "that may be the sweetest yet oddest thing that anyone has ever said to me." She pushed Nico gently to the bed and started to unbutton his shirt. The unexpected weight of her entire body on his chest combined with kisses to his neck made him gasp, as it did in real life as well.

"Nico ... Nico ... are you still with me, Nico?" asked the reporter who reached across and grabbed his arm.

"Oh yeah, no, wait, yeah, I'm sorry ... what were you asking again?" said Nico who was a bit confused.

"Nothing, I wasn't asking you anything. You were just talking about how you dropped out of your graduate engineering program in 2002 and a couple regrets, then you just sort of faded. But never mind," said the reporter patiently, "I should have directed you elsewhere several minutes ago. You were starting to get a bit too personal beyond the shooting."

"Oh, I see ... sorry," said Nico who realized that he had no idea what he said during his day dreaming, then further realized that at some point, Father O'Toole and the Bishop had joined him and the reporter in the room.

"Okay, not a big deal. Let's just get back on track here and let me ask you one final question: Do you think that what happened last Sunday, specifically, the fact that neither you nor Father O'Toole was shot was the direct result of divine intervention? In other words, do you believe a miracle occurred last Sunday?"

Nico intentionally paused before answering the question. He looked up at Father O'Toole and the Bishop and with a partial wink, he turned to Chris Michaels and said, "My conclusion doesn't matter. You know, only the Vatican can determine if a miracle occurred or not. But, truthfully, I do not need the Vatican to tell me what to believe. In the same way, who am I to tell others what they should believe. In my heart, I know what happened. You write the story. When the people read about the events, they can choose to believe or not believe. God gave us all free will, right?"

"Well, Nico, what would you say to somebody who reads this story and concludes that whatever happened to you, it was not a miracle," questioned the reporter.

"I dunno … maybe I will try harder next time?" said Nico jokingly. The reporter chuckled at the same time his audio recorder clicked off.

"Wow. I didn't think an hour could go by so fast. Well, like I said, I can't promise you that this story will get published. But honestly, I have a pretty good feeling it will. I think people really want to read about this story from a firsthand account. I am heading back to my hotel and if I can work hard, I think I can get a first draft to my editor this evening. With any luck and not a lot of editing that is needed, hopefully it can get published tomorrow," said the reporter. He put his two notebooks and his recorder into a work bag and excused himself. "Father, Bishop, thank you again for this opportunity. And thank you for allowing me to use the rectory. It has been a pleasure. Truly, it has."

Nico waived to the reporter as he exited the living room. He continued to smile as he looked at the reporter's business card still in his hand from the moment the two first met. He eventually stood up and grabbed his motorcycle helmet. The Bishop and Father O'Toole remained speechless and motionless. He turned to the both of them and said as he exited the room, "Good day, boys. We'll talk again soon."

Nico walked out of the room with tall posture and a slight spring in his step. Perhaps getting through an unwanted interview to make Father O'Toole happy was enough to make him feel good. Or maybe telling his story to an objective person who neither judged him nor gave him follow-up direction was what did it? Regardless, Nico appeared very confident after his interview concluded, and he certainly looked much better than when he first walked into the rectory.

The Bishop and Father O'Toole continued to stand motionless and in silence for several minutes after Nico had left. "Thomas, you were there. Is that .... what he said .... is that what really happened?" asked the Bishop quietly.

"I don't know. I just don't know anymore ... He and I ... we never really had a chance to talk, you know, just us. I guess ... I guess he never really had a chance to debrief or decompress." said Father O'Toole.

"Keep an eye on him, Thomas. And keep him on a short leash. I am already having regrets about allowing this interview to happen," said the Bishop scornfully.

Chapter twenty-five

All things considered, Nico truly felt good following the interview. He even smiled a bit when he jumped onto his motorcycle and fired it up.

Nico did not think about anything in particular during the ride home. Instead, he purposely observed things around him. He chose to take the extended way home. As he cruised through downtown, he felt the warm rays of the sun as they reflected off the tall, glass skyscrapers. As he slowly cruised through the Northside, he noticed how bright yellow the football stadium was without people in it. He also watched as families gathered around the beautiful fountain at Point State Park for some urban picnicking and river fishing. Crossing a bridge to ride into his part of the city, he noticed a lone rower out on what seemed to be a river of glass with only its tiny wake that caused ripples. Nico wondered how long the rowers would be able to continue their sport until the weather would eventually take a turn for the worse, bringing in the cold and the wind. Finally getting back to his own neighborhood, he listened to the sound of the leaves rustling under his motorcycle as they just started to fall from the trees. Other trees, however, still tenuously possessed their leaves which turned from green or brown to bright red, orange and yellow.

Nico's head felt clear and he was at peace. But despite his current and possibly temporary state of serenity, he clearly was not thinking at all. He parked his motorcycle behind his apartment in its usual spot. Instead of taking the fire escape into his apartment, Nico walked around to the front, oblivious for some reason, of the gathering of people that continued to grow larger over the past week. He was immediately spotted by one elderly woman who, as quickly as was possible for her, approached him with tears of both joy and pain. Nico realized his mistake immediately, but he also realized that he could not simply turn around and go into his apartment from a different direction. He fell back upon his upbringing in the presence of adults older than him.

"Hello, ma'am. I am Nico Rossi," he said respectfully.

"Oh, dear Lord. Bless you. God is with you. My back hurts so much ... so much. I can barely stand at times."

Nico placed his hands upon the old woman's back and gently rubbed it, not in an affectionate way, but just enough so that she felt what he was doing. "Ma'am, you need to go home. It isn't good for you to be on your feet all day standing here in front of this old apartment. I will pray for you, I promise. But you need to stay off your feet and you need rest," said Nico with genuine concern and candor.

The old lady raised her head and with more tears in her eyes, she strained to get the words "Thank you" past her lips.

A second gentleman approached Nico with a picture in his hand. The picture was small and folded as if it had been carried in his wallet for quite a while. The older man was large with a barrel chest and several military-style tattoos on both of his arms, but he approached Nico like a scared child. "My grandson ... he is extremely sick. He is right across the street, in the children's hospital. He is only six years old." The old man could not keep it together anymore as he grabbed Nico in a huge bear hug. Tears streamed down his face, and Nico felt them against his neck.

The bear hug made it difficult to speak, but Nico eventually forced the words out. "What is your grandson's name?"

"Kevin ... his name is Kevin."

"Go be with your family. Go be with Kevin. I will pray for all of you and tonight I will light candles for Kevin," said Nico compassionately.

Nico then proceeded to meet, speak to and address everyone who had gathered in front of his apartment. One by one, they eventually met with Nico, then dispersed back to their own lives of quiet desperation. Nico finally entered his apartment. He went straight into his bedroom and looked at his old digital alarm clock, which read 7:30 PM. Nico took his shoes off, then fell face down on his bed, above his covers while still fully dressed. In an instant, he was in deep sleep. No wine, no prescription sleeping pills, just deep, deep sleep.

Chapter twenty-six

The blazing alarm clock startled Nico as it had been many, many months since he was awakend by it. Normally, he shut it off well in advance of the 6:30 AM start time. He began his day as usual with his coffee, shower, and boring teaching clothes. After his shower, he peeked out of his bathroom window and saw that his following had started to assemble. He knew that he had to avoid them or else he would not make it in to teach that day.

As he sipped on his coffee and ate his waffles, Nico noticed that today he felt different. He was still tired, but his head was a bit clearer than usual for this hour. Perhaps it was the lack of wine and prescription meds before going to bed, or maybe it was just from real sleep, and lots of it. In any event, Nico was happy that he slept well and despite his minor fatigue, he was relaxed.

When Nico arrived at his school, the principal met him at the door. He walked Nico into his office and shut the door behind him. Nico took a seat in a chair at the front of the principal's desk while the principal stood behind it and asked Nico for a small favor.

"I … I just don't get it," said a confused Nico. "I am not sure what you want me to say. I mean, I'm not an expert on any of that stuff. You need a social worker or sociologist or something. I teach math."

"I understand how you feel. I know you are not an expert. But just look at this unique situation, look at it from my perspective as the person who runs the school. Here, we have one of our very own teachers who was involved in a shooting that occurred in a church. News coverage has extended beyond local into national. I would have to believe that this whole topic is being discussed at dinner tables and at homes all across the country, but especially here. We can't simply ignore it and pretend that nothing happened. That would be a disservice to all the students and their parents," said the principal.

Nico tried his best to squirm out of what he was being asked to do. "I do understand your perspective. And not to sound like a complete kiss-ass, I think that you do a nice job running the school. We have very few problems with the students and they are far better behaved compared to students in the other schools. That is why I am confused as to why you want to use me to deliver a lesson when you could be using a professional. I mean, when we do anti-bullying and internet safety, we bring in the pros, we don't use teachers. Why do you not want to bring in a professional for this one?"

The principal sat and listened to what Nico said. Nico did make sense and was logical in his argument. "Mr. Rossi, I am using my professional judgment on this one. I thought about bringing in the pros, but this situation, your situation … our situation …. it's unique, to say the least. Yes, you are right, we bring in the anti-bullying team and the internet safety team to give their lessons to the students in the hopes that we get ahead of those problems before they develop here. Fortunately, due either to those programs or sheer good luck, we have not had any of those issues to resolve. But now, we are forced to deal with this issue of societal violence that just landed on our doorstep."

"Yeah, but in a church, not here in school. It wasn't a school shooting."

The principal walked from behind his desk, moved his chair beside Nico, and sat down at eyelevel with him. "Agreed, nothing has happened here yet, thank God. But just look at it like this. Everybody thinks that school shootings happen at other schools. Nobody ever believes that they can happen at their school until it is too late. Now, right, again, there hasn't been a school shooting here. But everyone knows that school shootings are a possibility. And I am certain that parents and children are talking about violence a lot more and wondering how long will it be before it happens in a school, in our school, since it just happened in a neighborhood church." The principal paused for a moment, then continued. "Mr. Rossi … Nico … you must be the one to deliver the message. Everyone knows you."

"Yeah, I've heard that before."

"You are a victim, or were almost a victim. If the students can see that you are not afraid, then I will remain hopeful that they will believe that they are safe and will also not be afraid to be here."

"But here's the thing, how can we tell students that a school shooting won't occur? We can't promise them that?"

The principal stood, opened the blinds on his office window, and peered out into the school parking lot where buses of school children were unloading. After he took a sip of coffee, he turned back to Nico. "Maybe that is our disconnect here, Mr. Rossi. I am not asking you to tell students that we will guarantee their protection while they are in school with one hundred percent certainty. What I want you to say ... the message that I want to be conveyed is that we, as a school, as teachers and administrators, along with their parents, are doing everything humanly possible to keep them safe. We are trying. We are more than trying. Maybe we can't keep them safe with absolute certainty and the kids might be smart enough to know that. But what is important is that they know we are trying very hard. That is the message that must be sent. We have to say something about what happened. We can't ignore it. Violence, unfortunately, is part of our world and simply trying to ignore it ... well, we just can't sit back and do nothing on this one. Nico, this must come from you. Please."

The bell for homeroom rang. Nico stood up from the chair. "Fine, okay, whatever. You want me to be the messenger, I will be the messenger."

"Good. And thank you," said the principal with a smile on his face. Nico walked out of the office to his homeroom.

The entire day, Nico was distracted. He kept thinking about what he was going to say, about how he would be received. Would the students think he was a phony? Would they even pay attention?

Before the bell for the last period rang through the school, the principal spoke over the intercom and informed everyone that the last period of the day would be canceled in lieu of a presentation and assembly in the school auditorium. Even though the topic of the assembly was still unknown, cheers erupted from the students in every classroom.

The principal spoke with Nico briefly before he introduced him. Students fidgeted in their chairs and were noisy, as was to be expected, from the excitement caused by the simple change of pace. "Just be calm. Go to the microphone and ask for their attention. If they continue to be disruptive, I will intervene," said the principal, who was quite pleased with himself as he believed he was teaching Nico how to address a crowd of students.

The principal took center stage. After a few moments of trying to get the students to be silent, he simply spoke loudly over them. When he informed them that Mr. Rossi would be the speaker, the students broke into applause. The applause grew louder as Nico walked across the stage. Nico approached the microphone at the podium and cleared his throat. Every student immediately focused their attention on him. "Hi … Hello, students … friends. Most of you know me, I am Ni … Mr. Rossi. Ah … I … ah … I'm here today to talk to you guys and girls about safety in school." Nico continued to try to gather his thoughts. It felt strange talking to a complete auditorium in absolute silence. It was so completely silent that the microphone picked up the sound of his notes as he shuffled through them. He continued with more confidence. "Okay, listen students, we all live in a world that can sometimes be incredibly violent, mean, and angry. It is unfortunate, but that is just the reality of our world, sometimes. All of us, your teachers, principals, and especially your moms and dads, wish that our world was more peaceful than it is. But I would be a bad teacher … in fact, I would be a liar if I didn't tell you that sometimes, bad things can happen to good people. I was reminded of that the other day when I was sitting in church …"

As Nico began his lecture, his mind slipped once again to a time from his youth when he was the same age of the students who sat in front of him. He recalled playing basketball with one of his good friends Bret.

"So, what are you going to be when you grow up, besides a basketball player?" asked Bret.

"I am going to use all the money I make from pro basketball to make solar powered cars," said a proud, young Nico.

"Why solar cars, why not just regular cars?"

"'Cause a lot of people can't afford regular cars. Gas costs a lot of money and sometimes when the cars break down, they can't afford to get them fixed. So, solar cars would save them a lot of money since the sun is free and they wouldn't have to pay for gas."

"Well, what if it isn't sunny? What if it is raining or snowy?" asked Bret.

"I thought about that. Not sure just yet what to do. But you know how we have those solar lights in our yard? They get their batteries all charged up during the day from the sun, then they shine at night. Maybe that is how it can work. The cars can get all charged up all day in the sun, when it is sunny, like filling up a gas tank, and when the people need to drive them, they will be ready. They just have to sit in the sun at some point, at least for a little bit."

As his daydream flashback ended, Nico refocused on his presentation and concluded. "So, just keep in mind that you guys … all of you sitting out there … you are the ones who are ultimately responsible for keeping the school safe. The teachers, your parents, we can all help, but it is your job as a student to make a safe environment. And it is not hard to do. Don't fight. Don't bicker. Don't bully. Blessed are the peacemakers, for they are the children of God. If you do those little things, then you are making sure that your school will be as safe as possible." Nico shuffled his notes together and concluded his presentation. "Does anyone have any questions?"

A very young student who sat near the front of the auditorium stood up. "Are you God?"

Nico chuckled. "Am I God? Ha! Noooooo. How old do you think I am?" The other students in the auditorium chuckled a bit as well.

Another older student stood up. "Are you Jesus Christ?"

Nico thought for a second before answering that question. "Am I Jesus Christ? Well, yes, sort of. It's like this: when I was a little boy, younger than you guys, my priest told me that Jesus Christ is in me. And He is in all of you as well. So, when we go about our business every day, just remember that Christ is in us and we need to act like He would act. So be nice to one another. Treat one another with kindness. That's all you have to do."

A final student stood up. "Did Jesus Christ stop those bullets from hitting you?"

After an even longer pause, Nico responded, "Yes, yes, He did."

The final bell for the end of the day rang. The students got up from their seats and exited the auditorium in a quiet and organized manner. Nico didn't say a word to anyone following his presentation. He simply exited the school and jumped onto his motorcycle. He knew that he needed another long ride on the bike to clear his head. He was somewhat bothered by the fact that none of the questions asked to him following the presentation had anything to do with school safety. Instead, the students wanted to know about him, about who he was. Perhaps his presentation was ineffective, he thought to himself. Or maybe, the students were just asking more important questions?

Riding his motorcycle was more important to Nico than ever before. He used to view it simply as a rather inexpensive means of getting from point A to point B, but now, it was more crucial than just transportation. Besides giving him time to himself, it gave him anonymity from the helmet with a half-visor he wore. In addition, he also wore a Gator Mask over the lower portion of his face since the autumn weather had started to cool. The combination made him unrecognizable.

As he rode up and down the city streets in no real direction, he thought about the people who gathered in front of his apartment. He hadn't really had the chance to evaluate the situation yesterday since he fell right asleep then went to school right after waking up. The group that first gathered and woke him up with their singing was small. But the group that had assembled last night was much larger, maybe as many as forty or so people. They resembled an actual small congregation. Most of them were senior citizens, however, there were a few people there who were closer in age to him.

And he just couldn't shake the encounter he had with the old man who wanted prayers for his grandson. Even as he rode his bike, Nico still felt that man's tears that rolled onto his own face and down his neck and the immense bear hug of thanks the grandfather bestowed upon him.

Even though that encounter was quite intimate, compared to the other people whom Nico met that evening, he recognized a common thread that ran between the grandfather and the rest of the group. Each one of them reeked of pure desperation. Every person there found himself or herself in a situation that only a miracle could remedy, or so they believed. In truth, all of them would accept the miracle they were seeking from any source, but for some reason, they all sought their miracles from him. Maybe their religion had failed them? Or maybe, their desperation was the best explanation? Desperate people take desperate measures. That was certainly true and there is nothing exceptional, let alone miraculous, about that fact.

His continuous replaying of the first true encounter with the gathering, combined with his own questions raised in his mind, did not get Nico closer to any real answer that made logical sense to him. It was just so strange, so surreal. He decided to let that issue alone as he moved onto the events of earlier today. He remembered every word that came out of his mouth in his address to the elementary student body. *Did I say the right things? Did I effectively communicate a positive message to the children? Was I being helpful or did I further add to the students' confusion regarding the shooting in the Church? And what was up with the boy who asked if I was Jesus Christ? Was he being sincere or was he just trying to get a laugh from his friends? I mean, even for an elementary school student, that question is just ridiculous, right? But nobody laughed. Look, I would know if I were Jesus Christ, wouldn't I?* Nico thought to himself as he continued to cruise on his motorcycle.

But nightfall was now upon him and even with the warm bike engine and his Gator Mask, he started to feel a little cold. He decided it was time to go back home.

One thing was for sure, he did not feel like talking to anyone now, especially desperate seniors who wanted miracles. Nico killed the engine on his bike about two blocks from the rear of his apartment. He walked the bike the rest of the way and after it was parked, he quickly scaled the fire escape and entered his apartment. He left all the lights off, immediately went to the window and slowly pulled the blinds back just enough so he could see outside. To his amazement, nobody was there. Nico first thought it was rather late and cool outside, at least by senior citizen standards. But then Nico remembered: it was Monday night. And this week, the Steelers were playing in the Monday Night Football game. That was it. Had to be. At least some institutions in this town took precedence over miracles.

Chapter twenty-seven

Monday Night Football was just what Nico needed. He was tired of replaying past events in his head ad nauseam. Nico chuckled to himself when he thought about what was worse—losing focus during the day and slipping unconsciously into a painful flashback or intentionally forcing himself to do so? Both were equally disturbing for different reasons. Hopefully Big Ben would take his mind away from this entire situation, at least for a short time.

Nico lay down on the couch and stayed there for the entire game. He then watched the brief post-game, followed by the evening news, and eventually the late-night show. It was 1:30 AM. before he knew it. Nico thought about going to bed, but he didn't feel tired. Perhaps his body had not adjusted to the enormous amount of sleep he had the night before, or maybe, he was just hungry. It dawned on him that he hadn't had much to eat all day. He skipped lunch to prepare his remarks for the students. And he was so engrossed in recapping events on his motorcycle that dinner never came to mind.

There were a couple of diners and chain restaurants open at that hour, but to go there would require him to get back onto his motorcycle. And that task was too much of a burden at this point in the evening. Toaster waffles with peanut butter or microwave popcorn did not seem appealing either. He decided to go to the only place that he could quickly walk to—a small, somewhat dingy, Chinese restaurant that seemed to be open twenty-four hours a day. It was operated by a husband and wife and presumably, their daughter. They lived in an apartment connected to the back of the restaurant, which gave them the ability to work shifts around the clock.

Nico put on his coat and hat and headed out the door. He felt stiff from the long motorcycle ride followed by another long period of minimal movement during the football game. He trudged toward the Chinese restaurant and just before he arrived, a young girl's voice stopped him where he stood.

"Hey mister, do you want to party?"

As he turned his head, he saw a pair of skinny legs in fishnet stockings and rather large high heels. "Excuse me?" he replied.

"I said, do you want to party?" said a shaky voice after a sniffle or two. A young girl awkwardly approached him from behind the shadows cast upon the building by the streetlight.

"How much?"

"Well … how much you got?" asked the young girl who did everything she could to keep from crying.

"Oh no. I don't bid against myself. That is not how this works. You aren't very good at this job, are you?"

"Sorry. I'm … sorry. Look, forget I said anything," said the young girl as she started to walk away.

"Hey, hey, you don't have to be sorry. And you don't have to go. Just stop. Stop right there. I don't know if you are shaking because you're nervous or because you're cold, but when was the last time you ate anything?"

"I … I …"

"No matter. Look, I don't want to party. But I could use a date. Let me buy you some food. C'mon. For real, no games." The young girl did not say a word. She just hung her head and slowly started to walk back toward Nico. Nico grabbed her arm as she wobbled unsteadily in her attempt to walk in her heels.

"What's your name?"

"Jessie."

"Jessie, like short for Jessica?" asked Nico. The girl nodded her head. "Okay, then … Jessie. I'm Nico."

Jessie and Nico entered the restaurant and they were the only two people there, besides the husband, wife and presumptive daughter. Nico approached the counter and gave his order. "I'll have the lo mein noodles and one egg roll and my friend will have the General Tso chicken. Ginger ale for me and hot green tea for her."

"Okay one noodle, one egg roll, one Tso chicken, ginger ale, and tea. Sit down and I will bring your food," said the young girl behind the counter.

Nico helped Jessie to a table in the rear of the restaurant. As he peered around, he saw that there was one broken window which was seemingly repaired with clear packing tape and the loud hum and buzz coming from above indicated that several ballasts were bad, explaining why only half the lights functioned. Just when Nico thought that his life could not get stranger—once he realized that he was sitting at a table with a girl named Jessie underneath loud buzzing ballasts—he had a feeling that the best of the weird was yet to come.

The mirrored wall opposite his table was intact, but it was dirty and cloudy. Both lights above the table Nico chose were not working. Under different circumstances, the lighting might have been described as semi-romantic.

A lot of commotion came from the back kitchen. It just sounded like noise, but Nico could tell that the workers were talking to one another. The talking got faster and louder in a short amount of time. Weird, Nico thought. The order was rather simple and it should not have caused such agitation. Nico stopped checking out the restaurant and refocused on Jessie.

"So, what brings you out on this fine evening?" asked Nico sarcastically.

"I need money. That's all," said Jessie as she attempted composure.

"You need dope money?"

"No, I need electric bill and gas money. I'm not on dope."

"You live by yourself?"

"No, I live with my mom … She's the junkie, at least now she is," said Jessie who held back the tears.

"Sorry to hear that. What about your father?"

"Ha! That son-of-a-bitch left us a few years ago. Ran away with some slut. Nobody knows exactly where he is now … somewhere in this city … but he ain't around. That's for sure. I haven't seen him in almost three years. Just me and mom."

Nico stared at Jessie. His stare was intense, but somehow also warm. "How did you get that mark on your face? Your pimp slap you around a bit?"

Jessie could no longer control herself and started to cry. Nico grabbed for some napkins and handed them to her. "Hey, hey, look, I'm sorry. You know, this is none of my business …"

"One ginger ale, one hot tea. Your food will be ready in five minutes," said the young Chinese girl as she placed the drinks on the table.

"Just relax. Drink this tea. It should make you feel a little better." As Jessie sipped her tea, Nico again noticed more ruckus from the kitchen. The sounds of pots and pans banging around filled the restaurant. *How hard is it to cook noodles and reheat chicken?* Nico thought to himself.

"I don't have a pimp. I'm not really a hooker. I never … I never did this before. I don't know what I was thinking."

Again, Nico said nothing. His initially warm stare turned quickly into a sad, sympathetic stare and his lack of talking started to make Jessie feel a bit uncomfortable.

"Look, mister, it's like this: My mom used to have a real job. But the company she worked for went broke and everyone got laid off. So, my mom started to work every night at this filthy bar in the West End until she could find a new job. The creep owner paid her a little bit of cash, but mostly, she worked for tips. About a year ago, she got hurt trying to change a keg out by herself. The owner gave her some pills to get her through the night. Next night, she showed up for work, but was in more pain. So, she got more pills. And this same shit kept goin' until the fuckin' owner said that if she wanted pills from him, she would have to pay for them. So, she did. Pretty soon, she was working just for pill money. Then some asshole in the bar found out about what she was doing and he told her that he could get her something better for cheaper."

"So that is how she made the jump to H?"

"Yep, pretty much. She couldn't really work anymore once she started to use, so her asshole boss fired her. Now, she is *dating* that drug dealer because it's the only way she can score dope without money. All she does is lie on the couch until she needs a fix. Then he comes over."

"I am sorry. You shouldn't have to deal with that nonsense. There are some things you can do …"

"Oh, I tried. I fucking tried my ass off! Last Saturday, I walked to that filthy bar and I found the owner. I asked him to hire me in place of my mom. He just laughed at me. He said my mom is trash. And he said that 'the apple don't fall far from the tree, so that makes me trash too.' I don't know what made me madder, calling me and my mom trash or a whole bar full of drunks laughing at me. I mean, I was like, what the fuck, dude? It is your fault she got hurt and hooked on drugs in the first place. But he didn't care. He just laughed more … asshole. So, I went back home and when I got there, my mom was all whacked-out on the couch. Her scumbag drug dealer was all like, 'Yo, where you been, little bitch? Go cook us some food!' And I was all like, 'Fuck you, dude. You ain't my boss.' So he grabs me up, but I bit his hand. That got him royally pissed and he took a swing at me. I blocked most of it, but it still caught me a little … as you can see. So, I ran into my room and locked the door. He's all like pounding on my door and kicking it and screaming, 'Come out here, you little bitch, I'm gonna teach you some manners. So, I grabbed my backpack and just started throwing clothes into it."

"Well, at least you grabbed your hooker attire."

"Look, man, I didn't know what I was grabbing. These are the only fishnets I have and I never wore them. They must have been with these shoes …"

"That you were planning to wear for prom, now weren't you? Jesus, you are still in high school, aren't you?"

"Yeah … how did you know … how did you know I would wear them to my prom?"

Nico said nothing. He just rubbed his head and thought to himself, *how do I keep getting in these situations?*

"Anyways, he kept beating on my door. I thought for sure he was going to break it down. I just grabbed a blanket off my bed and climbed out my bedroom window. I jumped on a bus and I headed over here. I only had enough money on me for a one zone bus ride and this was as far as one zone could take me. I stayed in the park all night. I tried to sleep, but I was too worried that the homeless people or junkies in that park would do something to me if they found me asleep. But I stayed there all today and tonight. Then I got so cold and hungry and had no money. So, I thought hooking was a good idea. I

135

changed into these clothes behind some trees in the park and I came over here. You were the first person to walk past me tonight."

"Okay, okay, enough. You poor kid. Look, there is a lot you can do in this situation that doesn't require you to hook or beg, all you have to do …"

Before he could finish his sentence, all three employees of the Chinese restaurant approached the table where Nico and Jessie sat. They brought an entire banquet of food. Nico was shocked as he got up from the table and stepped a couple feet away from it.

"Whoa, whoa, whoa, I didn't order … any of this," he said with confusion.

"No. You take the food and eat. No charge. On house," said the girl who desperately tried to translate her father's commands as he spoke in Chinese.

"No, that is not right. I will pay you for what I ordered. No problem. Just the noodles, General Tso chicken and an egg roll. I am sorry if you didn't understand me at first …"

As the father spoke quickly in Chinese, his young daughter made her best efforts to quickly translate. "You take all of it and eat. You don't pay with money. My family needs a miracle."

"What!" exclaimed Nico.

"You pay with miracle. Father needs miracle, mother need miracle," exclaimed the young girl.

"I don't have a miracle in my wallet. I will pay with cash," said a frustrated and confused Nico.

"Oh my God! You are the miracle man everyone is talking about. My God, now I feel even dumber," said Jessie, who put her hands over her face in shock and embarrassment.

Nico slowly continued to back away from the table. "I don't understand? What miracle, what do you want?"

Both parents now spoke loudly in Chinese at the same time as each bowed to Nico. "My father needs a miracle, needs more customers … not enough money and many bills to pay."

"You need more customers! You don't need a miracle for that … You need an SBA loan. Fix the windows and put some curtains on them. Fix the lights. Replace the floor. Make the place look better.

Get real plates with real silverware instead of all this plastic. That is all you have to do to get more customers."

"You eat your food, then you pay with miracle," said the girl as she tried to speak English above her parents' Chinese commands.

"Look, I am sorry if you don't understand how things work in this country. But here, I order food and you bring me what I ordered. Then I will pay you for what it cost."

"My father says it costs a miracle. Sit and eat and give us a miracle, not money." The parents of the girl then directly approached Nico. The mother grabbed his arm and fell to her knees. The father grabbed his other hand and shook it vigorously.

"Alright, okay, look, enough. Fine. You know what," said Nico as he pulled away from the parents and continued to back up, "Look, no promises. But I will say some prayers tomorrow and maybe you'll get your wish …"

The doors of the restaurant then sprang open as a group of about ten people, all wearing Steelers shirts and hats, entered. They were all obviously drunk. Nico looked at his watch. It was 2:10 a.m. These people must have been watching Monday Night Football in one of the local bars, then decided to close the bar down. Now, they all had beer munchies and they were trying to sober up before they attempted to drive home. The young girl darted back behind the counter to take their orders. Nico looked at the Chinese man and woman, who both were bowing very deeply to him. He continued to back up until he was stopped, rather abruptly, by the wall. At that moment, after roughly bumping into the wall, the burned-out lights above his head ignited and bathed Nico in a flood of white fluorescent glow.

To Nico, everyone and everything in the restaurant just stopped. He looked about at the frozen drunks, the frozen Chinese restaurateurs, the frozen wanna-be prostitute. He looked at the dirty mirrored wall opposite him and he saw himself drenched in the light. Moments, seconds, minutes or hours seemed to pass like an instant before him, but that frozen moment in time, however long it lasted, ended when all the unlit lights in the entire restaurant came back to life in full force. The door flew open again as five more people staggered in from the street. The woman kissed Nico's hand and the man kissed his cheek, and bowed their heads as they backed away and headed to the kitchen to start cooking. Nico turned back and looked at Jessie, who was speechless. He went back to the table where she sat with a look of confusion and admiration upon her young face.

"I'm sorry, I had no idea who you were," said Jessie.

"Never mind that. Listen, fix yourself. Take care of this problem tomorrow. Here is what you must do ..." Nico then stood up and pulled out his wallet. "Here is seventeen dollars. I am sorry, that is all I have until payday at the end of the week. But it is enough to get you back home. Now, when your mother is on the couch, all smacked-up tomorrow, call 9-1-1. Tell them that your mother is on drugs and she is threatening to kill herself."

"Um, well ... wait ... why ... I mean, that is a lie. I can't lie to 9-1-1 cops, they'll arrest me," said a very confused Jessie.

"No, it's not a lie. Is anyone forcing your mother to shoot smack? I mean, is anybody physically forcing it into her arms?"

"No, she pretty much does it herself. I don't get it," said Jessie.

"Okay. And what will happen if she continues to shoot dope?"

"She will die or get killed, I guess, right?" said Jessie.

"Exactly, there you have it. She just lacks the wherewithal to express her slow suicide attempt verbally. It is not a lie, it is just a liberal interpretation of the situation. The cops will come and they'll take her to Western Psych. She'll detox there and maybe they can get her into treatment. Then Youth Services is going to speak to you, probably at the same time the cops are there. You tell them you are a senior in high school and you can take care of yourself. Most likely, they will let you stay at your house."

"And if they don't?"

"If they don't, they'll put you in somebody's house temporarily and at least you will be safe and you can eat and finish out your school year. You will see your mom again as soon as she gets into a program."

"What about the asshole drug dealer? What if he is there?"

"Easy, just don't let him see you call the cops. But after you do make that call, you tell him that cops are on their way. He will run away, fast. You will never see him again. He won't want to be anywhere near you when the cops show up. And make sure you tell Youth Services about your dad. They will track him down and get money out of him."

Despite the utter chaos around him, Nico was cool and focused, not like everyone else in the place, who either scrambled to make food, take orders or was drunk. He momentarily sat and used chopsticks to shovel some noodles and a few pieces of chicken into a bowl, which he took with him, along with a plastic fork.

"I ... I don't know what to say," said Jessie.

"Nothing to say. Just do as I told you. Take whatever food you don't eat tonight with you in case you can stay in your place after you call the cops. It should last you a few days. Oh yeah, last thing, quit swearing so much. You are a pretty girl, but it makes you seem ugly when you talk like that."

Nico slipped out of the restaurant amidst the commotion and went home while he ate his food along the way. After he walked about a block, he turned and looked back. The lights from the Chinese restaurant illuminated the whole street as people continued to leave the local bars and enter the restaurant like moths to the flame.

Nico finished his food by the time he made it back to his apartment. Again, he simply took off his clothes, crawled into bed and immediately fell asleep. The alarm clock woke him in the morning.

Wil 3

Chapter twenty-eight

Teaching elementary students the next day proved to be a challenge for Nico. They weren't unruly and the material wasn't difficult, it was just that Nico felt different. He didn't Monday-morning quarterback what he experienced in the Chinese restaurant. In fact, he didn't think anything of that at all. And he didn't struggle with losing his focus and falling into a bad flashback memory, either. Quite the opposite. He felt physically good. He felt rested and healthy. His mind was not full of clouds from insomnia or pills and booze. Maybe he just couldn't handle feeling rested and healthy because it was so out of his norm? Maybe he just wasn't used to operating under these conditions? Whatever caused him to feel this way was uncertain, but nonetheless, this new state of consciousness bothered him greatly, more so than his usual sleepwalking mindset he had grown accustomed to.

By the end of the school day, Nico didn't feel any better. He just sat at his desk and stared out over his empty classroom. He decided that maybe his principal was right, after all. Maybe he did experience trauma and he was starting to feel the effects of it? Maybe his poor mental health had delayed the onset at first, but now, his head was not as cloudy anymore. "Great," Nico said out loud to himself in the empty classroom, "I cleared my mind only so that I could fully feel and appreciate trauma. Perfect."

Nico was not opportunistic by nature, but now he figured he should utilize the opportunity to get more rest. He left his classroom and walked to the principal's office. He sat down with the principal and explained that perhaps the weight of the entire situation was too much for him to bear and that maybe the principal was right with his initial assessment. He explained he was starting to feel tired and maybe even slightly confused. He needed time off from teaching so that he could settle down a bit.

The principal, as expected, agreed with Nico. After the brief conversation, the principal began to prepare the necessary paperwork for Nico to take a medical sabbatical. A sabbatical for a permanent substitute teacher was not allowed, but under the circumstances, the principal saw fit to bend the rules a little. Nico went back to his empty classroom and reviewed all his lesson plans to make sure that his house was in order for whomever would replace him as the new long-term substitute teacher. Nico was still an engineer and all his lesson plans were written as would be expected of an engineer. They were precise and complete and not in need of the slightest revisions. Mostly, Nico pursued this task just to kill time until Lucy arrived home from work. Shortly after 5:00 PM, Nico got up from his desk, turned the lights off in his classroom and left the school for the last time. He fired up his motorcycle and rode to Lucy's apartment without first calling in advance.

Lucy opened the door after hearing the heavy knock. "Sorry to arrive unannounced, but I need to talk to you," said Nico, who appeared flustered. "May I come in?" Lucy opened the door for him and Nico entered her apartment. He noticed that there was an open Bible on Lucy's coffee table and several candles were lit around the living room.

"Nico, I am sorry that you are not happy with how our relationship has evolved. But I do honestly love you, I just can't have sex with you anymore. It's just not right ..."

"Shh. That's okay, that's okay. Not what I am here for, not what we need to talk ... what I need to talk to you about." Nico took a seat on the couch and motioned for Lucy to join him. She reluctantly did so, but kept a noticeable distance from him. Nico reached out and grabbed both her hands. He fought with himself to get the words out of his mouth as he trembled slightly. "Luce, you are smart. I respect you, a lot. I respect your opinions on all sorts of stuff ... it's just ..." Nico tried to gather himself as he could feel his composure starting to slip. With a slight quiver in his lip and the hint of a tear in his eye, he started the conversation. "Do you actually believe that I may ... I am responsible for a miracle? Do you actually believe that I really may be more than just a second-grade teacher?"

Lucy moved closer to Nico and gently started to rub his arm affectionately. The conversation was one-sided initially as Nico did most of the talking. Eventually, Lucy offered some of her own opinions. Throughout the conversation, she continued to hold Nico's hand. Her warm, friendly touch comforted Nico. As he continued to pour his soul out to her, he could feel the weight on his shoulders and the stress in his head start to alleviate. The feelings he experienced were familiar, although he hadn't felt that way in many years. But it was the same way he felt as a young boy after having just completed a confession to a priest. Not that he was ever extraordinarily sinful—his confessions were pretty mundane and his nickel-dime sins were probably not any different than those being confessed by other boys his age. Still, he always felt good and clean after having confessed and being absolved. Confession, he always thought, was a gift and one of the best aspects of being a Catholic. He always thought that confession should be promoted and not dreaded as just another Catholic obligation. Nico experienced that feeling again, but this time, it was better. It was more. He felt complete.

Although confessing to Lucy made him feel better, he could tell that he was starting to overwhelm her. After all, he talked about many heavy topics including his prior relationship with Jessica LaRue. Lucy never asked much about Nico's life prior to her dating him and Nico wasn't the type of person to simply volunteer information, especially information concerning such deep and troubling details about his prior shortcomings, even though those mistakes were directly responsible for making him into the person who sat there with Lucy now.

But the concerning, troubled look on Lucy's face was undeniable and it signaled time to wrap it up. Nico gave her a huge hug that was warm and loving, like a parent would hug a child. She smiled, although it seemed to Nico to be forced.

"I'm sorry, Luce, for making your ears bleed for almost two hours now. But thank you, thank you for listening. I am truly grateful that you are in my life," said Nico as he got up from the couch and started to put on his jacket. Lucy again said nothing and tried to force a smile. Her demeanor bothered Nico. "Lucy, I know this was a lot to unload on you. I'm sure it was much more than you expected, maybe even more than you could handle. But I would be a bad friend if I didn't ask … what is it that is troubling you?"

Lucy sat up straight, then sat back and put her hands over her face as she rubbed her forehead. "Nico … sweetie … I'm just … I'm so worried about you. I mean, you have been incredibly hurt in the past and I'm scared that it's not over yet. I really feel like the worst is yet to come. I don't know; I can't really explain it. I just have this sense about it, about you … just a feeling I really can't explain."

"Is that why you never answered my question? Is that why you never told me who you think I am?"

"That's just it, Nico, it doesn't matter what I think."

"Oh, yes it does. It most certainly does. If your opinion didn't matter to me, then why would I come over here to talk to you about it?"

"No, Nico. You are wrong. Why can't you see that? Nobody's opinion matters. Whatever this journey or this cause or this trip, whatever it is that you are on now, you are by yourself. Nobody else is with you. I don't know if they can be. I know I can't. So, stop worrying about what other people think about you or who they think you are. It doesn't matter. Who do you think you are, Nico? That is the only thing that matters now. And I am just worried … I'm scared, Nico, I'm scared that this trip doesn't end well for you. I just don't want to see you get hurt anymore, but as long as you continue on this path, I just feel that more pain … more suffering … I feel like you won't be able to avoid it, Nico. And it breaks my heart to see you suffer like that," said Lucy as tears started to roll down her cheek.

Nico was moved by Lucy's words as well as the genuine love and concern that she shared with him. And he never expected such a profound response from her. He paused for several moments and thought about what she said before he responded.

"Lucy, you believe what it says in that book, right? It says that Jesus was hung on a cross where He died so that one day, He would come back to save all who believed in Him, right? Well, if I was already killed once, then how much pain and suffering could possibly lie ahead?" Lucy started to quietly cry upon hearing those words. "I am sorry to leave you like this, Luce, sorry to have upset you so much. But now, there is something that I must do and it can't wait. I love you too, Lucy."

Nico zipped his jacket and closed the door behind him. He jumped onto his motorcycle and rode to the jail. Although it was past visiting hours and though Nico wasn't an attorney, for whatever reason, the jail guards allowed Nico to have a contact visit with Dylan Ray after visiting hours. Nico waited in the visiting room by himself for about ten minutes until Dylan Ray was brought in to meet him. Nico stood up as Dylan entered the room. Dylan Ray was shocked to see Nico standing there by himself. He started to walk toward the very small conference table when Nico gestured to him to stay there. Nico simply said to Dylan, "Mr. Ray, I forgive you. I forgive you for what you did in the church. I know that you didn't mean it and I know that you are truly sorry. I know you were just confused from getting mixed signals of some kind. I forgive you wholeheartedly." The initial shock of unexpectedly seeing Nico wore off Dylan Ray quickly and upon hearing Nico's words, was replaced by the intense feeling of having been forgiven for his indiscretion. Dylan Ray fell to his knees and started to weep.

"Thank you my Lord, thank you my Lord."

Nico said nothing more, removed himself from the jail, and rode home. He parked his motorcycle behind his apartment, then walked around to the front of it to meet his following.

Wil 3

Chapter twenty-nine

After he parked his bike, Nico approached his gathering from the rear. When Nico was about twenty feet away, he spotted a tiny, frail little boy holding the hand of a much older man. Nico stopped for a moment before proceeding.

"Hello, Kevin, how are you feeling today?"

The little boy turned around, as did his grandfather who had an enormous smile and tears of joy all over his face. "You know my name? How do you know my name?" asked the little boy with natural childlike curiosity.

Nico took a knee right beside him. "Well, Kevin, I prayed for you. We all prayed for you. Your grandfather most of all. We all thank God that you are here."

"Truly, it is a miracle. God bless you, son, God bless you. CANDLE Syndrome. It was … diagnosed … then, it just … it just disappeared … with no medical explanation," said Kevin's grandfather as he fought through his tears.

"No sweat, pap. It was your faith, not mine. And those are some pretty talented doctors over there. I am sure that they had a lot to do with it," replied Nico.

Nico made his way through the congregation until he reached the front. He hopped up onto a step and explained that he was very busy this evening and could not stay long. He then proceeded to mingle with those in attendance for about an hour before he made his way into his apartment by the front door.

Once inside, Nico called Chris Michaels from *The New York Times*. "Chris … er … Mr. Michaels, hi, this is Nico Rossi … Oh, yes, I read it. I thought it was very good, personally speaking. It was accurate and detail-oriented, but never drew a conclusion. I liked it … Yeah, well, actually, I am calling to see if you are interested in writing a follow-up piece? I have a few things on my mind. Was wondering if you would be interested in hearing them … Great. Yes, this weekend is fine. … We, ahh, can't use the rectory again. My apartment will be best, but, you may have trouble parking … You will see, but no big deal. See you then."

Nico hung up his phone after his brief conversation and proceeded to his window. Slowly, he pulled the drape away just enough to see his congregation which gradually started to disperse. As they left, members of the group hugged one another, shook hands heartily, and although Nico was not a lip reader, he could clearly see the words being conveyed by different people as they would clasp their hands together, look to the heavens and say, "Thank you, God." As people continued to leave, Nico saw, for the first time, that someone had erected a makeshift structure that resembled an altar. It was placed to the side of his stoop. Apparently, there were too many people standing in front of it that Nico failed to notice it on his way into his apartment that evening. Behind the altar was a wooden cross mounted to the railing by some type of wire, close to the front wall of the apartment building.

Chapter thirty

When Nico reached out to Chris Michaels for a followup article, Chris accepted the offer without hesitation. The interview with Nico impacted Chris in an unexpected way that he could not fully understand. Chris knew his article in *The New York Times* was excellent and from a journalistic standpoint, it may have been one of his finest pieces. The linear model of non-editorialized journalism clearly and accurately conveyed Nico's experience with the church shooting, yet it failed to convey any of the intangibles that Chris felt when he was in Nico's presence. As Chris drove home following the interview, he reflected more upon how he felt when he was with Nico and less about the church shooting. But how could he memorialize those feelings on paper when even he was at a loss to understand just exactly what those feelings were? Chris was certain that there was more to this story and more to Nico Rossi that must be told. The failed assassination attempt in the church, though extraordinary by anyone's standards, was too inadequate to be the defining moment of Nico Rossi's life.

When Chris turned onto Nico's street, he saw a sizeable group of people on the sidewalk and street in the direction he was going. Sure enough, as he slowly drove to Nico's apartment, he confirmed that the large group of people was assembled in front of Nico's place. He continued to stare at the group as he crept past them. Eventually, he saw what he believed was Nico's head and shoulders slightly elevated above the crowd. Nico faced them as they looked at Nico with their backs to the street. Chris continued his route until he found a parking space about five blocks away from Nico's apartment.

Chris walked toward Nico's apartment, but stayed about thirty feet or so back from the crowd and took a position that gave him a clear view of the entire scene from across the street. He was utterly amazed and dumbfounded at what he saw.

Nico was dressed in all black and was, in fact, slightly elevated above the crowd. He spoke to those who gathered, but Chris' distance did not allow him to clearly hear Nico's words. However, the attitude and the intent were unmistakable. Chris watched in amazement as Nico conducted some sort of Mass. It was more than a prayer service, clearly more than any type of social gathering. The crowd would silence themselves as Nico spoke, then in unison shouted "Amen" in response. At least that part was clear. This process repeated for a short time until the entire group knelt on the street. Nico stood before them with outstretched arms and blessed them one last time as a final "Amen" emanated from the crowd. The crowd then rose to their feet and began to disperse as Chris watched Nico enter his apartment building.

A flood of questions and thoughts rushed into his Chris' head as he fervently attempted to jot down thoughts on his notepad. He looked up after he filled three pages of notes to find the street was completely empty and silent. Although still a few minutes early for their meeting, Chris could no longer wait to speak with Nico. He jogged across the empty street and entered the building through the front door.

Nico opened the door after hearing a knock and before he could say anything, Chris blurted out, "What in God's name is going on out there?"

Nico backed away from the door to let Chris enter the apartment. Turning back to him with a very matter-of-fact tone, he said, "God's name ... my name ... whatever. How are you doing, Mr. Michaels? Find my place easy enough?"

Chris was stunned by Nico's demeanor, which was vastly different from the first time they spoke. Nico's confidence emanated from his body, yet he acted and moved in such a nonchalant fashion that it was unnerving. "I saw a part of that ... ahh ... performance out there. And, man, I don't even know where to start," said a befuddled Chris Michaels who quickly flipped through his recent notes. "I mean, what are those people doing? What are you doing?" asked Chris, who in a million years never expected to witness such a spectacle.

"Please, take a seat, Mr. Michaels. I know you had a long drive. I appreciate you taking the time to come speak with me on the weekend. Would you like a cup of coffee or something else? I know the amenities here are not as comfortable as the rectory, but I hope you don't mind too much," said Nico warmly as a polite host would say.

"Yes. Yes, I would like coffee. Black. Please. That would be great." As Chris Michaels sat on Nico's couch and waited for his coffee, he felt embarrassed that his first two leadoff questions were nothing more than absolute blind shots in the dark with only the hope of hitting something. He also could not help to notice how he himself felt at that moment. He remembered his initial sense of disbelief when he first waited to interview Nico a few weeks ago in regard to a miracle of some kind. But that disbelief was based upon normal skepticism. The kind of skepticism that rational people might feel when they are told to investigate the story of a potential miraculous situation. But the disbelief he was now experiencing was not based upon normal skepticism. In fact, it wasn't based upon anything normal at all. It was disbelief based upon … upon … lunacy? Blasphemy? Absurdity? Occult? Maybe paranormal? Again, Chris was dismayed and disappointed that a journalist of his experience could not find the words to appropriately capture the essence of what he just witnessed or how it made him feel to see it. Fortunately, the coffee arrived quickly. Chris thought it best to refrain from self-examination and just get to the story, or whatever it was that he came to Bloomfield for.

"Thank you for the coffee. Should we begin?" asked Chris.

"Don't you want to start your recorder?" asked Nico politely.

"Sure. Yes. Okay. Recorder is now on … here we go."

"Well, Okay then. Go ahead … shoot."

Chris Michaels was again taken aback by Nico's odd word choice. "Nico, it has been a little less than a month since we last spoke and clearly … obviously, I have noticed things have changed since that time. You have changed. Before we get to you, why don't we start with what I just saw outside of your apartment. What exactly was that?"

"Oh that. Well, yeah, that is a bit tough to explain. You just kind of have to be a part of it to understand."

"I saw it. I saw you praying or preaching. I saw the people respond to you. I saw it and I still don't understand it."

"You witnessed it, but you were not a part of it. I'm sure it looks strange."

"Okay, fair enough. I am not, was not, a part of it. What was it that I was not a part of?" asked Chris.

"Well, I guess it started shortly after the shooting. A group of four or five senior citizens showed up in front of my apartment every morning to sing hymns. From there, it grew into many people of all ages. It got to the point that it was becoming disruptive, so I had to tell them that there are only certain times of the day when they can gather."

"So, you created a schedule?"

"I guess you can say that. Once a day, there is a gathering. Sometimes the times change a bit, but at least that keeps the disruption to a minimum. I wish there was more time for healing, but we are limited by the demands of regular life as well."

"Okay, I see, sort of. But why you? Why not their church?"

"Oh, that's simple. They come to me because they are all in search of some sort of miracle in their own life. Something their church can't provide."

"Is that your game now? Handing out miracles curbside? Or is this a grassroots beginning to a career as a faith healer?"

"Maybe. I don't know. I can't say with certainty where it all leads or how it ends," said Nico.

"Well, have you performed additional miracles since we last spoke? Stop any more bullets midair lately?"

"See, I told you that you wouldn't understand if you weren't a part of it." Nico sat up straight on his chair across from Chris Michaels. He put his coffee down on the table and looked directly at Chris as he continued to speak. "Like I said, I do not have the power to understand with certainty what exactly is happening now. I do understand, however, that God has a plan and it involves me and I am just trying my best to comply with His assignment." Nico took another sip of coffee as Chris Michaels listened. "As far as miracles are concerned, I know that I am not responsible. Only God provides miracles. Whether He is using me as a tool for that or not … well, I just try to do what He asks. Look, if you talked to any of those people who were out there, they would all tell you that miracles are happening every day and all around them."

"So, you are granting the miracles they are seeking?" asked Chris.

"No. I don't promise results. What I do is I listen to them. I listen to their pleas and I pray with them. I remind them, as I remind myself, that God never burdens anyone with more than he can handle. I offer that advice, I offer prayer and a kind word. That is all I do. Whatever happens, happens. But to be honest, the fact that I am listening to them so intimately, well, to those people, that is miraculous. I am just showing people how to open their hearts and see all the miracles that surround them daily," said Nico quite proudly.

Nico picked up his coffee mug and continued to drink as Chris paused to review his notes. "Let's talk about you. You have seemed to turn one hundred and eighty degrees in a short time. You seem calm. Confident. You look rested."

"You are right. I am. Maybe the shooting did change me, it just took some time to sink in, I suppose. But hey, nothing out of the ordinary about a person changing after nearly being murdered."

"True. But most people who suffer from trauma become withdrawn, maybe anxious or depressed. You have gone in the opposite direction."

"Well, I am no psychologist, but I would suggest that people all handle extraordinary situations differently, depending on who they are and their background. I guess I am handling it how I am handling it, good or bad. I don't know what I should be doing differently. Got any suggestions?"

"I got nothing. And I mean, I am not suggesting that you are bad or you are doing anything wrong. I am just trying to grasp what's happening here and how it all got started. Trauma is unique. But I have interviewed hundreds of people who experienced all types of different trauma and I have never known anyone who was involved in a violent, traumatic situation to turn around and rocket off in the complete opposite direction. In your case, it seems like you got better?"

"Seems like it, huh?" said Nico as he drank some more coffee. "Let me ask you Mr. Michaels, have you ever met a trauma victim who was thirty feet away from a lunatic shooting a gun who then watched bullets inexplicably fall to the ground in slow motion and land five feet away from the target?" asked Nico.

"No. Honestly, you are the first."

"Okay, me neither. So then, is it fair to call the shooting situation traumatic?"

"I ... well ... maybe not ... I ... I don't know what you are getting at," said Chris Michaels.

As Nico readied himself, Chris noticed every aspect of Nico Rossi had completely changed. He was exacting in his movements and he spoke with the precision one would expect from an engineer.

"You said that since the shooting, I have changed. Agreed. Then you said the way I changed isn't consistent with your experience of how other people changed post-trauma. Finally, to bolster your premise, you indicated that you have spoken with numerous people who experienced trauma, which made you conclude that my metamorphosis is somewhat unique compared to those people. Did I get that all correct?"

"Yes ... it seems so ... I just ... I don't get it," said Chris Michaels.

"Okay, bear with me. It will make sense in a minute when you break it down logically," said Nico. He took the yellow notepad from Chris's hand and turned to a clean sheet of paper, wrote down his words, then showed them to Chris when finished. "Premise one: People who nearly get shot will experience trauma. Premise two: People who experience trauma will suffer negative psychological consequences. Conclusion: A person who survives almost being shot may become withdrawn, anxious, or depressed from the resulting trauma of the incident." Nico looked at Chris who continued to stare at the notebook.

"I know, I know, not as tight as it could be, but I think you understand. So, now let's take your analysis and plug my fact pattern into it, shall we? One: I was involved in a violent shooting. Two: I experienced trauma. But three: I did not and am not presently suffering from depression, anxiety, or some other adverse mental state. Well, what can we conclude from this exercise? Two things: First, maybe your logic is flawed? Probably not that simple. I mean, the evidence supporting your theory, although anecdotal, is vast. I don't doubt that you have been in contact with numerous people who have experienced trauma and though not scientific, it's sufficient and supports your logical conclusion. But it still doesn't apply to my situation. So, if your logic is good but your conclusion is erroneous, as it pertains to me, it suggests that your premise is faulty, not your conclusion."

Chris Michaels felt nauseated and no longer drank his coffee. He listened to what Nico said and continued to stare at the yellow notebook. Maybe the stress of this whole situation was more than Nico could handle and he was finally starting to crack up? But the certainty and exact nature of Nico's demonstration made him think otherwise. People who lost it were generally more vague and chaotic in his experience.

After looking intently at Chris Michaels for almost a minute, Nico finally spoke again. He picked up the notebook from the table, crossed out the word trauma and replaced it with miracle. "Change your premise, Chris. Change your premise."

Chris stared at it for a moment, then wrote below: "Premise one: People who are intended targets of a shooting, who inexplicably do not get shot, experience a miracle. Premise two: People who experience a miracle will change for the better. Conclusion: Nico's positive change in demeanor and mentality can be explained from experiencing a miracle, not trauma." It was though a lightbulb had turned on in his head. He put the tablet down on the table and did not say a word. Nico looked it over.

"It is a bit wordy, but all the important elements are there. Do you get it now?" asked Nico sincerely.

"Wow. Yeah, I do. I get it. So, let me get this straight, Nico. And I want to be clear about this. When we first spoke, you were not willing to say that a miracle occurred. Now, you are taking the position that all signs point to divine, miraculous intervention as the only explanation as to why neither you nor the priest were killed in church that day. And because you experienced a miracle and not trauma, you, your style, your attitude, almost everything about you, has changed for the better. Is that a correct conclusion to make, professor?"

"Well, I can't argue with logic. But you are still focusing on the least important aspect of this entire situation," said Nico.

"I see, just when I thought we were getting somewhere, you go back into riddle mode. Okay, no more games, Nico. Tell me what I need to hear. What am I here for? What should be my focus?"

"I apologize, Mr. Michaels. I am not trying to waste your time or play games, I'm just trying to get you to understand a little bit about me so you can make sense of the whole picture. I guess since you didn't know me before the shooting, you will never get a true picture. And, you are right, I didn't ask you to come here to talk about miracles or if they exist or how many angels can dance on the head of a pin, or any of that stuff. I will get to the point.

"See, people are free to believe in miracles or not, but what is most important is the effect, or rather, the aftermath. All those people who gather, I was just like them before the shooting. In fact, I was probably much worse than any one single person who comes here. I now understand what Thoreau meant by people leading lives of quiet desperation. I know firsthand because deep down, I used to be miserable, bored, no direction and I just went with the flow. And the whole time I was so consumed with past regrets and mistakes that you would have thought I was Irish. No offense, Irishman."

"None taken."

"Now, I am confident. I am driven. I have focus once again. The fact that neither of us were killed that day was only part of the miracle. How I feel and what I am capable of now achieving, that is the true miracle in my life. And there is no other explanation for feeling this way. Not in science, in math or even philosophy. None. Eliminate all other possible explanations and only a miracle is left standing. So yes, I believe that only a miracle could give me this power."

"Okay, so now you are driven and you have a sense of purpose, but for what? Bootleg church service in the street?"

"Well, that is kind of a pessimistic categorization, but yes, you are right. But there's a healing process, too."

"So, you are starting a career as a faith healer. That is shocking. I mean, I know you are a man of faith, but you are also a man of science and math. You don't seem to me to be the kind that would believe in faith healing," said Chris Michaels with a disappointed tone to his voice.

"Yes, I am a faith healer. But not like what you are thinking. I am not like those charlatans on TV that take people's money to cure their cancer. That's not me. I am not a faith healer, but rather I am a healer of people's faith."

"Semantics now?"

"Hardly. World of difference. Go back to the numbers and look at statistics which show that, regardless of denomination, Church attendance is falling. Every year it falls more. Now Church officials want to say that attendance is falling because society is becoming worse, becoming more violent, too much instant gratification and the Church doesn't fit into that rubric. That explanation is over simplistic and those people outside of my apartment prove that isn't true."

"How so? In what ways?" asked Chris Michaels as he picked up his notebook.

"Speaking about the Catholic Church, as it is the only Church I have ever really been a part of, it is failing, it is losing parishioners, and it isn't attracting new ones because it has completely lost touch with the people. It's not about failure to adapt to a new, ever-changing society, but rather, its failure to address people's most basic spiritual need—the desire to know that there is more to this life than quiet desperation. They need to know that God in His infinite wisdom has not abandoned them and they still matter. They need to believe that He put them here with a purpose and for a purpose. And all purpose is important, none is too small. You don't have to win a Nobel Prize to make a difference in the lives of others.

"People need strong faith first so they can find their ultimate purpose in this world. Without faith, people's beliefs tend to be limited only to their next paycheck, or their health insurance, or the chance to win Powerball. But as faith is restored, people see that their life does matter and they naturally pursue their real purpose with renewed spirit. Faith is where it begins, but alone, is not enough. Faith without purpose is as useless as a gun without bullets, so to speak. But faith leads to purpose, and strong faith is the engine that drives purpose. And that is what I do. I heal their faith and from there, they find their purpose.

"They come to me, I hold their hands, I put my arm on their shoulder. I pray with them. If they think I am a miracle on two legs, great, so be it, if it helps to open their hearts. And when their faith is healed through me, they start to see everyday miracles in their own lives as they pursue their purpose and they get out of their ruts. That is what I do now, Chris. That is what God wants me to do. I don't know why or where this is all going, but I know that is what I must do—be a healer of people's faith. That is my purpose. And my faith drives it."

Before Chris could respond or ask further questions, Nico launched into an assault against the Catholic Church and its policies. Chris Michaels did the best he could to keep up with him and mostly just listened and took notes.

"The easiest thing the Catholic Church could do is start to preach acceptance and tolerance, especially in the gay community. I mean, on one hand, you have the Church saying that God made every man and woman in his image. But I guess that doesn't apply to homosexuals, right? If God didn't make them, who did? Or maybe God did make them, He just took them out of the oven a few minutes too soon? No, no, that can't be. God doesn't make mistakes. Obviously, they were made by God, but clearly, they turned their backs on Him with their lifestyle choices, those heathen bastards. And just for the record, I am not gay," chuckled Nico.

"I was starting to wonder. You have mentioned a girlfriend, but I have never seen her," quipped Chris.

Nico then became quiet and still as he reflected. "Chris, it's like this: When I was in grad school, I had this one professor who was absolutely the most brilliant man and the best teacher I ever had. He was also gay. I mean, not Freddie Mercury flaming or anything like that. He was very distinguished and kind. Truly, one of the few genuinely compassionate people that I have ever known. Anyways, I found myself in a bad situation. Only this professor came to my rescue. It seemed like everyone else turned their back on me, at least that was how I felt. To this day, he is the kindest man I have ever known." Nico took another long pause and remained still as he completed his thought. "Now, you can't tell me, no priest in any Church, no Bishop, no Pope, can ever tell me that man does not deserve a place in heaven just because he is gay. There is no possibility that God would turn His back on that man, not a chance. If I die and go to heaven and I find that my professor friend is not there simply for no other reason than for being gay, well, then from my perspective, heaven is not perfect. If that place isn't perfect, then it is not heaven."

"Are you saying that there is no such place as heaven. And I guess if you are, then hell must not exist either, right?" asked Chris Michaels.

"No, I believe in heaven, hell as well. But the Catholic Church's teaching of what heaven is, well, it's just plain wrong. You can't say that God created man in his own image, preach forgiveness and compassion, then exclude certain people just because they live the lifestyle and manner in which God created them, which happens to be against the teaching of the Church. You just can't have it both ways."

"Your friend, your professor from grad school … do you still keep in touch? Did you ever have discussion of this nature with him?"

"Yeah … um, well, I meant to. I wanted to. I kind of had to … gather myself a bit. When I was better, I tried to reach out to him, just to let him know how much I appreciated him in my life. But he died. He died about a month or so after helping me and I never knew because I wasn't around anymore. Part of my regret, I guess. Now I can't even thank him, let alone repay him for what he did for me. Well, at least that is how I used to think. Maybe now I can do something."

While the interview continued, another meeting had just started across town. All Nico's good friends once again gathered in James's apartment. Everyone from the last party was there as well as additional people who decided to join. Lucy, usually the quietest of the group, had become the leader of discussion on various passages from the Bible. There was passionate discussion, but not argument, no cheap shots, no loud music and no beer. Just a Bible and a good talk.

Nico's intensity grew stronger as the interview progressed. The indescribable feeling that Chris Michaels experienced following the first interview was overshadowed by the power and desire to affect change that now radiated from Nico's being.

"Well, why can't priests get married, Chris? Why not? It's no wonder there are so many pedophiles in the Catholic Church. It was the Church's own policy of not allowing priests to marry that opened the door for these predators in the first place. Disguised as a priest, no one will suspect them of being gay, God forbid. But then problems occur when they can't act naturally. Altar boys become targets, psychological manipulation, they get caught, the Diocese covers it up, it happens repeatedly in a vicious cycle. It is a cycle that would end, abruptly, if priests could marry."

"Wow. I am, uh, almost speechless. Tell me, are these thoughts recent revelations from your new miraculous lifestyle or have you thought these things for some time?" questioned Chris Michaels.

"I guess a little of both. Now, I am doing simply what God asks me to do. I am going to get a message out there. I am going to heal people's faith," said Nico.

"Okay, last question. The changes you just proposed, don't you think that people will say that is just are watering down religion?" asked Chris Michaels.

"I suppose, but should they? The changes I suggested are just changes in the message and the delivery—a focus more on faith and love and kindness, not regiment. Why keep a failed institution in a state of continual decline instead of adopting change that will make things better for all involved? Better for the parishioners, better for the priests, for the Diocese and for the community at large, many of whom are not Catholic. Why is it when change and adaptation are proposed, people dig in their heels to keep what in all honesty needs an upgrade? Perfect example—slavery. Slavery was an institution that built our country initially. But, aside from the few, hardcore pure racists and neo-Nazis, you would be hard pressed to find anyone of moderate intelligence who could argue that our country took a turn for the worse when slavery was abolished. Last time I checked, the first African American just finished two terms in the Whitehouse."

"True, I get what you are saying. But didn't it take four years of a brutal civil war to accomplish that end?"

"Yes, it did. Would you rather the North not have entered that war?"

"That is not what I am saying. What I mean is that anytime anyone tries to make a substantial change to any deeply-rooted institution, religious or otherwise, many times nothing short of a war will bring about the changes sought."

"I agree."

"So, are you calling for a civil war, of sorts, against organized religion?"

"Maybe I am, if need be," said Nico, very calmly.

Chris Michaels sat stunned and silent. The loud click of his recorder coming to an end snapped him out of his bewildered pause. "Well, Nico, thank you. Thank you for your time. Thank you for inviting me into your home. I have a lot of writing to do now if this story is to be printed by Monday. One final, last question … and we are completely off the record now … Do you, do you believe you are Jesus Christ?"

"Huh, I get that a lot these days. The only thing I will say is that when Jesus Christ returns to Earth, he won't be recognized by anybody. And he will probably be quickly jailed for being a rabble-rouser. Father O'Toole taught me that years ago."

Wil 3

Chapter thirty-one

While Nico was busy putting the Catholic Church on blast, the police station buzzed with activity. In an isolated part of the precinct, Detectives Kelly and Martin worked alongside many other law enforcement officers in between several empty pizza boxes, empty coffee cups and cheap suit jackets that were strewn about the room. Large sheets of butcher paper were taped together to form a small billboard at the front of the room. On the paper was a picture of the altar, the location of Father O'Toole at the time of the shooting, Nico Rossi's location, the location of the shooter and the resting place of the bullets.

Detective Martin continued desperately to try to find a logical explanation for both Dylan Ray's actions and for his failure. "What about the two actual bullets that were fired? Isn't it possible that these two bullets simply did not have enough gunpowder in them? Wouldn't that explain why they were only able to go ten feet?"

"Maybe, but not really," said Detective Kelly from his chair.

"What do you mean?" said Martin.

"Look, Benny, I went over that possibility with the scientist boys in crime lab. Lack of gunpowder is just not a possibility."

"Not a possibility! Not a possibility! Of course, it's a possibility. Anything is possible ..." an agitated Detective Martin said. He immediately could tell what he was about to say and tried his best to cut that sentence off.

Detective Kelly calmly continued. "Okay, well, crime lab explained it to me like this, I'll do my best to repeat it: See, the process to make bullets is extremely precise. These things aren't put together by men on an assembly line, it's done with machines and computers. That way, every shell casing is the same size, every bullet is the same weight, every primer is placed in the right spot and in this case, the exact same amount of gunpowder is used in every shell. If there is any slight deviation in this process, let's just say like if one of those machines starts to malfunction or break down, different computers catch it and sound the alarm. Well, let's just suppose that the high-tech computer monitoring system isn't working either. The finished bullets still go through quality control. And that's the thing— if part of this process fails, it will fail repeatedly for the whole lot. It's not just going to fail on two bullets while the rest of them, before and after, are fine. Now, I interrogated Ray, and he said that he hit the targets when he was practicing and the targets were at fifteen yards. He never said that he saw any bullets stop short and fall in front of the target. To suggest that the machine putting the gunpowder in failed, but only on two bullets, and it went unnoticed by the computers that monitor as well as people in quality control, and that those two specific failed bullets just so happened to be the exact same two bullets that were shot by Ray in the Church, well … I know that priest is Irish, but ain't no Irishman ever alive who was that lucky."

Detective Martin just stood motionless as Kelly continued. "Besides, all witnesses we talked to said that they heard the loud shots. Some said four shots, some five. We know that only two were fired. The other sounds were echoes you would expect to hear if a gun was shot inside an old stone church. If the gunpowder was short, the bullet may not travel, but there would also not be a loud sound from the gunshot. It certainly would not have been loud enough to echo two or three times either. But what do I know? I'm just a grumpy old beat cop without a beat."

After he listened to the explanation, and after endless days of staring at the paper billboard, Detective Martin snapped. "It just doesn't make any fucking sense!" The room fell silent and activity stopped. A smirk came over Detective Kelly's face as he slowly got up from the folding chair. He put his Styrofoam cup of coffee down and approached the paper. As he stood in front of the paper billboard, he pulled a laminated picture of Jesus Christ from his shirt pocket and taped it to the spot that showed where Nico Rossi stood. He turned around and said to all in the room, "Now it makes sense," as he sipped from a pocket flask and headed back to his seat.

Chapter thirty-two

Monday morning brought complete chaos to the church. Father O'Toole's office resembled more of a war room at a battle front than an office that ran a church. If the protestors and attempted assassination didn't cause complete chaos, the second article in *The New York Times* certainly finished the job.

"Blasphemy! One hundred percent blasphemy! Did you see what your boy said? And why was he even talking to this reporter again? Didn't I tell you to keep him on a tight leash?" screamed the Bishop as he slammed down a copy of *The New York Times* onto Father O'Toole's desk.

"Margaret, Margaret, dearie, please take messages or send all calls to voicemail. Whatever you think is best, but I cannot be disturbed while the Bishop is here," said the priest as he hung up the phone. "Well, I can't be with him twenty-four hours a day. I do have a parish to run, hospitals to visit, people to bury, marry and …"

"Don't try to blame your negligence on the fact that you are busy. I thought that I was clear to make this situation your priority," scolded the Bishop.

"I have many priorities, your Eminence."

The Bishop paced madly throughout the small office, often at times bumping roughly into one of his assistants. "We are going to have to issue a response immediately."

"Forgive my ignorance, but if we respond … if we issue a statement … won't we just draw even more attention to this exact divide that he is pointing out?"

"What divide, Thomas? Where? I see no divide. There is no divide. These issues, these maniacal statements are the opinion of one person. It is nothing but a mindless rant not subject to any type of meaningful debate. There is no divide!" screamed the Bishop once more as he ordered his assistants into action. "Get a response typed up. I want to review the first draft within the next two hours."

Phones rang continuously outside the office while the secretary struggled to field so many calls. "Careful, Bishop. With all due respect, do you want to start a war of words with this guy? Clearly, he has the attention of a newspaper with nationwide circulation. We leave this alone, it might just die on the vine. But if we provoke him, well ... look, all I am saying is that even though his opinions are clearly disagreeable, maybe even unfortunate or misguided, his argument is well thought out and seems to be quite supported," said the priest calmly in an effort to ease the tensions a bit.

"Supported only by his opinion formed in his sick mind, not by traditional Church teachings or beliefs. Did you read this article? Did you see what he has said? Homosexuals should be welcomed into the Church ... Priests should be allowed and encouraged to marry. Here is the best one of them all, 'Overturning *Roe v. Wade* and making abortion illegal will not stop abortions from occurring. Rather, it will open a blackmarket for abortions to occur in a less than sterile, hospital environment thereby putting the mother in great danger as well. Only through education first, then prayer and faith will abortion ever cease to exist. Instead of pressuring legislators, endorsing political candidates and protesting abortion clinics, the Catholic Church should focus their energy and resources into educating children at a very early age about safe sex practices to avoid unwanted pregnancies. And if the Catholic Church was truly pro-life, they would encourage the development of stem cell research. What could be more pro-life than curing someone who would have otherwise died from a disease that could have been saved by stem cell treatment?' This is insanity. He's completely turned his back on the sanctity of life in every possible way!" yelled the Bishop as he threw the newspaper across the room.

"Well, at least he didn't go into his rant about how Roberto Clemente should be the next person to receive sainthood."

The Bishop suddenly stopped pacing and looked at Father O'Toole with a venomous stare. "Wait a minute ... just hold on here. Thomas, you agree with this boy, don't you?" Father O'Toole said nothing. He just sat in his chair and tried to continue to deflect as best he could, though he realized that this would now be his problem as well. "Now I get it. Now I understand. This mess, this whole entire unfortunate situation is all your doing and I should have known. I was made aware of your history and your radical approach to ministry. But I figured that all stemmed from the fact that you were a young priest in the sixties, full of piss and vinegar just like the rest of the youth, priest included. I just thought you mellowed out in your old age."

"Bishop, I make no apologies for my past. What has been said, what has been done, that is all behind me now. You are right, I am an old man. I simply want to serve my parish, my Bishop, my Pope and retire peacefully. I got no agenda." said Father O'Toole.

"You say that. You want me to believe that ... but it isn't true, is it, Thomas? You, sir, are the cause of all these problems. This whole situation rests on your shoulders." The Bishop moved closer to Father O'Toole, who remained seated in his chair. The Bishop put both of his hands onto Father O'Toole's desk and lowered himself to eye level. "You, with all of your preaching and supposed ministry are what caused those protestors to show up in the first place. You have driven good people from this parish and replaced them with a firestorm of protestors and a miracle boy that blasphemes the Church through *The New York Times*. You, sir, with all of your preaching about forgiving women who have abortions and acceptance of homosexuals."

Father O'Toole jumped up from his chair and got into the face of the Bishop like a homerun king who just got called out on a bad third strike. "Are you listening to what you are saying, man? Am I to believe that you are finding fault with a ministry that emphasizes forgiveness of sin and compassion to others? What is wrong with that? I thought that was what priests were supposed to be doing?"

"Your semantics won't work on me, Thomas. Maybe they worked on that boy who you brainwashed—"

"Brainwashed!?!"

"Yes, brainwashed, Thomas. That is what you did. I hope you are proud of that. Add it to your list of accomplishments. You know damn well that there is a difference between offering forgiveness of sin versus completely turning your back on fundamental principles that our Church was founded upon. Give me a break!"

"Well, you can't have it both ways," shouted the old priest.

"Exactly. That is the first thing that you have said that I can agree with," shouted the Bishop back at O'Toole.

"So, what would his Eminence like me to do about it, huh? I mean, I can't fire the boy, he doesn't work here. He is only a volunteer. And if I tell him that his services to this parish are no longer needed, well, that might only fuel the fire."

The Bishop turned away from Father O'Toole's desk and knocked his chair over as he took a seat on the office couch. One of his assistants brought him a glass of water. "What do I want you to do? I will tell you, Thomas. You can stop with all this nonsense about abortions and homosexuals. No more of it. Ever. Start there. Preach a traditional message. That would at least be a start."

"Fall in line, soldier. Is that it? That is what you are telling me, to fall in line?"

"Exactly, Thomas. As your superior, I am ordering you to fall in line."

"And if I disobey the order, what are you going to do about it? Court martial me?"

"Believe me, Thomas, if this situation were even slightly different, I would personally take your collar myself for what you have created. However, I have no interest in trying to find a priest to replace you, which we are short on these days, in case you haven't had time to notice, what with all your 'ministry' and whatnot."

"So, that's it, huh? It's a business move. It is cheaper to keep me than to replace me, so here I stand."

The Bishop jumped up from the couch. "Oh, get off your high-horse, Thomas! You know damn well what I am saying. Ministry is not free. The cost of running a Church, of running a parish, of running a Diocese grows more and more expensive every year. And right now, we are short on both priests and money. So, I can sit here and tell you that it is all about religion, but without the money, the message fails to be delivered. You know that is a fact. But if you wanted to resign and collect on your pension, well, you won't get any disagreement from me." The Bishop was winded and sat down with both of his hands on his face. His assistants remained standing perfectly still with terror on their collective faces. They never saw the Bishop so irate and they certainly had never heard anyone speak to the Bishop with such utter defiance like Father O'Toole.

Father O'Toole took a deep breath and eventually exhaled as he opened his desk drawer and took out a bottle of scotch. The slight squeak from the cork being twisted off was heard in the room, as was the sound of more than a mouthful poured into an empty coffee mug. He stood up and moved to his window as he looked up and down the Strip District while he slowly sipped his drink, neat with no ice and interesting notes of coffee residue. After a couple minutes in silence, he sat back at his desk. The Bishop continued to sit on the couch with his hands on his face. Father O'Toole realized this discussion was way too heated and the brakes needed to be applied immediately before one of them said or did something that couldn't be undone.

"I have no interest in retirement. And I am sorry. Clearly, this entire situation is upsetting to everyone, and I seem to be making things worse. I do not want to argue and fight about it anymore. I will do what is necessary, your Eminence. I will do what you ask of me so that we can fix this problem," said the old priest apologetically.

"Thank you, Father O'Toole. I am also sorry. Perhaps I was a bit rough on you. You are right, I am not here every day, I cannot truly appreciate the cross that you bear. I was wrong to suggest that you brainwashed this boy. I know in your heart that your intentions are good. I know that your history, though disagreeable at times, has always been the product of meaningful intentions. Maybe this boy simply got the wrong idea? Only God knows."

"See, that is just it … Nico, this person who you call a boy…well, he is, compared to both of us. He is just a boy, a boy with a litany of his own problems. Why then are you so threatened by him? Maybe sticking our heads in the sand may actually be the best way to handle this mess?"

"He threatens all of us, Thomas. All that has gone on for hundreds of years, the very fabric, the very foundation and principles on which this Church stands on. You may think I am being dramatic, but every avalanche starts with a single snowflake. This boy is being worshiped, quite literally, and he certainly has the attention of *The New York Times*. He has even captured the attention of the Holy Father himself. You and me, we have worked our whole lives to serve our God and our Church. Look, I can admit that our Church does have its fair share of problems. Every major organization does and we are no different in that regard. But deep down, we both believe in the inherent good of our Church. We wouldn't be here today if we didn't feel that way. If I didn't believe that, I never would have entered the priesthood. I never would have continued to grow, both in my beliefs and in my professional development, to become a Bishop if I didn't truly believe in the good that we do. But I most certainly will not stand idly by and watch everything that I, that we, have worked for all these years get destroyed because one boy thinks he's a miracle man who wants to tell us what is best. It will not happen," said the Bishop sternly.

"But Bishop, with all due respect, have you been so consumed with operations, budgets, bureaucracy and me likewise, consumed by my own beliefs and my sermons ... have our hearts hardened so much that there is a distinct possibility that a miracle happened? That it happened right here, right under our noses, and we missed it? We are missing it now. We are planning response and damage control and the like and we are not celebrating a true miracle?" questioned O'Toole.

"Sometimes, Thomas, the business of a Church does overshadow the faith and I, too, need to be reminded that we are holy men, servants of God, first and foremost. I get what you are saying and with that, I cannot disagree. Officially speaking, I can't declare a miracle occurred any more than you can. That is the sole responsibility of the Vatican. Fortunately, the Vatican is sending its Council to Pittsburgh in a few weeks from now. I want you to meet them with me at the airport."

"The Vatican Council is coming here? So soon! I mean, I expected them eventually, but I thought these things, these investigations, take time, don't they?" asked Father O'Toole, who poured another drink.

"Yes, they will be here in about a month, if that. Perhaps now you can understand the cross that I bear." The Bishop signaled to one of his assistants with the two-fingers sideways sign. "May I, Thomas?"

"Yes, of course, forgive my manners," said Father O'Toole as he poured a slight drink of scotch, approximately two sideways fingers in length, for the Bishop. The two shared a quick drink.

"Now, between you and me, Thomas, personally, I would like nothing more than to believe that a miracle happened. Lord knows, the people certainly could use a miracle or two. I just hate all the baggage that comes with these things. But look, if you want to approach your ministry a bit differently as a result of what has transpired … If you want to focus on God's love for His people and His presence, which has been shown through a miracle that occurred in your very own church, well, let's say that I would not fault you for jumping the gun before an official declaration is made known. Let's just say that I would welcome that change of pace as compared to your normal sermon. And you know what, I know that coming from you, it will be genuine. So, Father O'Toole, can I count on you to cooperate with the Vatican Council? We need you, Thomas. We need you to deal with Mr. Rossi and put this matter to rest now, before the Vatican Council arrives."

"Indeed, sir, indeed," said Father O'Toole humbly.

The Bishop raised his glass and swallowed the mouthful of scotch, "Top of the morning to you, Father."

"And the rest of the day to you, sir," replied Father O'Toole as the Bishop gathered his assistants and proceeded out of the rectory office.

Father O'Toole sat still in his tattered leather chair as the Bishop and his entourage exited the rectory office. As he gazed out the window and watched the men get into their car and drive away, Father O'Toole remained motionless at his desk. Eventually and without any real cause, he peered down toward his feet and opened a small desk drawer at the bottom part of his desk. The drawer squeaked loudly as the priest pulled hard to open the drawer that had been closed for many years. A stack of seemingly unimportant papers, old receipts and some newspaper clippings were removed and pushed aside as Father O'Toole pulled out an old baseball glove which had an even older baseball inside of it. Father O'Toole wasn't quite sure that he had put on his glove since the day he removed it following his career-ending injury. Remarkably, the glove still fit well. Its once-brown appearance had faded to gray and the leather cracked a bit after not being oiled for several decades. But it wasn't yet brittle and the way it felt on his hand comforted to the old priest. He started to slowly throw the ball into his glove and eventually, he threw a little harder. The unmistakable sound of a baseball slamming into a leather glove brought a momentary smile to his face. "Sweetest sound in the world," said Father O'Toole to himself.

Looking down into the drawer, Father O'Toole noticed a piece of construction paper with faded writing that was written in crayon or marker. He wasn't sure exactly what it was, but upon closer inspection, he remembered what sat in that drawer. He removed his baseball glove from his hand and placed it softly on his desk before he picked up the old construction paper, which was a cover sheet stapled onto three pieces of lined paper. The very faded cover page read, "Bob Feller, by Tommy O'Toole." Father O'Toole gently turned the musty-smelling pages and he was amazed that the pencil writing was still quite legible. After the very brief read, he turned it over to discover a note that was written in red pen, presumably by his teacher, which he had forgotten about. The note said, "Excellent job, Tommy. Your father sure would have been proud of this fine work. A+."

Father O'Toole gently put the report back into his desk drawer. He then took his old mitt from his desk, opened it up and placed it over his entire face. He inhaled deeply through his nose. He had not smelled such a thing for decades. It was an amazing smell that both calmed him and terrified him simultaneously as ancient, buried memories flooded back into his head. It was haunting and beautiful and remarkable and painful. He smelled the courage and hope he once had. He smelled opportunity for escape from shanty town that old glove once afforded him when he wore it in younger days. But more than anything, he smelled every piece of cobblestone, mud, oil, and stagnant puddle water of the shanty town. That smell was unmistakable—it smelled like his father.

He took the glove from his face and held it tightly to his chest in the manner that his father would hold him after he returned from "work." He never really remembered many of his father's exact words, but the feeling he had when he sat on his father's lap came back to him in vivid definition as if it happened yesterday. He had never forgotten about shanty town, or baseball, or his lost brothers and especially, his father. He had never forgotten about pain and loss and suffering and dirt poor poverty that few people ever experience in their lifetime. It seemed that those feelings, too, were placed into a drawer and covered over with useless papers inside of an old desk in his mind.

Unfortunately, the drawer in his mind had opened and the painful emotion spilled over its sides in waves. As he continued to hold his old baseball glove tight to his chest like a small boy, he thought about his girlfriend from his Army days. Regret is a common affliction suffered by many Irish, but surprisingly, that was one typical trait the old priest avoided for most of his life, until now. Perhaps it was due to his near-death experience and the subsequently refocused examination of his own mortality? Or maybe it was the fact that he was never given any time off from the church to relax or decompress after the shooting? Instead, because of the shooting, he now worked more hours per day per week than he ever worked during his life, and maybe all that work had left him fatigued and had stolen his mind's ability to keep such painful memories suppressed from his conscience.

His thoughts traveled to his old girlfriend he once loved when he was in the Army. He remembered how sure he was of his decision to leave her and enter the priesthood. He believed he had received his true calling and that God had spoken directly to him. A tear formed when he remembered how miserable he felt when he broke his girlfriend's heart and how he was only able to move past that terrible feeling because he was so sure his path, his destiny, was unavoidable. Now, these miserable thoughts of days past made him think that maybe, just maybe, he was wrong. Maybe he should never have left her. If he hadn't left her, now he might have been happily married with sons of his own. No guarantee that his boys would have made the big leagues, but he certainly would have enjoyed playing catch with them in a nice suburban backyard.

Father O'Toole's thoughts grew darker as he lamented over his ancient decision to become a priest. *What change have I really affected? Whose lives have I truly made easier? Or better? I've done nothing but chase my tail in circles and piss into the wind for my entire adult life. Maybe I would have been a better dad than a priest? Maybe I should not have become a priest? Maybe I am not a priest now, maybe I never really was? If I wouldn't have become a priest, none of this disaster would have happened. I gave up a chance to have a family so that I could become a priest, but I did nothing more than agitate people and cause chaos.*

A single tear rolled down the beaten Irishman's face. Growing up in suffering and constant pain, combined with ministry to the sick and dying, left the priest unable to cry since his mid-thirties. But now, he couldn't stop.

He looked outside at the expensive green condominiums which covered up the sandlot where he used to play baseball and where his brother and many others were killed in the great explosion. He remembered throwing baseballs at old tin cans and how free he felt when he ran the bases by himself after the other kids left. He remembered Father Cox and how he never saw him again once he said goodbye, until he was buried. He started to softly sob a bit. He cried for his mother he never knew and his father he barely knew. He cried for the constant, unending struggle. He cried for his old girlfriend and the lives of his children that he never got to have. He cried, most of all, because he realized he made a wrong decision in becoming a priest.

If Father O'Toole wasn't completely broken at this point, he wasn't far from it.

The shrill siren of a ringing phone pierced his head and temporarily stopped his heartache. Father O'Toole's head spun, maybe from the bitter trip down memory lane or maybe from the scotch. Or perhaps it was because it was not quite yet lunchtime and he had already put in more than eight hours of work, including a vexatious meeting with the Bishop. Regardless, that morning's events had physically and mentally exhausted the old man. And at that point, the thought of the work and preparation necessary for the Vatican Council's arrival overwhelmed him. He felt the effect of all his years of hard living, but even a man half his age would be terrified of this situation and of the unknown that lied ahead. He wiped the tears from his eyes and face. He put his ball glove back into the drawer. He folded *The New York Times* and placed that in the drawer as well. Then he stood up from his desk and marched off to his bedroom for a nap.

Wil 3

Chapter thirty-three

Father O'Toole woke up for dinner. His nap turned into a sleep. All the extra work created by the miracle, then by the second article in *The New York Times*, combined with the rest of his normal duties, had resulted in Father O'Toole keeping a twenty-four-hour-a-day schedule like a college student in finals week. He went to his desk, reviewed the voluminous phone messages, sent a few emails, but by this point, he was hungry and a little hung over. Before gearing up for another full night of work, he thought it might be best to grab some dinner. Maybe Nico would want food as well and maybe it was a good opportunity for the two to get together?

Nightfall came sooner as autumn steadily moved closer to winter. Street lights illuminated the blocks leading to Nico's apartment. Father O'Toole, however, noticed that there was an unusually bright hue emanating from the street near Nico's apartment. "Probably just my eyes, still full of tears for the love of Pete," he muttered to himself under his breath.

Father O'Toole was lucky enough to find one space about a block away from Nico's apartment. He quickly pulled in and upon exiting his car, he realized his eyes were just fine and there definitely was some type of lighting system in place that made the street bright. Perhaps electrical or gas work was being done and the workers were simply working through the night to get the job finished? As he walked up the block further, he saw a many people had gathered in front of Nico's apartment. The lights were makeshift floodlights hung from the building which illuminated what appeared to be an altar.

Father O'Toole continued to walk toward Nico's apartment, but stayed on the other side of the street. His usual all-black outfit, less the collar, allowed him to navigate among the building shadows and not be seen. From his vantage across the street, he saw, to his absolute dismay, that Nico stood behind an altar as the floodlights shined down on him while he conducted a Mass in the street. After about fifteen minutes of bewildered observation, he felt a strong tap on his shoulder. He turned around and found Detective Kelly standing there.

"Mind if I have a few words with you, Padre," said the detective politely. The detective put his arm around the priest as the two walked down the block in the direction opposite of the mass.

Soon, Nico concluded his Mass with a final blessing, to which all in attendance offered an enthusiastic "Amen!" Nico shook a few hands, gave a couple extra blessings, killed the floodlights and went inside into his apartment. He turned on the apartment lights as he moved to his window, drew the curtain slightly, and watched as the congregation started to leave. When he looked up momentarily from the street below, his eyes fixed upon the second-floor apartment across the street where the curtains had been left open. Nico looked inside the apartment and saw a leather couch. The sight of this couch sent him into an immediate flashback whereupon he was instantly transported back to the studio apartment that he once shared with Jessica in Philadelphia.

"Mail call! Mail call!" shouted Jessica very playfully. "Looks like somebody's grades came in the mail today."

"Ooo, ooo, ooo, lemme' see," said Nico, even more playfully.

"No no, me first." Jessica ripped open the letter in overly dramatic fashion. "Ha! You are such a nerd!"

Nico grabbed the report from her hand. "Yes! Just what I expected. I knew I caught fire at the end of that semester."

"We should celebrate ... Do you have plans tonight?" asked Jessica.

Nico paused for a moment and looked at her. "Yes, yes I do. I thought you knew that? I have dinner plans with my professor ... Look, it has been marked on the calendar for almost one month now?"

"I know, I know, I'm just teasing. I know you have plans. Maybe we can celebrate tomorrow or the weekend or something," said Jessica as she giggled.

"Jess, what is up with you? I mean, thank you for being happy and wanting to celebrate because I got good grades ... but it's not that big a deal. Pretty much what is expected of me. What's going on?

Hey, did you sell some of your art today? Is that why you are so happy and want to celebrate? What did you sell?" asked Nico.

"Better than that," said Jessica with a huge smile on her face.

"Better than selling art? What could be better than selling some of your art? Oh, don't tell me that you got commissioned to create something ... cool?"

Jessica approached Nico slowly and deliberately. She took his right hand and slowly brought it to her face, placing his palm on her cheek. She then moved his hand to her mouth as she slowly kissed it affectionately. Jessica then took his left hand and placed it on her belly as she turned her back to him and snuggled close. After enjoying a brief moment with Nico, she reached back and gently pulled his head forward and whispered in his ear, "I'm pregnant, Nico." Although she could not see his face, she was quite sure that his expression would be one of shock and disbelief.

Nico released his hands from her body and slowly took a couple steps back from her. "I ... I ... I thought you said that was impossible?" said Nico, now in a confirmed state of disbelief.

"Yeah, that is what I was told when I was very little, that it would be damn near impossible for me to ever get pregnant. And I've been on birth control long before I ever needed it just because it helps to keep me regular ... I don't know what to say, love. Never in a million years did I think this would be possible. Nico ... love ... it's a miracle."

"A miracle? Only God can give miracles. I thought you didn't believe in God," said Nico.

"No, I said I wasn't sure. I mean, you know I didn't grow up in a religious home. But now I am sure. I have never been more sure of anything in my life. This is a miracle. Thank God. Thank God for this miracle."

A billion thoughts raced through Nico's head as did feelings of joy, excitement and terror, but he remained calm. "I see," said Nico softly, "What do you think about this?"

"I think I love it, I think I love us, I think I love you," said Jessica very sweetly. "I don't think anything this perfect can come from anyone other than God ... although I am sure you may have had a small role. Nico, I love you so much and I am so in love with you. Now more than ever."

In the final seconds of his flashback daydream, Nico spoke out loud to an empty apartment full of nothing, "I love you too, Jessica. I love you so much," as tears ran down his face.

Bam! Bam! Bam! A knock at Nico's door thundered through the small apartment and immediately brought his flashback to an abrupt end. The flashbacks were nothing new, though it had been almost a week since the last had one. But this flashback was so vivid and so real that it took a moment until Nico regained his bearings. He then realized that he had been crying.

Bam! Bam! Bam! Another pounding knock at the door. Nico looked at his table and saw his jug of wine and sleeping pills. He walked past them and instead splashed water on his face from the bathroom to try to cover the tear tracts. "I'm coming. Give me a minute. Be right there," said Nico to his door. After he wiped his face dry and quickly combed his hair, he opened the door to Father O'Toole who stood there patiently.

"Hey, Father, how are ya'? I wasn't expecting to see you ... I thought it would be somebody else looking for prayers or something. C'mon in," said Nico, relieved that it wasn't somebody from his congregation. But upon uttering that phrase, Nico immediately felt embarrassed as he never shared his ministry with Father O'Toole.

"Well, I am always looking for prayers. If you got any to spare, send 'em my way," said the priest. "Say, you mind if I have a sip of your wine?"

"Mi casa es tu casa, Padre."

"Ahh ... Spanish. Beautiful, beautiful Romance language, second only to Gaelic," said the Priest with a snicker. He pulled out a mismatched wooden chair from the table and poured himself a mouthful of wine. After he took a sip and damn near choked, he did everything in his power to swallow it. "Nicholas, how old is this wine? It is awful."

"Oh yeah, sorry. I haven't had any of it for a while now. It probably turned to vinegar or is on its way. My bad. But hey, those sleeping pills are old, too, but they probably still work. Help yourself if you need to take the edge off," said Nico.

Father O'Toole's demeanor quickly changed when he sat down. Nico had hoped that the change in his appearance was relaxation caused by a brief rest enjoyed after a walk up two flights of stairs. Nico soon realized that it wasn't quite that simple.

"Oh well, look, I'm not here to have a drink; I was coming here to see if you wanted to grab a bite to eat. Maybe we could talk a bit, least now 'bout that new article in *The New York Times*. But Nicholas, what I just saw outside … I … I don't even know where to start, what to even say."

"What, what are you talking about, Father?" asked Nico in one final feeble attempt to avoid this inevitable conversation.

"Nicholas, you know … I just saw you … out there … holding a Mass, for the love of God," said Father O'Toole.

"Oh, you saw that … Good. But, I mean, I wouldn't call it a Mass. There are a lot of technicalities that are missing. It is more like a neighborhood prayer group."

"Neighborhood Prayer Group! Lacking technicalities! Nicholas, you were standing at an altar with a Crucifix behind you and you were handing out communion. That's not a prayer group."

"Well, I also hand out blessings, too. And some people even confess their sins to me if they are not too embarrassed. I don't ask them, they just sort of do it."

"See, that's just it. Nicholas, I shouldn't have to tell you, of all people … but what do … how … Nicholas, you're no priest! You just can't do that," said a flabbergasted Father O'Toole.

Nico paused for a moment and sat down in the chair beside Father O'Toole. "I suppose you are right. I mean, if I were a priest, I would have taken up a collection."

"Nicholas, this is no time for your sarcasm! You know damn well that what you are doing is wrong and frankly, it's insulting."

"Insulting? Insulting to who? By my count, there were at least one hundred people who were there tonight. Maybe more. They didn't seem to be the least bit insulted or offended."

"It is insulting to me, for one, and for the thousands of other holy men that studied tirelessly in school and seminary, became missionaries, got ordained ... you have just insulted all those people by your actions. How do you not see that? This isn't a job, it is a way of life, it's a calling. There are no shortcuts to becoming a priest."

"So that's it, huh? I can't be a priest because I have not been ordained. Okay, well, I guess that is just one of those technicalities that is lacking. But like I said, I don't need to be ordained to do what I do," said Nico whose mood changed from embarrassed to defiant.

"Yes, you do Nico. Those are the rules," said Father O'Toole, who could not believe that he had to argue with somebody whom he thought was extremely intelligent.

"Those rules were made by men. They may be religious men, but they are men all the same. I don't answer to any man anymore. Look, I grew up with the Church. I go to Mass every Sunday. I have received just about all the sacraments I need. I have listened to you and a dozen other priests preach the gospel every Sunday. The way I see it, I have at least twenty-five years of Catholic education under my belt, including my four years of college at Notre Dame. I am just practicing what I learned. Easy-peezy."

Father O'Toole started to become somewhat sympathetic. "Nico my boy ... God love ya' and your screwed-up little head. Look, I think it is wonderful if this is what you want to do. If you have received your calling, that is great. Nothing would make me happier or prouder. God himself knows that our faith could use a brilliant mind and kind soul such as you to lead the flock. You might ... You might even be the one to make changes. Real changes. Changes like we talked about before, changes like what you told that reporter about. Lord knows I have tried. But you, Nico, you could succeed where I have failed. But let me help you. Let me help you do it the right way instead of doing whatever it is you call what you are doing out there."

"No. Sorry. No time for that. Those people need my help now. They don't have time to wait until I become official. And sorry again. I thought you knew me better."

"Well, what? I don't understand?"

"I am sorry that you think this is all about me. Like this was my choice or something. Like I woke up one morning and said, 'Hey, you know what, I think I will almost get shot and killed today and soon, I, too, can be a priest. I can even have my own street congregation.' Ridiculous. If this choice was mine … if I had any choice, I'd be engineering right now. I'd be parenting. That would be my choice." Nico stood up and felt himself becoming emotional with the thoughts and feelings of his recent flashback fresh in his mind.

"We can get there, Nico. We can do that. Together. Let me help you. With my help, you can get that back …"

Nico's sadness turned to anger and hostility. "How? How Father, how is that possible? Yeah, get it back for me, get all of it back for me. That would be a miracle beyond biblical proportions. Where is Fucking Lazarus when you need him?"

"You see, there it is, Nico. There it is. You are so angry. God knows, you have ample reason to be angry. I can't tell you how long to hold onto your anger and when to let it go. But that is what I can try to help you with. Let go of your anger so you can live your life. If that means being a priest now, then I will help you. If that means being an engineer, that is great. But, this transformation … How can you go from hating God for so long to wanting to be a priest so quickly that you don't want to follow the right path? I just don't understand."

"I don't know how it could happen so quickly. Maybe you should ask St. Paul," said Nico snipingly.

"Don't lecture me, son. We are both past that," said Father O'Toole who was also upset by this point.

"And don't patronize me, Father. You know damn well there is more than just being an engineer. I know I can always go back to that. My degree wasn't taken from me. My brain still works the numbers quite well, I'm sure."

"You can't live your life blaming yourself for things …"

"There you go again, Father. Why do you keep insisting that I have a choice here? Look, this is not my choice. Pick an expression, I don't care—either these are the cards I have been dealt, or this is the cross that I have to bear or even more to the point, my Father has spoken to me. Any of those will suffice. But in any event, my Father has spoken to me and I am simply doing as He asks."

"Jesus, Nico, Jesus," muttered Father O'Toole slightly above a whisper. "When you say your 'Father' has spoken to you … do you mean your Father, the Creator, specifically, or more general, like our Father who art in heaven?"

"What do you think I mean, Padre?"

"Oh Jesus, Nico. That is what you truly believe? In your heart of hearts and above all … you actually believe that you are the Resurrection?"

After pausing a few moments, Nico responded, "Maybe that is why I don't find all of the formalities of becoming a priest quite as necessary as you did."

Father O'Toole was stunned beyond belief and his gift of gab was nearly rendered useless. "Son, I love you very much. I always have. You are the closest thing that I will ever have to having my own son … I cried for you, son. I cried for days on end when I found out about Philadelphia. When I heard you were coming back, I thanked God. I wasn't happy, but I was relieved. I thought being back here would help your spirit heal. Since you've been back, I have done everything in my power to try to help you find your way. If you want to talk about miracles, then let's talk about miracles. Don't you think it is odd that since the shooting, you and I have never discussed what happened from the standpoint of a miracle? We talked about it only as a way to deal with … with the immediate situation. But we never talked about what happened to us … what that shooting did. I mean, it is almost like each of us are scared to know what the other is thinking. Well, I'm not scared, Nico. And I do think a miracle occurred. Absolutely. No doubt in my mind. Only God could have saved me. Only God could have saved us. So, let's talk about miracles, my good boy. But as for you being the literal Son of God … you, the Resurrection, Jesus Christ himself and in the flesh … How Nico, how?"

"How? Why? I don't know," said Nico who was as defiant as ever and unmoved by Father O'Toole's heartfelt words. "But you, you Father O'Toole, you were the one that told me that if Jesus Christ came back in our lifetime, he would be locked up in a mental ward. You said that. You believe that. You said that everyone has lost so much faith that Jesus Christ would not be recognized. So why do you think that somehow you know more than anyone else, huh? How is it that you think you will be able to spot Jesus when the rest of us can't? How can you be so positive to know that I'm not the One? You, along with everyone else, have lost your faith."

Father O'Toole slammed his arthritic fist on the table and caused the old jug of wine to wobble. "How dare, you, Nicholas! How dare you! My faith is not an issue, it has never been questioned."

Nico realized how much he had upset Father O'Toole. He tried his best to de-escalate the situation as he pulled a chair up and sat at the table with him. "Father, maybe I am wrong. Maybe the mistake I made was not including you in this ... in this ... journey. And I get it, I do. I see how my actions are offensive to you and other professionals. But I'm just asking you to look past that, forget about that for one minute. Forget about the altar and the street congregation and just look at the result. Because you know, before the shooting, I was just like all those people who you saw gathered tonight. I will admit it—I had no faith. I also had no direction or purpose. But after I accepted that miracle, and it took a while, but after I accepted it, my faith started to come back to me. And so much so that I have to question if I ever had it at any point in my life before the shooting. But now, I can feel it, almost physically feel it. As my faith continued to grow exponentially stronger, I started to notice the hundreds of miracles that happen every day to each one of us. We are surrounded by constant miracles by the minute. But because we lack faith, we also lack the vision to see them or the wisdom to recognize them. You know, I never intended this ... this whole ... ministry. I never reached out to anyone, they all reached out to me. I never stood on the soapbox, but the soapbox was literally brought to my front door. My faith would not let me ignore it. How could I turn my back on those people? How could I ignore my Father?"

Father O'Toole sat and continued to listen to Nico. "Don't focus on the means, Father, just look at the result. What I am giving those people is hope. I am giving them hope that there is a God out there who listens, who cares, who performs miracles in their lives every day. Okay, so maybe He's not a Catholic God or a Jewish God or any other denomination, but He is there and is listening to His people. And look, the absolute truth is that a few of those people aren't even sure that they believe in God just yet, but all of them believe in me and in what I can do to help them. And they all leave with hope. And the more hope that they have, the greater their faith becomes. It gets healed first, then it grows. Isn't that what is important? Isn't that exactly what you tried to do for me when I came back here? Isn't that what ministry is all about? Healing peoples' faith and giving them cause and reason to believe in something much greater than themselves?"

Father O'Toole could not help but be impressed with his thought process and organization, even if he wasn't sure of the stability of Nico's mind.

"Father, people have lost their faith because they have absolutely nothing to believe in anymore. Our churches close constantly, more scandals with Church leadership develop and more priests are getting arrested for diddling altar boys. As for those TV preachers, more and more of them go to Federal prison each year for stealing from the very people they conned in the first place. And the government? Forget it. Not a politician alive today who anyone genuinely believes is not in it for himself. Sports superstars? Not anymore—wife beaters, drug users, narcissists and they have no loyalty, except to themselves. There is just absolutely nothing for anyone to believe in anymore ... and because of that, people have lost their faith ... Until they see me. Until I hug them or shake their hand or pray with them. Almost instantly, their faith is restored. Now tell me Father, what is so wrong about what I am doing?"

Father O'Toole said nothing. He felt a mix of anger, frustration, and complete defeat. Slowly, he stood up from his chair. "Well, today the Good Lord has given me a day where I can win no argument of any kind. I guess He has a sense of humor and enjoys seeing me bang my head against a wall."

The heartbroken priest spoke one last time to Nico. "Nico, in three or four weeks, representatives from the Vatican Council will be at our parish on direct orders from his Holiness himself. They will be investigating the church shooting to determine if a miracle occurred. I am sure they want to talk to you and to me ... But Nico ... son, you must be careful. The Bishop is deeply involved in this process and there is no doubt that you made an enemy in him. And you know how he can be. He already feels extremely threatened by you and he doesn't even know the half of it, apparently. I don't know how the Vatican is perceiving things, but that recent article in the paper certainly didn't help. If you continue down this path, I will not be able to help you. If they see what I just saw, well, at best, they will call you a kook and will excommunicate you from the church. When that happens, there will be no more talk of miracles and all of this is for naught."

Nico did not reply. Rather, he half-smiled and shrugged his shoulders. "So be it, I tried," said Father O'Toole as he turned and headed for the door.

"Father," said Nico, "I never told you about my nightmares before. Would you like to hear about them?"

Father O'Toole slowly turned around and took his seat again at the small table as Nico continued.

"My insomnia—I don't ever think it was caused by stress, or anxiety or regret. I think it is more from fear ... fear of the dream that I constantly had, night after night. Maybe all that stuff caused it? Who knows? But it always the same. I am going fishing, by myself, but I am not sure exactly where I am going. I climb and hike and soon, I start to get tired. I keep thinking I should turn around and go back home, but something keeps driving, keeps pushing me to continue. Eventually, I make my way to this very small lake, or maybe it is a big pond. The water is breathtakingly beautiful—clean, it is clear, it is peaceful. Trout break water all over the place and birds soar above. It is the most beautiful place God ever created. I pull out my ultralight rod and get ready to fish, but then see my family and friends all standing on the shore about twenty feet from me. They are talking to one another, but not fishing. For some reason, they don't know I'm there. Well, I'm not concerned about why they are there or what they're doing because I want to fish in this incredible lake. Almost instantly, I hook a fish of some kind. Turns out, it is an absolute monster.

The first thought in my head is what is going on? There should not be such a large fish in this tiny lake and my rod is too small to handle it. But I stay with it and try my best to land it, but it's stripping line off my reel like crazy. Then I see them, all my friends and family, on the shore. They're all criticizing me and saying that I don't know what I am doing. Suddenly, the fish I hooked changes direction and starts to swim back at me to the shore. I frantically reel and reel to try to keep up with it. But then it veers off and heads for a tree trunk that is partially submerged in the water. I know that if it gets into the tree, the line will get wrapped around it and will snap. I try my best, but the fish gets hung up on the sunken tree trunk. So, I drop my rod and start running toward it. I just want to see what kind of a fish I hooked before the line breaks. I get to the fallen tree, I start to slowly walk down the trunk until it meets the water, then I look over for the fish. At that moment, an incredibly large snake shoots out of the water right at me. I stick out my hands and arms and try to push it away, but it wraps itself around my waist. I make a fist and punch the snake, but it takes my breath away while it grows larger the whole time. I try to yell for my family and friends, but they still can't hear me. They don't notice me or the enormous snake that is about to swallow me. Just when I feel my last breath leave my lungs, this enormous snake opens his mouth and gets ready to finish me. As I stare into the complete blackness of the snake's mouth, the last thought that goes through my mind is that I can't believe that my people were not here to help me. I can't believe that they did not notice the life and death struggle that I was going through … And at that point, I wake up. Usually, in a cold sweat. Sometimes screaming. Or crying. Two or three nights of not sleeping follows."

Nico's voice weakened more and more as he told the story of his reoccurring nightmare. A trickle of sweat formed on the side of his head and started to roll down his face. Father O'Toole said nothing.

"You know, that dream never made sense to me until after the shooting. I know now that I have been beating myself up saying, why me, why me, for several years and why didn't anyone help me when I needed it. But then I realized that I shouldn't be the one asking for help, I should be the one giving help. I shouldn't be asking, 'why me,' I should be asking 'why not me?' I understand my calling. Now, I sleep peacefully. And I haven't had the nightmare since I have accepted the miracle and accepted that maybe, just maybe, there is something more to me that has yet to be revealed. Father, I love you very much. I do. You know that. And when I said that you lost your faith, I wasn't being critical in the least and I'm sorry if I upset you. But it's the truth. If you had faith even the size of a mustard seed, then you would believe that what I am saying might be possible, just possible … even if you aren't convinced, you could still see a potential. But you already concluded that 'it ain't me, babe'. You're so sure that I am just Nico, a little insomniac, part-time altar boy and nothing more. Faith, Father, faith will allow you to see things differently. Let me help you. For all the help you have given me, let me be the one to help you now. Let me heal your faith. Follow me. Please."

Father O'Toole just gave Nico a look that was a cross between disbelief and despair, which was quite a look to achieve, even for an aged and beaten-down Irishman. He nodded to Nico and walked out of the apartment. Nico sat there still as he listened to Father O'Toole's footsteps echo down his hallway.

Father O'Toole returned to the rectory and went straight to his bedroom. He opened his closet and pushed hanging outfits past one after another until he saw an old Army uniform. He pulled it out of his closet and laid it on his bureau. He then crawled into bed and went to sleep. No brushing of teeth, no changing into pajamas, no evening prayer … just sleep.

Chapter thirty-four

Nico felt terrible the next morning after he awoke. It was an emotional hangover more painful than any that followed his worst night of binge drinking. He sat on his bed for a long time thinking about the terrible conversation from the night before and the horrendous way it all ended with Father O'Toole shuffling out of the apartment with not so much as a goodbye nod.

Father O'Toole was right about one thing: Nico was so accustomed to being numb for so long that he forgot what it was like to feel anything, let alone incredible sadness. He hadn't felt that bad since Philadelphia. And, like before, he realized that he had nobody to blame but himself. He should have known that Father O'Toole would be offended by his actions and maybe if he had only talked to him ahead of time, maybe if he would have included him on the journey instead of going rogue, maybe this whole situation could have been less painful? More manageable? Maybe Father O'Toole would have understood his point of view and just maybe, Nico would have had his support?

The entire day, Nico tried desperately to shake the feelings of remorse for having inflicted so much pain upon his closest friend. He couldn't care less about newspaper articles or even the Vatican Council. But having upset Father O'Toole as much as he did bothered him tremendously.

As the day progressed, his guilt started to lessen. He constantly reminded himself, as he told the priest, that he never asked for any of this mess and that he was just doing what God had asked of him. Eventually, voices from the street below indicated to Nico that his flock was starting to assemble. He knew that the message and the healing had to be the priority and his own feelings or the feelings of Father O'Toole had to take a back seat. He readied himself, focused and prepared to meet his people.

Nico took his place in front of his congregation, though he couldn't completely shake all his ill feelings which still slightly lingered. It was like a dull headache or a sore muscle—he knew it was there, but he was determined to push through it. Perhaps that was why his normal message of miracles and hope was slightly deviated that night.

"Friends, love is of the upmost importance and forgiveness is right beside it. We all want to love one another. We strive to love our enemies as much as we love our family. We all yearn to grow our ability to forgive one another as well. We were all created by God and designed to love and to forgive others in the same way as God loves us and forgives us for our many, many shortcomings. Mind you, these divine characteristics, these gifts from God, take work. They do not come easy.

Many people say, 'don't sweat the small stuff.' That is great advice for stress management, but for loving and forgiving one another, the small stuff is what's most important. To grow our capacity for love and forgiveness, we must focus on the details, our intricacies, our quirks, our unique characteristics that God has bestowed upon us that truly show our divine qualities. By recognizing these divine qualities in others, we are recognizing God's presence. And when God's presence is recognized, the door to love and forgiveness gets thrown wide open."

Nico started to feel light-headed. He paused for a moment and took a drink from a bottle of water. He tried to continue as the crowd remained silent. "We must focus on details … we must be patient …" Nico thought he was going to faint. He grabbed the makeshift altar with both hands, then lapsed into a flashback that took him back to Philadelphia.

"Look, Jess, I know you are stressed and anxious and so am I. But I don't have any time to look for houses or apartments. Finals are right around the corner. Besides, in a year, school will be done and I will have job offers. I will do everything I can to take a job around here, but who knows? But, once I know my salary, we will be able to get something nice. Maybe we can get a big house and move your studio in it? Or, maybe we get a smaller house and continue to rent this space? I am fine with either."

"Nico, this place is fine for us, but we can't raise a newborn in these conditions. It's dark, it's drafty. It gets filthy when I am painting or sculpting," said Jessica.

"Can we move some of your things? Or maybe you can get rid of some of the less important stuff?"

"Less important stuff!" yelled Jessica.

"You know what I mean. What if we just rearranged things and we could section off a corner. Then we can frame some walls and have them insulated. We can build a nursery."

"Can you do that?"

"No, not really. I could try to find someone, maybe?"

"I thought you were an engineer. You're telling me you can't frame a wall?"

"Yes, that's what I am telling you. I am an engineer, not an architect or carpenter. I can't hit a nail straight to save my life. And just so you know, I can't drive a locomotive either."

"Not funny, Nico," said Jessica as she quickly walked to the bed and threw herself down on it. "Even if we do build a nursery, that still is no way to raise a child. What is the child to do, Nico, spend all day in one room? It's a baby, Nico, it's your baby, not an animal in a zoo cage. A child can't be here. How do you even begin to baby-proof a place like this?"

"Look, Jess, I don't know. I don't have all the answers for this. Just try to be patient and you might have to make sacrifices ..."

"Sacrifices! Like what kind of sacrifices, Nico? What are you saying? You want me to stop doing my art and spend all day in a framed room with a newborn for a whole year?"

"I'm sorry, that is not what I meant, that came out wrong."

"No, that is exactly what you meant. Okay, well, fine. I will make sacrifices. What sacrifices are you making, Nico?"

Nico's level of agitation started to rise. He did not like being challenged by Jessica. "What sacrifices am I making? Well, for starters I am working my ass off to finish at the top of the class. Then I use every spare moment to network so I can get a great job. Once I land that job, we can have any kind of house you and I have always wanted."

"That is not a sacrifice, Nico; that is your career. And then what, huh? What are you going to do then? You're never here now and you're a student. What's it going to be like when you are working? When do you plan on being around?"

Nico could tell that nothing he could say would satisfy Jessica. He knew he needed to de-escalate the situation before it spun completely out of control. He slowly walked over to Jessica and sat on the bed. "Sweetie, I love you. You know that. You and this baby mean more to me than my career, even if it doesn't seem that way to you now. All I am saying is that if we can make this work until I get a job, we will both be rewarded for our patience, you especially. You will not need to bartend or waitress anymore. You will find time for your art and the baby and ..." A growing noise came from the street below and interrupted Nico's thought midsentence. He got up from the bed and went to the window to see what was happening.

"Nico, Nico, are you okay? Do you need a doctor?" asked an elderly woman who gently shook him. When Nico came to, he realized he was on one knee behind the altar with his head in his hand. He was unsure how long he had been like that or what he actually said to his following. He stood up and apologized. "Sorry, friends. Sorry. Look, I just don't feel well. I need some rest. I'm sorry, but I just can't do this tonight. Let me rest, and I will see you tomorrow evening." Nico turned and went straight into his apartment.

Chapter thirty-five

Nico sat at his table and tried to regain his composure. After a few minutes of resting, he walked into his bedroom. Boxes were roughly removed from his closet, with little concern for their contents, until he found the strange painting again. He brought it to his kitchen/living room and sat it on the table. He then went to the wall where a cheap print of *Starry Night* in an even cheaper frame hung, as this was his only décor in the apartment. Nico forcefully ripped the cheap print from the wall and flung it across the room. In its place, he hung the oil painting, which was both colorful, bright, and happy, and at the same time, was dark, painful and sick.

Once the painting was haphazardly fixed to the wall, Nico sat down at the table and stared at it. This time, instead of involuntarily falling into a daydream, he forced himself to remember. His stomach turned as he thought of the tiny, rat infested crack-house apartment, less the crack, that he rented for four months before moving from Philadelphia back to Pittsburgh. It was so disgusting and small, but he could no longer live with Jessica and that was the only apartment he could find that he could rent on a month-to-month basis. His current apartment was a penthouse compared to that hole.

He remembered being down to his last bottle of booze, which was enough to get him through one more night. He remembered packing his car with boxes—the same boxes that were now in the closet of his current apartment—which were never unpacked. Briefly, he considered unpacking those boxes now, but he was scared as to what he might find, so he thought better of it.

Nico's mind continued to methodically review the heartbreaking details as he recalled how he packed away his clothes after he sorted through them to find the cleanest, dirty ones to wear the next day to feign some sort of appearance upon his return to Pittsburgh. With all contents of the rat-hole apartment packed into his car, he remembered making the conscious decision to finish his last bottle of booze and pass out. Whatever time he woke up the next morning, he would drive home. Maybe he would shower first if he was up to that task.

Nico could not remember when he learned of Jessica's death or even how he learned of it, for that matter. Those months living in that apartment were a blur of alcohol and tears and he wasn't sure which had been more in supply. He certainly did not suffer from insomnia during that time. He mostly slept. A lot. If he was awake, which was rare, he would drink. A lot. Or cry. Or both. But now she was gone, too, and he no longer could stay in Philadelphia.

Despite the massive amount of alcohol he consumed that final evening, he remembered lying down on his floor with only a blanket and his arm for a pillow until he eventually passed out. He remembered the knock on his door that woke him the next day. He slowly got up from the floor and tried to push his long, unmanageable hair out of his eyes. The clouds and pain in his head no longer bothered him as he had grown used to that sort of minor inconvenience. When he opened the door, a delivery man from some local delivery company greeted him with profuse apologies.

"Mr. Rossi ... Mr. Nicholas Rossi. Are you Mr. Rossi?" asked the delivery man. Nico did not say a word, he just nodded. "I am so glad to finally find you. We have been trying to deliver this package for almost three months now. I apologize so much for how long it took. But the first delivery address we were given was wrong. Then we couldn't get ahold of the girl who brought this to us for delivery. Man, I am so sorry, and really, it is only pure luck that we found you. So, again, I am very, very sorry for the delay. But here, this package belongs to you."

Nico didn't say a word. He simply took the package back into his empty apartment and unwrapped it. Then he found the letter.

"The letter," Nico said out loud to himself, "Well, why let the pain stop now." Nico got up from the chair and approached the painting. He lifted it from the bottom slightly off the wall while he slid his other hand behind it until he felt an envelope. He slowly removed the envelope, which was taped to the back of the painting, and took it back to his seat at the table.

Tears immediately formed in his eyes as he tried to read it: *Dear Nico, I am sure that you can't understand why I did such a horrible thing and you probably never will. And maybe I'm not sure why I did it either. Maybe I was just scared or confused, but I know that I hurt you tremendously. I know you hate me right now and I can understand why. But I love you and I miss you terribly. I want to work through this. I want a fresh start. Please think about it, that is all I ask. I painted this picture for you when we first started dating. Now, I hope you now can understand its meaning. I am sorry. Please come back home. You can hang it up when you get here. Love, Jessica.*

Nico remembered putting the letter back into the envelope and putting it back onto the reverse side of the painting with the same tape. He recalled carelessly throwing it into his car just before driving to Pittsburgh.

Nico stood up one final time. He wiped the tears from his eyes and put the envelope and letter into the garbage. "This is where I must leave you, Jess. I am going in a different direction. Il mio cuore si spezza, l'amore. With that, he shuffled off to bed.

Wil 3

Chapter thirty-six

The weeks that followed for Father O'Toole and Nico came and went as one continuous never-ending day. Father O'Toole was transformed into a sad mix of worker bee, bureaucrat and damage control agent. The sheer amount of logistical work necessary to ensure a smooth arrival of the Vatican Council justified the hiring of additional support staff to aid him. But the Diocese purse strings were tight and Father O'Toole was tasked to handle all matters exclusively. "Maybe that's how they plan to get rid of me," said Father O'Toole to himself, "work me to death." Father O'Toole's spiritualism, which once defined him, had evacuated his body seemingly overnight. Luckily the natural void created in his soul was easily filled with his workload.

To make matters worse, Father O'Toole now faced with another problem—extremely low attendance at mass. Every week, fewer people came to church, even though active protests had stopped weeks ago. Father O'Toole had no time to determine why attendance was down or to contemplate how to fix it. He was too preoccupied with his immediate tasks.

Nico, on the other hand, continued to grow and move forward. Unlike Father O'Toole, Nico constantly thought about the miracle and the life-changing impact it had upon him. The miracle had become the centerpiece of his street ministry, which had grown so large that the numbers of his followers would have made any church drool. Nico quickly moved past the one fainting incident and with every one of his street sermons that followed, he appeared physically and spiritually stronger.

Nico rarely thought about Father O'Toole or anyone else, for that matter, who was in his rear-view mirror. His flashbacks had diminished to only one or two over the past few weeks. He was obsessed with getting his message out to more people and helping them heal their faith. Anything other than that was simply ignored. Still, he felt bad on Sundays when he was not at the church celebrating Mass with Father O'Toole. It had now been a month since Father O'Toole walked out of his apartment after he witnessed part of a street service. According to what O'Toole told him, the Vatican Council would be arriving sometime this week. Nico knew the Council would want to speak to him and perhaps, maybe more than just speak. He thought it would be a good idea to go to Mass today to clear the air with Father O'Toole. Maybe if he met him in church, the yelling and screaming would be kept to a minimum? But in the end, Nico decided not to attend the Mass, which eventually proved to be a big mistake.

Chapter thirty-seven

Father O'Toole did not know when he fell asleep, but fortunately, he woke up on his couch about twenty minutes before the start of Sunday mass. He quickly washed his face, combed his hair, and microwaved a mug filled with day-old coffee. After he slammed the scalding coffee and brushed his teeth, he walked to the church. Before he entered, something caught his eye. It was ... nothing. Absolutely nothing. He looked across the parking lot and saw only two cars parked there. Father O'Toole looked at his watch just to make sure he had the right day and time. Sure enough, it was Sunday morning, 8:55 AM.

Fewer than ten people were in attendance. He realized the attendance situation had gone from bad to worse to dire as the Vatican Council was scheduled to arrive in three days. Father O'Toole completely skipped the sermon that day and was back in the rectory by 9:30 AM.

As he sat in his kitchen and waited for fresh coffee to brew, Father O'Toole tried his best to brainstorm ideas. His back was against the wall and he knew it. The Bishop already concluded that all the recent problems St. Mary's was experiencing were his fault due to his ministry and his brainwashing of Nico Rossi. If Vatican Council showed up for Mass on Sunday and only ten people were in attendance, well, that might literally be the last nail in his coffin. He would never be rewarded or recognized for transforming a nearly defunct parish into something that had become vibrant and flourishing. But he knew he most certainly would get blamed for taking a once vibrant and flourishing parish and driving it into the ground.

The best idea Father O'Toole concocted involved the Diocese, which was disheartening. But he believed if he called the Diocese office on Monday morning and explained that perhaps the arrival of Vatican Council at St. Mary's had been under-emphasized, the Diocese PR. department would send out a blitz to all the Catholics throughout Pittsburgh. Maybe that way, parishioners who formerly attended on a regular basis would come back next Sunday, even if only for that day. Maybe non-parishioners would also have their interest piqued and attend? Maybe a media blitz and the luck of the Irish would be enough to have at least half of the pews filled for Vatican Council.

Father O'Toole thought of Nico as he sipped his coffee. Despite Nico's new obsession to achieve priesthood and his corresponding Jesus complex, deep down, Father O'Toole missed seeing Nico. He would have been a good person to be sitting at the table now. He might have had some good ideas as to why attendance had fallen so drastically and what could be done about it in short order. Father O'Toole never told Nico not to come back and likewise, Nico never said that he quit. The two just parted ways following a very intense scene and now, both were too stubborn to lose their stare-down.

It was time to make amends, thought Father O'Toole. He was certain the Vatican Council would want to speak with Nico and it was probably better for all involved if he and Nico made nice prior to their arrival. And talking to him would be good—maybe he would have a suggestion as to how to solve the attendance dilemma.

After he finished his coffee, Father O'Toole put on a warm coat and hat and went out to his car. It was a bright and clear morning, which made it cold, even for late autumn. Father O'Toole started his car, then scraped the ice from his windshield for the first time of the season. "Ugh. Sign of things to come, no doubt," said Father O'Toole to himself.

It was a quick and easy drive to Nico's apartment as few motorists were on the road Sunday morning. When Father O'Toole turned onto Nico's street, he slammed the brakes. Although still three blocks away, he easily saw a large crowd, two or three times bigger than the previous crowd from a month ago, gathered in front of Nico's apartment. Father O'Toole pulled his car to the side of the road and walked toward the gathering. He was amazed at the number of people standing in the street, especially on such a cold morning. Normally, there wouldn't be a crowd of that size in Bloomfield unless it was during the "Little Italy Days" festival that was held in the summer.

As he walked farther, he heard prayer coming from the crowd. He looked for Nico, and though he could not see him, he was certain that he was there and leading from the front. The prayer became louder and more recognizable the closer that he got to the group. Father O'Toole stopped just short of them when he recognized several of his regular parishioners in attendance at the street service. Mixed in between them were also former parishioners turned protestors who prayed in unison with everyone else. Several other people and faces Father O'Toole didn't recognize had huddled together in the mass of people as well.

"Yeah … Nico probably would have an explanation as to why attendance has been down," said a somber Father O'Toole.

Father O'Toole was there only a minute, but that was plenty. He had seen enough. He felt disgusted, humiliated and betrayed. A lump formed in his throat and it was choking the life out of him. Besides being physically exhausted, stressed and anxious, Father O'Toole was now completely heartbroken as well.

How could you, Nico? After all I did for you. I took you in when everyone else pushed you away. I gave you a place to stay until you got an apartment. I fed you. I used a big favor to get you a teaching job when you had absolutely nothing else. This is how you repay me? Steal my congregation. Ruin my reputation. Make me look like a fool in front of Vatican Council. Destroy my legacy.

Father O'Toole was a proud man. Not in the sinful biblical sense, but in the honest sense of pride in accomplishment. And rightfully so. He may have had some regret that he didn't change the world into the vision of what he thought it could be when he was an idealistic young man. But his failure wasn't from lack of effort on his part. His pride in his work ethic and in the fact that he never backed down from a fight when the fight was right genuinely was something to be proud of. He was also proud that he was a survivor, especially when no one else in his family survived the turmoil of the shanty town that raised him.

And that was what upset him the most. Father O'Toole was the last of his family. He had no other family or children of his own to carry on his work, inside or outside the Church. Nobody would be left to think fondly of him or even remember him once he was gone. O'Toole believed that Nico, that sellout, was his last shot. Father O'Toole's legacy was his entire life's work to build a better church that responded better to the needs of the people. And now, that legacy was in ruins, like the crumbling factories and mills that also were once part of shanty town.

Father O'Toole knew that when Nico's street ministry eventually was discovered, the Bishop would strip him of his collar. If that happened, he would simply be buried as just another old, dead Irishman who almost was ... somebody, at best. What's worse, Father O'Toole thought to himself—having his legacy destroyed by his closest ally or sacrificing any meaningful personal life to build what turned out to be the wrong legacy in the first place?

The gathering broke into "How Great Thou Art" just as Father O'Toole made it to his car. "Sure, son, sure. How great thou art ..."

Chapter thirty-eight

Nico was aware the Vatican Council arrived on Wednesday and that they would be staying with Father O'Toole at the rectory. Nonetheless, Nico's ministry and message remained the priority. He did, however, remain vigilant and was prepared to address them if they happened to suddenly appear. But he was determined not to let the muckety-mucks from the Vatican disrupt the growing momentum of his cause.

At first, Father O'Toole thought that having the Vatican Council so close to him would be annoying, like a team of micro-managers constantly looking over his shoulder. It turned out to be not nearly so intrusive. Most often, the Council's investigation seemed to him to be nothing more than polite conversation. After a couple of days with them, Father O'Toole even started to enjoy their company as their presence seemed more like a peer-to-peer relationship than a Boss of all Bosses/subordinate relationship. They did, however, ask about Nico quite often. He could not tell if his little white lies were perceived as such or not. But when asked about Nico, Father O'Toole simply said that he had not heard from him in almost a month and he did not know where he was.

Father O'Toole also told them that he tried to call Nico several times, but was only able to leave voicemails. He even told the Council that he called Nico's school, but was told by a secretary that Nico had taken a sabbatical. That part, at least, was true. But despite the lack of direct communication, he was certain that he knew where Nico was and what Nico was doing. As much as he did not like and did not understand what Nico had become, Father O'Toole would not dare take the Council there for fear of what they would see and for fear of what they would do to the both of them afterward.

The old Irishman was tired, worn out, and defeated. He had no fight left in him anymore. In the few rare moments of peace and quiet, he sometimes attempted to make sense of this situation and how things had gotten so far out of control. During those times, he thought that it might be best if he just suggested that he and the group pay Nico a visit. Upon arrival and discovery of the obvious, he could feign shock and plead ignorance, then let the chips fall as they may. At least that course of action would give him some control over the situation, if not the outcome. But he decided not to take those steps. Occasionally, he thought that his inaction was nothing more than a subconscious attempt to continue to protect Nico as best as he still could. No, that wasn't it, either. Father O'Toole, consciously or otherwise, had enough with Nico and with the whole situation. He simply needed everything to just end.

Chapter thirty-nine

It was early Sunday morning and daybreak was upon the City of Pittsburgh. It was a typical overcast fall morning with the sun still hidden behind the clouds and smog that hung over the city. Detectives Kelly and Martin sat in their car parked on the street across from St. Mary's Church for the best vantage point of the main church entrance. Not a word was spoken for several minutes and even the car radio was off. The only noise heard was the occasional crackle that came across the police scanner, which was minimal at that time of morning. Both detectives just sipped on their hot, strong coffee from the local café— the only source of activity at that time of day.

Detective Kelly started to feel the ache in his bones and the tired in his body. The combination of the cold autumn morning combined with the ungodly early hour that they had arrived forced him to review his mental calendar to tally the days until he could hang up his gun and badge for one last time. Yet being in the car at that time caused him to think, if just for a moment, that he was a bit lucky to be there. The club kids who go to the Strip had long since left for home. The dockworkers shift had ended and all the noise associated with produce trucks and honest labor had come to a halt. And it was still too early for churchgoers and shoppers to arrive and cause hustle and bustle congestion. For the time being, the Strip District was calm. And Detective Kelly was perfectly content with enjoying the moment of peace, however long it lasted. God knows, peaceful moments had been few and far between for anyone to enjoy since the shooting at St. Mary's.

Detective Martin, on the other hand, was not enjoying the peace and serenity. He was agitated. Fidgety. He gnawed on his take-out coffee cup in between sips. He appeared as though he hadn't slept in a couple of weeks, but the younger detective showed no signs of fatigue or slowing down. After he finished his coffee and a failed attempt at origami on the cup, Detective Martin could no longer keep silent.

"Today is the day, Kelly. Today, we take him down," said Detective Martin very coldly.

"Rossi?" asked Kelly.

"Yeah, Rossi. Who else you think I'm talking about?"

"Okay … why?" replied Kelly.

"What do you mean 'why'? Why not? Today is the day."

"I see … what charge you arresting him on?"

"What charge? What are you, sick or something? How about conspiracy and attempted murder for starters, then we can go from there after we meet with the DA."

"Alright … What's your evidence?"

Detective Martin's agitation grew. "What do you mean, what's my evidence! You know damn well we haven't got any evidence yet. That is why he needs to be arrested."

"Okay, well, you don't have any evidence of a crime, but you are still going to arrest him. Don't you see any slight problem with that?"

"Damn it Kelly, whose side are you on! We must arrest him so that we can get our evidence. Pretty simple. Look, this whole … ordeal, this whole situation … it was orchestrated, it was planned, it involves Rossi, Dylan Ray and maybe the priest, too, who knows? I could care less as to why they did it … who cares what their motives were. That doesn't matter. This whole shooting bullshit doesn't just happen, it has to be perfectly planned. I talked to Rossi a bunch. I tried to squeeze him a little, but nothing works. Why? Because he is free. He is on the outside looking in. He is comfortable. We slap some chrome on his wrists and put him in the ACJ with real killers and bad guys, maybe he is not so comfortable then. Maybe he starts to tell the truth a little more."

"Not gonna' happen," said Kelly very matter-of-factly.

Detective Martin chuckled a bit. "Okay, okay … Well … that is my idea. Nothing else has worked, so we gotta' try something, right? And I mean, you haven't exactly come up with any great ideas yourself. No explanation coming from you this whole time. So, tell me, why you so sure that Rossi won't crack if he has to spend some time in jail?"

"Nothing there to crack and he won't sit in jail. For starters, Rossi and Ray's stories line up almost exactly. And it is just too bizarre, ya' know? If those two were going to make up a story, don't you think they would make up something that was slightly more believable?"

"See, that is just it. You just proved my point. Their stories line up. Isn't that what you would expect to see from the same people who planned this shooting together? Matching stories. The fact that they may not be believable isn't my concern. I can't help it if they suck at storytelling. So, anything else to add, besides the fact that you are continuing to support my position to arrest Rossi now?"

Detective Kelly's moment of serenity ceased. He slightly arched his back for a good crack then sat up tall in his seat. "I guess you are right, Benny. I got nothing, really. Nothing but the intuition of a soon-to-be retired beat cop. And clearly that's not good enough for you. But hey, don't mind the fact that I have been working these streets since you were getting private squash lessons in a country club."

Detective Martin chuckled again. "Okay, okay, calm down with your indignation. Yes, I value cop's intuition, especially yours. You know that. But what about me, huh? When do I get to play the intuition card? Do I have to start crossing out days until I retire before I can get credit for my intuition? And look, yeah, you've been working cases, more than I have. Can't argue with that. But not this case. I am the one working this case. I'm the one on the street, I'm talking to the witness. Don't get me wrong, you are doing your fair share. I'm not saying you are sitting on your hands …"

"Better not be saying that," said Kelly sternly.

"I'm not. But you know, being a quarterback coordinating between CSI and crime lab and the brass and the DA … Yeah, that is a lot of hard work and necessary to get convictions. But it is not the same as being on the street. You haven't even talked to Rossi, not once. I got firsthand accounts …"

"You got firsthand accounts of absolutely nothing."

"Yeah, you're right. So far that is true. That is why I want to arrest him. Let's flip the script on him and shake things up a bit."

"So, your mind is made up. Doesn't matter what I say, you don't want to hear it. Unless I agree with you that he should be arrested."

"Seriously man, what has gotten into you? When did you change? It really sounds like you believe this Rossi kid and you believe that he has nothing to do with this mess."

"What I believe and what we can prove are two different things. Don't ever make that mistake of confusing personal belief with proof in court," said Kelly.

"Oh, so now you are deciding to be a cop again, huh? Now you are going to lecture me, is that it? Fine. You just go ahead believing whatever the hell you want to believe while I keep trying to prove the elements of a crime, specifically conspiracy and attempted murder. And look, oh wise and sage senior detective, not you, not any brass, not any crime scene investigator, certainly no DA, nobody has given me any help here. No ideas are coming from anybody. All I see is a bunch of so-called law enforcement officers chasing their tails in a circle. Look, if anyone has a better idea, I'm all ears. But if not, well, I'm the lead on this case and I'm making the call, Jesus H. Christ, Kelly."

"Jesus Christ, huh? Maybe so, Benny, maybe so."

Detective Martin started to laugh. Out loud. He didn't mean to sound so maniacal, but the combination of his own lack of sleep with his endless frustration produced the laugh of a mad man in an insane asylum. "Please, Kelly, please … please don't tell me that you believe in this miracle nonsense now. Not you. Not now," said Detective Martin as he continued to laugh.

Detective Kelly did not say a word. He didn't need to. He just stared at Detective Martin in silence. "Didn't you … didn't you just say that beliefs don't matter, what matters is proof? Didn't you just say that, Kelly?"

"That is not really what I said …"

"Doesn't matter. But tell me this, Detective Kelly, speaking of God and Jesus and whatnot, tell me, when I was taking private squash lessons at my country club and you were working the streets, tell me, did you ever see God? I mean, out here, out on these streets.

Did you ever see God working through people out here? All the murders, all the child abusers, the rapists, the junkies, the crackheads, the gangbangers, the wise guys ... tell me, Detective Kelly, where was God when all that shit was happening? Where was God when that mother sold her kids for dope? Tell me one time when you saw God at work, doing ... well, doing anything good to help anybody ... tell me just one time you saw it and I promise you, I swear to God and St. Michael the Archangel, that if you show me just one time when God was here, then maybe I will believe that it's possible a miracle occurred. Just one time, that's all I ask."

Detective Kelly felt the frustration seeping from Detective Martin's body. He heard his words, but also felt them as they smacked him in the chest. Kelly replied with caution, but also with certainty. "I see God every day, Ben. I see God every time I sit in this car and watch you work. I see God working through you. You know, when I was your age and I was the driver, policing was different. I would have my partner, whoever it was that month, I had a lot of partners back then, but they were all the same. We'd drive down the street, see a guy, see some situation, jump out of the car, grab the guy up, hand out some stick time. Then we'd throw him in the back of a paddy wagon, bang him around a little more in there. The idea was that if you roughed enough of 'em up, they will eventually learn not to fuck up anymore. That was policing. That is how I was taught to do it. But not you, Ben, you are different. You are kind to people. You are thorough, attentive to detail, no stone left unturned. You are not like those guys, my old partners. You are better. Way better. You try to help people first and always. Your heart is in the right place. You should be proud to be the kind of detective you are. You know, I haven't partnered with anyone as long as I have partnered with you. I appreciate you. Every day. I am proud to be your partner. I do see God working through you. So there. Does that count?"

Detective Martin sat in disbelief. He never expected in a million years to hear Detective Kelly say such nice things about him. Kelly hardly spoke more than a few sentences a day to him. And when he did talk, the discussion usually involved where to eat lunch. Detective Martin was stunned.

"Well … thank you, I think. You know, I am proud to be your partner as well. So, partner, help me out. Give me something. Tell me what you think we should do?"

"Let 'em go, Ben, let him go."

"Can't do that, Kell. You know I can't. I think … I feel … like we are so close, I think he will crack if we can just make him uncomfortable."

"You have to let him go. Not because I said so … Hell, a part of me might believe that he does have something to do with this. But look, you gotta' forget about him because it is the right play."

"What do you mean, the 'right play?' I don't get it, what's our play?"

Detective Kelly gulped down the last mouthful of coffee and threw the empty cup on the floor.

"Look, Ben, you arrest this guy, he is going to be swamped by the best attorneys in the city, all of them offering their services for free, right? Disguised pro-bono work in exchange for a lot of media coverage, maybe even national media coverage. We bring Rossi before a judge on conspiracy or attempted murder and the judge says, 'What's your evidence?' What are we going to say? Ahhhh, nothing now, your honor, but we are real close. Bullshit. Any number of defense attorneys will easily say, 'look, your honor, Mr. Rossi was five feet away from the target of this hit. He isn't a conspirator, he is a victim. The state got nothin' in terms of evidence, you can't hold him here without any evidence.' Case dismissed. Now the DA will be all kind of pissed-off at us and any chance of prosecuting Rossi if and when evidence does appear has just gotten flushed down the toilet. Let him go, Ben. Go with the sure thing, see where it leads. We got Dylan Ray dead to rights. Let him sit in jail for a few months. See if he starts to crack a bit. Once he realizes how bad things will turn out for him, maybe he will give up Rossi. Maybe he will start talking if he thinks he can cut a deal? At least we get a conviction on the shooter. If he is weak, well maybe he will rat out Rossi."

"I hear ya' Kelly, I do … You are right, you know, you are right. It's just … It just doesn't sit well with me, know what I mean? I can't explain it other than he feels too involved in this to skate, that's all."

"I know. Look, I don't discount your intuition. You got a lot years to go to catch up to me, but I know you ain't no rookie either. But why now? Why here? You could have popped this guy at his apartment, at his school, any number of places. Why here and now? You trying to say something?"

"Yeah, Kell, maybe I am trying to say something. Look, everybody around us, including you, apparently, has found religion in one way or another since this case started. Well, maybe I have too. Maybe I found, no wait … I am certain that I have also found my religion. You know what part I found? I found the part where it is written that God said you should have no other gods but me. You shall not worship false idols. Rossi is a false idol. Parading around here pretending to cure people with church services out in the street. Oh yeah, I know about them. I read your reports, too. No stone left unturned, remember? We take him down now. We cuff him in front of his followers and show them that he is nothing but a snake oil salesman, we put him in jail, then when everyone abandons him, he will level with us. He will tell us what's up at that point."

Detective Kelly said nothing. The only advantage he had over his partner was experience. He certainly wasn't smarter and he was not as good at police work and he knew that. He no longer wanted to argue, so he gave in, sort of.

"Okay, fine. Your mind is made up, clearly. Let's just … do this … humor me, please. If Rossi shows up today, then he is here for church. Let him have his Mass. At the end of Mass, you think he still needs to go, we do it then, okay?"

Detective Martin thought about Kelly's suggestion for a moment. "Ok. Sure Kelly. Sure. I can do that. We'll pop him after the Mass is over. He will be here. I am certain of that," said Detective Martin as he stared down at the weekly issue of *The Pittsburgh Catholic* newspaper which announced, via headline, that certain members of the Vatican Council would be on hand to celebrate the 9:00 a.m. Sunday mass today at St. Mary's.

Wil 3

Chapter forty

Detective Martin was correct. Nico Rossi would be there. In fact, he already was. Nico arrived at the church and entered through the back door out of the sight of the detectives. While all his close friends and followers were sleeping and while Kelly and Martin argued in their car, Nico Rossi had been in church praying intensely. The two candles lit by the altar were the only source of light in the otherwise dark church. Nico was dressed in all black, like a priest, except without the collar. His long hair had been cut short and business-like in the same fashion as when he was a grad student.

The more Nico prayed, the more intense his prayer had become. Sweat started to trickle down his face. Eventually, he lifted his head from prayer to wipe the sweat from his forehead when his eyes locked onto the candles, which caused him to immediately go into another flashback.

Nico stood in the doorway of the studio apartment that he shared with his pregnant girlfriend, Jessica LaRue. He opened the door, but was stopped in his tracks at the sight of Jessica, who sat on the couch crying. Two candles were lit on the end table beside the couch.

"Sweetheart! What is wrong? Are you okay?" asked Nico with panic in his voice.

"Stay away from me! Just stay away! Don't come any closer," yelled Jessica loudly. Nico was stunned because it was the first time that he had ever heard her raise her voice not from exuberance or joy.

"What? Why? What is wrong? Jessica, you are scaring me." Nico started to come through the door, but Jessica screamed again, even louder. "Stay back, do you hear me, stay back!"

"Are you sick? Are you okay, is the baby okay?" asked Nico who was now frightened. "My car is right outside, we can go right to the hospital now."

"No, Nico, no. You don't get it. I just came from the hospital."

"What? Why didn't you call me? I could have taken you ... I could have met you there ... I could have ..."

"No, no you couldn't. You wouldn't. You would never," sobbed Jessica, "Nico ... I had an abortion."

Nico stood there. Speechless. Jessica continued to sob. Eventually, he went down to one knee while still in the doorway. He wasn't praying, he just didn't think he could stand any more.

"You say that you love me, but you don't, you don't really love me. You love your career and I am just a waitress with a paint brush. I have appointments with doctors and you don't go because you can't miss class. You network with professors and business people and I fall asleep before you get home. I'm sick all morning, but you are already gone. You don't need me or a child ..."

At that point, a bright light came over Nico's face, which caused him to raise his arm to block it. The sun had risen and broke through the clouds over the Strip District. The flashback ended. Nico was a sweaty mess. "I was doing that for you, for us ... for our child. Why couldn't you see that?" said Nico out loud in the empty church.

Nico left the pew and jogged to the restroom to wash his face and comb his hair. He then returned to his pew and just sat there. However, there was no time to reflect as he could hear the door behind the altar being unlocked and soon, he was joined by Father O'Toole, the Bishop and a few members of the Vatican Council.

"Nicholas! What are you doing here ... so early?" said Father O'Toole. Nico stood up and approached the group.

"Just thought I'd get a little quiet time in. Oh, yeah, I used the key you gave me awhile back, remember?" Nico pulled out a rather large church key that was in his front pocket.

"Young man, is that priest attire that you are wearing?" asked the Bishop who was immediately angered by Nico's appearance.

"Well, no. Brooks Brothers, actually. Tailor made Brooks Brothers, but I went with a mock turtle neck instead of a collar. Kind of my twenty-first century take on fashion that is a bit dated."

The Vatican Council immediately started to speak to one another in Italian. Father O'Toole said nothing and started to pull at his own collar to loosen it a bit.

"Just what is the meaning of this?" asked the angry and embarrassed Bishop.

"The meaning of what, your Excellency? Me praying in church?"

"Do not play games with me. You know what I am talking about. What is the meaning of your outfit, dressing like a priest?"

Nico responded, somewhat defiant, "Oh, I'm sorry, I wasn't aware that this Church had a dress code … I certainly wasn't expecting the Spanish Inquisition." Nico then jumped near the Vatican Council and shouted, "Nobody expects the Spanish Inquisition … C'mon, guys, you missed your cue!"

"Enough, Nicholas, enough! Back there, now!" screamed Father O'Toole as he pointed his bent, arthritic finger to the backroom behind the altar. Nico led the way and the rest of the group followed. After they entered, Nico took a seat on a folding chair while the rest of the group huddled together on the opposite side of the room. Nico tried to pretend that he was not interested in what they were saying, though he strained his hardest to hear the discussion. Despite all best efforts, Nico couldn't tell what they were talking about, but he had a hunch. He could tell that Father O'Toole was embarrassed and perhaps apologetic at times. Clearly the Bishop was outraged and was risking a stroke if he didn't calm down. And the Italian being spoken by the council wasn't quite audible, but what little he could hear seemed to be in a much calmer tone. After several minutes of discussion, the priest, the Bishop and the Vatican Council approached Nico. He stood up from his chair and met them half way.

The Bishop was the first to start in on Nico. "Son, I do not know who you think you are …"

"Oh, please don't ask him that question, your Eminence," blurted Father O'Toole.

"The Vatican Council did not come all the way from Rome to Pittsburgh to see you make an absolute mockery of two thousand years of religion," scolded the Bishop.

"Thank you. I can assure you, sir, that is not my intention," said Nico calmly.

"Well, then just what is your intention?"

"I am just here today to spread the good word. No different than any of you are here for today."

"How, by pretending that you are a priest now," asked the Bishop.

"I am not pretending. I am all that has ever come before me. Nothing more, nothing less."

"See, absolute blasphemy! This is an outrage. Thomas, do something!"

"Maybe it is an outrage to you, your Eminence, but not to them," quickly replied Nico before Father O'Toole could even get a word in.

"Not to who? Who is not outraged by your blasphemous and disrespectful conduct?"

"My followers," said Nico who remained remarkably calm.

"Your followers? What followers," yelled the Bishop as he threw open the office door that led to the church. "I see nobody."

"They're just waiting. That's all."

"Waiting! Waiting for what?"

"They're waiting for me to take my rightful place … they are waiting for me to lead them," said Nico. Upon hearing that, Father O'Toole rolled his eyes and muttered something under his breath. The Vatican Council continued to speak to each other in Italian.

"Nonsense! Absolute nonsense! This is insane. You, young man, are not a priest. An outfit does not make you a priest."

"I know, I know, I heard this lecture before … go to seminary, get ordained … I know, but I don't agree," said Nico quite defiantly.

"You don't agree? So, what? I don't care. Those are the rules. I run this parish, not you. You are not a priest. You cannot celebrate Mass. In fact … in fact, you are done. No more of you on the altar, volunteer or not, there is no further need of your service. Here or in any other parish if I have my way. Now Thomas, it is time for Mass. Do your job and lead us, if I am not asking too much," scolded the Bishop.

"Yes, your Eminence."

Father O'Toole led the Bishop and the Vatican Council to the rear of the church while Nico remained seated in the office behind the altar. Father O'Toole checked to make sure all the church doors were unlocked, which they were. However, not one single person was seated in the church. It was even worse than Father O'Toole thought was possible.

Nonetheless, the opening hymn started to play and on cue, Father O'Toole led the group down the aisle. Upon approaching the altar at the front of the church, all parties genuflected in unison and took their positions. When the opening hymn concluded, O'Toole took center stage and readied himself to speak to an empty church as if nothing was out of the ordinary. An old voice just slightly louder than a whisper came from one of the Council. "Aspettare, Aspettare."

The group reconvened in the back room once more. Again, they huddled opposite of Nico who remained seated the entire time. Eventually, one of the members of the Vatican Council approached Nico. Nico stood to greet him and bowed his head slightly as he addressed the group in Italian. "Mi dispiace, non sto cercando di offenderti."

"There is nothing for you to be sorry about, my son. You did not ask for this," said a member of the council. And with those words, Nico felt an extraordinary burden being lifted from his shoulders. He smiled a little at first, then a much larger smile that couldn't be contained followed. Tears of joy filled his eyes.

"What is it that you would like me to do?" asked Nico.

"Lead us in worship, Figlio, lead us in worship," said the council member.

Nico bowed his head, then quickly walked to the back of the church ahead of the older gentlemen. He threw open the doors and appeared before a large group of his followers who had assembled just outside. "This morning, I will put all the demons to rest," yelled Nico at the large group of people who crowded the sidewalk and street in front of the main church entrance. Upon seeing and hearing Nico, his followers, along with both detectives, stormed into the church and scrambled to find seats.

The Bishop, Father O'Toole and the Vatican Council finally made it to the back of the church to join Nico. "Ave Maria" began to play loudly on the pipe organ while more people tried to get inside.

Within minutes, there was not an empty seat to be found, including the second-floor balcony seating, which was only ever utilized on Christmas Eve Mass and sometimes Easter Sunday. The church looked amazing. The gray morning turned to unusually sunny for Pittsburgh as the sun's rays absolutely flooded the church with brilliant stained glass colored lights.

Nico stood in the front of the holy men, and as he turned to face them, he said with focus in his eyes once again, "Questa mattina, ho mettera tutti i demoni per riposare!" Nico then began the march to the altar at the front of the church. He walked down the aisle with a swagger and purpose that resembled more of a veteran boxer's walk into a ring than a priest who was about to celebrate a mass. The Bishop carried his Shepard's Staff behind Nico. O'Toole carried the readings in the book adorned with the gold cover. The members of the Vatican Council brought up the rear. When they made it to the altar, all genuflected again in unison and took their places.

Father O'Toole moved closer to the office door and was somewhat off the altar as he started to unbutton his vestments. At that moment, he thought of Father Cox. Almost every day of his life as far back as he could remember, he kept Father Cox in his prayers. Father Cox's guidance and upbringing continued to be a remarkably strong influence in O'Toole's life even as he grew older. Father O'Toole often prayed directly to him just like a saint. However, Father O'Toole realized that he failed to pray to Father Cox, or even think much about him, since the shooting. But now, Father Cox's words were just as clear and direct in his head as though he was standing right beside him. He remembered what Father Cox once told him about his own father: "Tommy, no matter how much faith a man has, no matter how hard he tries or what efforts he puts forth, sometimes a man will just hit a breaking point. Once that happens, a man is like a ship lost at sea and only the grace of God Almighty can give him shelter." Father O'Toole said one final prayer to Father Cox and prayed that he would help him to find shelter.

When the "Ave Maria" ended, Nico walked behind the altar, instead of the lectern, to address the congregation. "Brothers and sisters in Christ, on behalf of his Excellency, our Bishop, on behalf of our beloved pastor Father O'Toole and members of the Vatican Council who so graciously traveled from Rome to be with us today in celebration, I welcome you to worship today on this beautiful Sunday morning." As Nico began to speak, he looked down at the front row. He could see Detective Martin and Detective Kelly sitting there, ironically enough, right beside his girlfriend or ex-girlfriend, Lucy. As Nico continued to look at them, he watched Lucy morph into Jessica right before his eyes. He felt another flashback coming on, but he fought it off and continued with his opening address. "Brothers and sisters, as we worship here together today, please know, please understand, it is your faith that brought you here today. It is our faith that binds us to one another and it is our faith that will bring us all salvation ..."

BANG! A gunshot rang out! People screamed and ran. The church was instantly thrown into absolute chaos. Detectives Martin and Kelly pulled their guns out from under their coats and tried to survey the situation. A second church shooting just occurred in the same exact church. This time, however, the sheer number of people in attendance caused even greater confusion than the first shooting.

A single bullet hit Nico squarely in his left chest and knocked him to the ground. After hitting the floor, Nico opened his eyes to see Father O'Toole, who stood about twenty feet from him. He was dressed in a military policeman's uniform. At his side was a standard issue Colt .38 service revolver with smoke still coming from the barrel. A few moments later, Detective Kelly made his way to the altar and removed the gun from Father O'Toole, who put up no resistance. Nico closed his eyes and waited to die.

Wil 3

Epilogue

The first thing I noticed when I was on the ground at the altar was how absolutely clear my head was. I mean it, really. It was like I never had insomnia, I never took a drink or a pill, no psychosis ever touched me. I was just extremely focused with a level of clarity I had never experienced before. How tragic, I thought, that I would experience this feeling only one time in my life and in my closing moments, nonetheless. First I thought that maybe this feeling was a product of being shot. You know, biological and chemical processes that I never really understood. Maybe the bullet in my body was so intrusive that my body focused all attention and resources there, which made my head really clear. Or maybe, this feeling was God's final gift to me, whether I deserved it or not. Kind of like, "Here is your parting gift, thanks for playing the game." Then I thought about that old movie *Caddy Shack* and how Bill Murray's character described what it was like to caddie for the Dalai Lama. Although the Lama never tipped him when he finished caddying the round, the Lama told him that on his death bed, he would receive total consciousness. Perhaps Bill Murray's character was more of a theologian than anyone gave him credit for? God, how fucked up am I? Who else gets shot and finds humor in their last dying moments? I wish I could have found more humor in life when I was alive and well.

I felt my body getting warmer. I thought bodies were supposed to cool when they die? I expected the marble floor to be cold. Maybe it was? I was just getting warmer. Perhaps that is just what happens after you get shot or are ready to die. I had no experience with either, so I just tried to ready myself for whatever it was that was going to happen next. I knew I could open my eyes if I still wanted to, but I was just too scared for that. Not sure what I would see and at that point, so I decided to not look anymore. I know I sounded like an old man, but in my short life, I decided that I had seen enough, so my eyes would stay shut.

As I continued waiting to die, I thought about Jessica. I think she was my one true love. I remembered how good I felt the first time she kissed me and how that feeling never seemed to fade, until the end. How amazing it was to instantly fall in love, to recognize that it was true love and not just desire or excitement, and for that feeling to stay strong. At least it stayed that way for me. That was the stuff of once in a lifetime, man, and it was great.

Would she be in heaven, I wondered? Would I see her again? I mean, she had two major strikes against her. As for her suicide, well, Catholics believe that people who kill themselves don't go to heaven, they go to hell. I always hated that belief, more than any other, that principle is just terrible. No other religion in the world shares that belief. It simply didn't make any sense whatsoever, unless the Catholic bureaucracy realized that if parishioners shared that belief, then they would continue to contribute to the weekly collection plate. But if they kill themselves, well, you can't turn that spigot back on. I mean, seriously, suicide victims going to hell is just a big middle finger to the mental health community. And what does that belief say about God? A person who is absolutely tortured by poor mental health, in and out of the hospitals, on and off medications, perhaps on and off drugs and alcohol, any kind of relationship with somebody is usually one of co-dependence and not one based upon love, and there's usually physical abuse at a very young age until the end, too. What an awful life. So now that person can't take it anymore and decides to go out peacefully with a cocktail of bourbon and sleeping pills. Now what? They suffer horrifically during their time on earth only to suffer eternal torment in the afterlife? Why would God create a person to suffer constantly on earth, then punish them further after they die? Shouldn't they be the ones rewarded with bliss in heaven?

I will remain confident that the Catholic Church put that notion out there to control their flock and that there was no actual merit to it. But the abortion, well, that may be a different story. Maybe in God's infinite wisdom, which at this moment still escapes me, He has some reason to look past that decision she made? Maybe that decision stemmed from poor mental health that caused a psychotic breakdown then suicide a short time later? Maybe it is all just part of one giant illness and God will be cool with that? I hope so, anyways. I hope she finds her way to heaven. I really want to see her again.

And my child, what about my child? I didn't even know if it was a boy or a girl. But the thought of meeting my child in heaven was comforting. Would I parent in heaven? Would I raise a child or would the child already be perfect? Would the child be an infant or would the child be age appropriate? Or maybe since the child was never born, it gets to pick what age to be in heaven? Who knows, but maybe the fact that I will meet and be with my child in heaven was my reward for getting shot and killed by a priest in a church?

It is really starting to heat up. My whole body and not just my face, is starting to get rather warm.

What about Father O'Toole? That poor old man. I loved him so much because he was more than a priest. He was a real, genuine person. One hundred percent emotion all the time. And whatever problems I may have encountered in my life, none came anywhere close to what he experienced. I always had clean clothes that fit. My roof never leaked. I always had plenty of food. What he experienced at a young age is unbelievable. And yet despite all that suffering, he truly was thankful to God. Every day. Even if he himself did not understand why he was made to suffer so much or why he was called to be a priest and not a father and husband.

Can I make a request? Not sure how this whole dying thing works, but do I get a final wish, like a prisoner gets one phone call? Well, God, if you are listening, my final request is that you not punish Father O'Toole for shooting me. I can see it now, it is all my fault. He needs to be forgiven. I turned into such a prick at the end that he really had no choice but to shoot me. I take the blame for that. I drove him mad, but not mad enough, I guess. That must have been his old officer's uniform he was wearing when he shot me. He wasn't in his vestments. I guess he still had enough respect for his profession to remove the priest clothes.

Jesus, is it hot! Holy shit, holy, holy, holy shit!! My God, now I am sorry! I know why I am hot. I'm not going to heaven, am I God? I am not going to see Jessica again, well, maybe I will see her, but I definitely won't see my child because I am going the other direction. That explains the heat. Now I am sorry, God, do you hear me? I am sorry. I hope you understand that my railing against the Catholic Church wasn't meant to offend you, or Jesus, Mary and Joseph for that matter. But I understand now my sin. I became a false prophet. I'm no prophet or Jesus reborn. But I believed that I was. Worse, I convinced others that I was. They believed in me. Those poor souls who thought I was a walking miracle provider. I allowed them to believe in me. I caused their sin. I caused Father O'Toole's sin, too. I most likely caused Jessica's—no, I did cause Jessica's sin as well. The blood of two innocent people and the eternal fate of Father O'Toole are on my hands. My God, what kind of an awful monster did I become that I was capable of spreading so much misery everywhere I went? I get it now, I see what I did, but what sucks most, I can see what I should have done. I can see how I could have used my influence for good instead of causing problems and heartache.

I feel cold hands on my neck. Is that Satan pulling me down for good? I can't take this heat anymore. I can't take these hands on my neck. I am opening my eyes while I still can …

As I opened my eyes, I saw—of all people—Detective Martin, checking my neck for a pulse. I sat up, which caused him to jump back. With my eyes wide open, I could see Father O'Toole and Detective Kelly standing about twenty feet from me. Detective Kelly was holding a gun in one hand and one handcuff in the other while the other handcuff was attached to Father O'Toole. I placed my hands on the floor at the altar. The floor was very warm. Of course, the hot water pipes run directly under the altar. The altar floor is always warm because of the heat from the pipes. The cold morning made the heating system turn on. I wasn't warm because I was dying and going to hell, I was warm because the floor was actually hot. I stood up and looked around. The entire church had emptied except for the people on the altar. My chest was throbbing with pain. It felt like someone hit me there with a hammer. I looked down at my shirt. There was a small hole in my pocket that I put my finger through. I reached into my pocket and I pulled out the church key. On the fat part of the key was a single bullet that had mushroomed out, but the bullet did not penetrate beyond the key. I held the key in front of me. St. Peter's Key, I guess. Detective Kelly dropped the gun he was holding. Father O'Toole dropped to his knees. I turned to Father O'Toole, the Bishop, and Vatican Council and with my fingers going through the hole in my shirt, I said, "Blessed are they who didn't see, yet still believe."

The end.

About the Author

Wil 3 is a father, an educator and a retired college assistant basketball coach who graduated from Washington and Jefferson College with a double major in Political Science and Secondary Education. He has worked as a teacher and curriculum developer in several school districts and post-secondary institutions. An advocate to end homelessness, Wil currently sits as a Board Member at "Hearts of the Homeless," a 501(c)3 non-profit and regularly volunteers at Light of Life  Mission in the North Side of Pittsburgh, PA. Prior to releasing *Heartly God?,* Wil authored several one-act plays that have been performed by various theater groups in Western Pennsylvania. *Heartly God?* is his first full-length novel. When not writing, Wil can be found trout fishing or on a stand-up paddleboard with his son Rider and occasionally practicing law, if time permits.

Heartly God?

Nico Rossi was an engineering wunderkind, until tragedy robbed him of his future. He limped home to Pittsburgh to work as a Catholic school teacher in the hope of rebuilding his spirit. Self -medication, toxic girlfriends and unrelenting insomnia all conspired to sabotage his healing ... until, one day, he found himself smack in the midst of a miracle.

Do miracles happen?

"Heartly God?" dives into this question. If they do happen, can we recognize them, or have we all become too bitter, too cynical, or too tired to notice? Can we believe in miracles if science and technology fail to explain events that are indisputable?

www.ingramcontent.com/pod-product-compliance
Lightning Source LLC
Chambersburg PA
CBHW071313250626

47159CB00004B/1412